LYING

to

CHILDREN

LYING

to

CHILDREN

ALEX SHAHLA

This is a work of fiction. Names, characters, places, and incidents are the products of the author's imagination or are used fictitiously. Any resemblance to actual events, locales, or persons, living or dead, is entirely coincidental.

Cover design by Lauren Harms

Published by Fitzwilde LLC

ISBN 978-0-997-79650-6 (eBook)

ISBN 978-0-997-79652-0 (Paperback)

For my parents

LYING TO CHILDREN

WHAT IS THIS?

Dear Annabelle and Peter,

Not all books start at the end, but this one does. Buckle up, because this is the director's cut to your childhoods, complete with behind-the-scenes footage and a running commentary by me, your loving father. Peter, your mother and I just returned home from dropping you off at college, and it seems only yesterday—two short years ago—we did the same thing for you, Annabelle. The baby birds have finally left the nest, and now I can start redecorating your rooms or—once your mother comes around to the idea of it—packing for our move to the Caribbean, where she and I will retire. That is, until we age to the point where we require routine medical attention, and then it's back to a city with a trauma-one hospital.

But seriously. Congratulations. You've reached the end of the Yellow Brick Road and what awaits is the joy of partying your way toward massive amounts of educational debt, followed by the misery of adulthood, where you'll discover there are repercussions for your actions beyond being grounded.

I know what you're thinking. Surely I don't need to write a book to tell you what you already know lies ahead. You're right. I don't.

But this book isn't about what lies ahead; it's about what happened in the past.

This is my side of the story. One day when you tell your future significant others, children, or therapists what horrible parents your mother and I were and how we ruined your lives, this book might help to exonerate us. It's what people who make mistakes call "context." And I've made plenty of mistakes, so I'm definitely in need of a lot of context. What follows is a series of vignettes — let's call them explanations for my actions, which often lack reason and always lack foresight — of what really happened while your mother and I were raising you.

This is your chance to pull back the curtain and see the Wizard at work, and, kids, don't be surprised to learn that Oz has a lot more flying monkeys and falling houses than you remember. Because…well…that's life.

No more smoke and mirrors. Just the truth, the whole truth, and nothing but the truth — as I remember it, which at times may be influenced by sleep deprivation — about all of the lies, deceit, and trickery that went into molding you into the humans you are today.

One last thing. Before you click your heels together three times and try to return home, make sure you call first. Your mother and I will be taking some much-needed vacation.

Oh yeah, and I love you.

Dad

THE LIES

1. Daddy Loves His Job

2. We Can't Have a Puppy

3. If I Kiss It, It Will Make It Better

4. If You Put a Tooth Under Your Pillow, a Magical Fairy
    Will Bring You Money

5. There Is a Bunny Who Brings You Presents on the Day
    Jesus Rose from the Dead

6. If You Eat Too Much Candy, Your Teeth Will Fall Out

7. You Can Be Anything You Want to Be

8. There Is a Jolly Fat Man Who Brings You Presents
    (Assembly Required)

9. The Dog Went to Live on a Farm with Your Goldfish Where
    They'll Have More Room to Run Around

10. Those Are Daddy's Cookies

11. The Enemy of Your Enemy Is Still Your Enemy

12. Daddy Loves Going to Grammy and Grandpa's House

13. The Doctor Is Not Going to Hurt You

14. Always Take the High Road, Because That's What I Did

15. I'm Happy You Moved Out of the House and Are Going to College

1

DADDY LOVES HIS JOB

Kids, I have not always been the happy-go-lucky man — who, I grant you, is neither overtly happy nor terribly go-lucky, but who instead worries about everything, including the impending zombie apocalypse, the very real threat of thermonuclear war, and the gag reflex induced by expired milk—you know today as your father. That's right. For a while there, my working life was tough, real tough. I was a housecat in a dog-eat-dog world. But like any cat, when I finished napping—the brief stint during my life when I marched aimlessly on my career path—I sharpened my claws and prepared to pounce, with your mother's help, of course.

To fully appreciate the depths of my struggle at work, we have to go back, to the time before you were born, or as your mother and I refer to it, the best and most profitable years of our lives. You see, unbeknownst to you (in part because you don't care, as children are naturally selfish beings), your mother and I did in fact have a life before you were born. Oh, yes. And not only did we have a life, but there was a time when other humans actually wanted to hang out and be seen with us in public.

Yes, our life was awesome. We were young and in love. And when you're young, everything is a breeze, because the cold, harsh, and bitter reality of life has not yet made your acquaintance. You're not yet strapped with the burden of mortgage payments, the IRS, car loans, credit card bills, petty thefts, or the IRS again—they come back every year. Plus, you can eat whatever you want and still lose weight. More importantly, you can drink whatever you want and still lose weight—whether it's beer, milkshakes, or beer milkshakes (I'm told these exist, though I've never had one). And finally, you can sleep through the night without having to get up multiple times to use the bathroom—and that, kids, well, that's the way life was meant to be lived.

If I endeavored now to spend a Friday night the way I spent any given Friday night during my early twenties, I would die, or at the very least be severely incapacitated. Scratch that; I would definitely die. When I was younger, I could outrun a locomotive, stop a speeding bullet, and leap tall buildings in a single bound.

Then I met my kryptonite: Father Time and my beloved children.

"But, Dad, your life couldn't have been that awesome! We see the way you fall asleep on the couch every Saturday afternoon and drool until Mom wakes you up. And that's after you've had only one sip of beer."

Au contraire. It was awesome. Here's a little background on Daddy. Daddy used to be in a band. Not a band like the Monkees…No. Wait. That dates me too much. New Kids on the Block? That's still a little bit dated, although Marky Mark turned into a pretty big star. Wasn't he in that? Or was it his cousin? Never mind, I don't care. Wait. I've got it. 'N Sync. Not like 'N Sync. No, Daddy was in a real band.

A boy band isn't a real band. It's a collection of slightly effeminate, prepubescent teens, in some cases from a country with a powerless monarchy, who don't have a valid driver's license among them. They can sing their way into your hearts, but they lack the necessary skills—and licensing—to pick up your dry cleaning. 'N Sync wasn't a band. Daddy could have kicked their butts while making Peter's lunch—unless it was a PB & J sandwich, because Daddy isn't superhuman and needs two hands to spread peanut butter, especially if it's crunchy—with one hand tied behind his back and the other holding a submachine gun. (I never said I would fight fair.)

My band was a real band. It was me and three of my college buddies who've all since suffered the same fate as me: marriage, mortgage, kids, and increased waistlines. The band was part of our short-lived golden era. We covered everything: the Who, the Clash, the Beatles, the…the…if a band's name started with "the," then we damn sure covered their songs. And before you strike back at me and suggest otherwise, no, the Beatles weren't a boy band. They were a real band. A little fatherly advice: Don't trust anyone who doesn't like the Beatles. Ever. They are lying. The Beatles made beautiful music and music beautiful.

I was living the dream. But like all dreams, it ended. I woke up in my late twenties, and instead of a leather jacket, bass guitar, and carpeted van, I found myself with a coffee-stained, short-sleeve white shirt, a tie clip, and a cubicle. I was a butterfly that had transformed into a caterpillar. If you had asked me when I was younger, I would have told you that I would rather face a firing squad than work an office job, but that's exactly where I ended up: looking down the barrel of a nine-to-five, with benefits, but no benefits worthy of bidding adieu to my life as a rock star (I'm applying the loosest definition of that term).

Annabelle, you of all people should know how much I loathed my job. Didn't you ever notice how I never actually brought you to work with me on Bring Your Daughter to Work Day? Let's recap. Here is a list of the places I took you on Bring Your Daughter to Work Day:

- the bowling alley
- the movie theater
- the mall food court (dads love the mall food court because it allows us to have our own version of tapas: free sample from the Chinese food vendor, cheeseburger, french fries, free sample from the Japanese food vendor, milkshake, slice of pepperoni pizza, chips and salsa, and top it all off with a frozen yogurt)
- Six Flags
- mini golf
- the mall food court again (see above; dads really love the mall food court)
- golf course (you were so good at finding my lost golf balls)

I worked at exactly none of those places. On Bring Your Daughter to Work Day, I always told my boss Daryl that I was taking you to the doctor. And he always appreciated that I was using what was in his mind a "worthless" and "inefficient" day to take a personal day. I never let him in on our secret.

Looking back on it now, it's a little disconcerting that you never questioned me about this. Annabelle. Honey. It's Bring Your Daughter to Work Day, not Bring Your Daughter to the Mall Food Court and Then Hit Trash Cans in Daryl's Neighborhood Day—not that I would ever take you to do that…But I did, and we did.

Free samples of kung pao chicken and Daryl's marinara-stained driveway aside, the moral of the story is that Daddy had dreams, and under the reign of Daryl, those dreams died. What do you think Daddy would rather have done? Go to work, where he was yelled at by his boss Daryl, who was less educated, less attractive—irrelevant but true—and a mouth-breathing idiot, or play at concerts, where he was worshipped by beautiful women and groupies? Let's see. Take constructive criticism from a nincompoop who got straight C's in college and routinely forgot how to use the fax machine, an out-of-date piece of technology that you kids will hopefully never have to deal with? Or take my chances with attractive groupies? Daryl? Or groupies?

Exactly.

"Wait, Dad, what was your job again? And why did you hate it so much?"

See above where I say that children are naturally selfish beings. How do you not know this? How do you not remember what I did for a living?

"No, Dad, seriously! Tell us!"

All right. Tom Brady—

"Daaaaaaaaaaaaaaaaaaad! Tell us!"

All in good time. Now, let me tell you my Tom Brady story.

"Ugh. Fine."

That's better.

Tom Brady—Annabelle, that's the guy who's married to Gisele Bündchen; Peter, that's the guy who's married to Gisele Bündchen. Why couldn't either one of you like football? And he's also the greatest quarterback to ever play the game of football. A couple of years ago I was watching a special about him called "The Brady 6." Despite being the greatest quarterback of all time, Tom Brady wasn't picked first in the NFL Draft. What's the NFL Draft, you ask? Remember when you kids used to play kickball and you always got chosen last? The same thing happened to Tom Brady. Six other quarterbacks were chosen before him. Don't you love him more now?

Sadly, I wasn't one of the six men chosen before Tom Brady, but I did watch the special on ESPN, and Tom Brady spoke about how hard it was to watch those six other quarterbacks, as well as other players, be selected before him. And finally, when he was picked, 199th overall, by the New England Patriots, a giant weight was lifted. He cheered. His parents cheered. And he said, "One day,

I'm going to be so good at football that a supermodel will want to marry me!"

He didn't say that. But his dream of being drafted had finally been realized, and in the special he said, "Finally! I don't have to be an insurance salesman!"

Well, crap.

No, I wasn't one of those six men chosen before Tom Brady. I wasn't even lucky enough to be one of the men chosen after him. Hell, I couldn't even have attended the draft as a fan if I had wanted to. Kids, I was an insurance salesman.

"Dad, that's not right. I just remembered. Aren't you a corporate something or whatever —"

I'm getting to that, Peter! Can I just finish my story?

As I was saying, I do love Tom Brady. I will always love Tom Brady. But he crossed the line with that comment about not having to sell insurance. Having said that…he wasn't wrong. Being an insurance salesman is no picnic. Or it's exactly like a picnic, but a picnic with ants — everywhere.

What's it like to sell insurance? Here's an average moment from my days as an insurance salesman: My boss Daryl hands me the latest batch of cold calls that need to be made, and I look down at the list, regretting all of my choices in life to that moment — a pretty standard occurrence during my workday.

"Get to work," Daryl says as he heads off to the kitchen to consume his third donut of the day. I mouth something obscene, and he pauses for a moment, making me question whether I said what I was thinking aloud. After he continues on his way, I vow that one day I will challenge him to a duel—swords or pistols. Then I look at the picture of your mother and you two on my desk to remind me why I endure this hell. My mood raised, I pick up my phone, ready to sell insurance.

Ring. Ring.

"Hello?" some poor guy on the other end answers.

"Hi! I'm calling to offer you a new deal that will reduce your insurance premiums by twenty-five percent!"

"How'd you get this number?"

"Yes, sir, that's right, I said twenty-five percent!"

"Don't you ever call here again!"

"Hello?"

Yup, he hung up. Multiply that by thirty, and that's one hour of work.

I was hung up on a lot. All the time. It takes an incredibly optimistic person to survive in that profession. The kind of optimism that borders on delusion. I am very clearly not that person. When it rains, I never think to myself, *Free car wash!* No, I think, *Traffic is going to be horrible*. However, I did eventually learn to use pessimism to my advantage. How? Like this:

Ring. Ring.

"Hello?"

"Did you turn the oven off, Tim?"

"This is a work number. How'd you get it? Who is this?"

"Did you turn the oven off?" I say it slower this time. Really let it sink into his head.

"I don't know who this is."

"You left the oven on, Tim, and now you have only two options: run home just in time to watch flames engulf your treasured family home, the one you and your lovely wife, Carol, spent your entire savings on, or buy fire insurance, which will prevent you and Carol from having to move back in with her parents. What's it going to be, Tim? Race home and arrive just in time to comb through the ashes of your life? Or purchase fire insurance just in case Carol forgot to turn off the oven this morning when she was making brownies for your daughter's bake sale?"

I look up from my desk and see Janine from accounting heading into the kitchen, and I know I have to lay my claim to that last donut unless I want to eat the leftovers your mother packed me for lunch. She makes great lunches, but nothing that could trump a chocolate glazed donut.

I place my hand over the receiver and call out, "That chocolate glaze is mine, Janine!"

Mark, another salesman, gives me a disapproving look.

"You stay away from it too, Mark!"

I take a moment and prepare myself before diving back into the call. It's rare that I ever break character, but I had to defend my claim to the chocolate glaze.

"So what's it gonna be, Tim?"

"Who are Mark and Janine?"

"Mark and Janine?" Crap. "They're...They're...They're a couple who didn't have fire insurance, and now they steal other people's food because they can't afford their own food. You don't want to end up like them, do you? A scavenger? The lowest level of the food chain?"

"I guess I don't."

"Then purchase the insurance."

"How much does it cost?"

And that's when I knew I had him. Hook, line, and sinker. I made many sales that way. I didn't sell insurance; I sold peace of mind. Oh, and if you're keeping score, Janine ate my donut.

I hated my job. I hated scaring people into buying insurance that they would never need. Even though I eventually found a way to be good at it, selling peace of mind to the Tims of the world didn't silence the voice inside of me that told me I was meant to do something different. I'd been ignoring that voice when I first took the job. Why? Two reasons. First, necessity. Sadly, student loans can't be discharged in bankruptcy. And second, your mother.

Yes, Daddy was in a band. It was a perfect world. A world where men envied me, women adored me, and children didn't exist. Then I met your mother and she ruined my life. The end. That's the end of the book. I hope you enjoyed it.

––––––––––––

Okay, fine. There's more to it than that. I'm not going to spend nine years telling you the story of how I met your mother like the TV show *How I Met Your Mother*, only to kill your mother off at the end. I actually liked the ending to that show—yes, I'm the one. Your mother is still alive and well, and will undoubtedly outlive me. The story of how I met your mother is short and simple. I was in college, barely, but still in college and doing better than my boss Daryl ever did. I met your mother at one of my band's shows and she was beautiful. I knew when I saw her that I had to talk to her after the show, and I did.

It was a short conversation. She loathed my band. Our first meeting was anything but love at first sight. She mocked my music, and I immediately hated her, just as any sensitive artist rife with insecurity and in dire need of approval would have. She had attacked my art; I was incredibly hurt, but I eventually got over it. After that first encounter, we parted ways.

It took me some time to realize it, but she was right. My band wasn't very good, but I was young and having fun. Peter Panning, if you will. I didn't want to grow up until something forced me to. That something was graduation. The band broke up after we left college, and every member got a real job. Robby, the band's drummer, now goes by Robert and is an ophthalmologist. Danny, the band's lead guitarist, now goes by Daniel and is an accountant. Andy, the band's lead singer, got a PhD in American history and is now a full tenured professor—he still goes by Andy because academia isn't the real world.

And me? The bass guitarist? I ran into your mother again at a mutual friend's party. At the time, I had a dead-end job working at a music store. The day after I ran into her, I quit my job and found a new one, selling insurance. Then I got your mother's number from the mutual friend and asked her out. She said yes, and we went out on our first date. We fell in love, got married, and had kids.

Peter, you once asked me, "Where do daddies and mommies go all day? Do they go to school?" Oh, Peter, my boy, no, daddies and mommies don't go to school. Daddies and mommies wish they went to school. No, Peter, they go to work. And work sucks. Or it can suck. But it's worth it. Yes, I hated my job. I always hated my job. But as far as I'm concerned, my days didn't start when I fought over donuts with Janine and Mark; they started when I came home from work every day and spent time with you.

Don't you feel bad now for all of those times you ate my cookies?

"Dad, if you hated your job so much, then why didn't you just quit?"

Because pacifiers cost money, son. That's why. Just quit? How could I just quit? I had bills to pay and mouths to feed.

But you're right. I hope you never lose that sense of idealism. And quit is exactly what I did. But I couldn't just walk away. You see, kids, I no longer had the heart of a child. It'd been ripped out of me, just like in *Indiana Jones and the Temple of Doom*. *Kali ma shakti de! Kali ma shakti de!* Why am I the only person who liked that installment in the franchise?

There's nothing wrong with selling insurance, but it just wasn't for me. I had veered off my path. And I was so unhappy with my job that I couldn't see a way out. I was a prisoner of my own misery, but your mother helped me escape. One night after a long day at work, she found me sitting with my head in my hands.

"Everything okay?" she asked.

"No."

She sat down next to me. "What's the matter?"

"Nothing. I just regret every decision I've ever made in my life. Except for you and the kids."

I was tired of living for the hours after work and on the weekends. I needed more fulfillment from my job. Correction: I needed fulfillment from my job. But I had forgotten how to try. I'd become complacent. Life will do that to you. Beat you down until you accept your lot in it. Don't fall victim to complacency.

Tom Brady didn't throw in the towel, and neither did I. I was never going to be happy selling insurance, but if I could go back and do it again, I would. Selling insurance played an important role in my life. Sometimes you have to do something you hate to find something you love. Incidentally, I think that's the essence of dating.

I didn't become a "corporate something or whatever" overnight. Remember, Lehman Brothers wasn't destroyed in a day. It took years of work by some of the brightest academic and financial minds to decay that sucker like a tooth. There's always a way out. That night your mother told me something I'll never forget.

"You have to see the bricks, not the wall," she said. "All you see is the wall."

She helped me see the bricks. I hated my job but couldn't envision myself getting a better one. I wasn't qualified to do anything else. Your mother made it simple for me.

"If you're not qualified, then get qualified," she said.

And I did. I started going to night school and eventually, after a couple of years and many sleepless nights spent studying more than

I've ever studied in my life, I earned my MBA. Then I applied to numerous employers, was rejected by most, accepted by some, and finally decided on one I loved. And after I secured gainful employment, I quit my job at the insurance company. I went to Daryl and told him I was leaving.

"Listen, Daryl. I just want you to know that I found a better job. Also, you've been a horrible boss who's never treated me with the respect that I deserve. So I'm leaving, and I'm taking all of the donuts with me. Even the jelly-filled ones! And I don't even like jelly donuts, but that's the kind of monster that working with you has turned me into."

I really wish that had happened, but Daryl got fired before I quit. It was really unfortunate, because I rehearsed several versions of my "I quit" speech before I left — that was the only version not laced with numerous expletives and that didn't end with my throwing something heavy at him.

Kids, learn to turn your misery into motivation. It's okay to feel sad, depressed, downtrodden, and beaten. Those are normal human emotions. But don't wallow in your self-pity. Get up off the mat. Sharpen your claws, and when you're ready, pounce. See the bricks, not the wall. It's a lesson I learned too late in life. It took me some time, but with your mother's help I was finally able to see my job for what it was — a step on my path. Not the end, but a stop on my journey to something better — to becoming a "corporate something or whatever."

2

WE CAN'T HAVE A PUPPY

Annabelle, I've never told you about the first time you ever spoke. I'm not sure that anything could have prepared me for that moment. You see, it was a big transition for me to get married and share my life with somebody. I no longer made decisions based solely upon what I wanted; I had another person's needs to consider. Then you came along and started speaking, and instead of having just one person to disagree with over my lifestyle choices, I had two. I wasn't ready for that. I was the consummate bachelor, an emperor trying for the first time to learn to live in a democracy.

Let me paint a picture for you of what my postcollege, premarriage life was like. Before your mother and I got hitched, I lived life according to my rules, and my rules were thus: I ate what I wanted, I drank what I wanted, and I cared for no other person except for my Labrador retriever, Steve. He and I lived in perfect harmony together. I didn't get in his way and he didn't get in mine. He never got angry with me, unless I came home late from work and missed feeding time. Things changed after I asked your mother to marry me. I sat him down one Friday afternoon to tell him the news:

"Steve," I said, "things are about to change, for the better. I've decided to get married. I would've told you first, but I know how you worry. Well…she said yes. And I promise you that everything is going to be okay. Nothing is going to change. Just because I love her, it doesn't mean I love you any less. And as for our life together, we're still going to have fun. I know she doesn't like when I give you table scraps, but people food is still on the menu. This is going to be good for us. Now you're going to have two humans looking after you."

I looked into his dark brown eyes, and I could tell that he didn't buy a word of what I was saying. The expression on his face said it all: "You're lying to me, human. But what's worse, you're lying to yourself." He was still young then, only two years old—his yellow coat still had that soft puppy feel—but he was wise beyond his years. He didn't believe me, and I should've listened to him. To this day, he's the smartest dog I've ever known.

———————————

I was wrong. So wrong. Things were not the same. Everything changed. Within a week of moving in with your mother, Steve and I were both on diets. She put Steve on organic dog food—he was never allowed table scraps, not even on the high holidays (i.e., three-day weekends and the Super Bowl). He did receive the occasional dog treat, provided that he was a "good boy." As for me, well, I learned to become a vegetarian. And it was hard. Real hard. I almost cried a couple of times.

"But, Dad, you've never been a vegetarian!"

Kids, if an animal didn't die in the making of my meal, then it's the same thing as being vegetarian. If I eat a salad for lunch, and said salad has no meat in it, then I count that as being vegetarian even if later that same day I have a T-bone steak for dinner. As for beer, I forgot its taste. If I had a drink, it was wine. I don't see the appeal in drinking a beverage that one must taste-test before consuming, but I learned to pretend to love it, which is more than I can say for salad.

We may have lost control over our dietary decisions, but Steve and I looked great. We were in the best shape of our lives. Still, Steve often sought refuge near the trash can, just in case any human food fell by the wayside, and I found myself fantasizing about the sound a beer bottle makes when opened. I wanted a beer. Desperately. Just one. Followed by five more. Okay, I wanted a six-pack. But no dice. Our life expectancies may have increased threefold, but what kind of lives were we living?

We'd been domesticated.

Fast-forward a couple of years into my marriage to your mother, and I was beginning to see my abdominal muscles for the first time since high school. Everyone I encountered from my past had one of two responses to my marriage: 1) that she was the best thing that ever happened to me; or 2) "I don't get it, why'd she marry you?" I considered myself blessed. As for Steve, well, even he realized that your mother was my better half. I think he started to like her more than me. The turncoat even began greeting her first when we came home.

Life was pretty good. Better than I ever could have expected. And then we had you, Annabelle. During the first year of your life, I never slept more than three hours in a row. I was fatigued. On edge.

Any time a person without children told me that they were tired, I wanted to punch them. *You don't know what tired means*, I'd think as I clenched my fist, ready to swing. But I held back. Who was I kidding? I was too tired to hit anyone, and even if I had made contact, it wouldn't have hurt. I lacked the energy needed for violence.

But I loved fatherhood. Every day was an adventure, and I couldn't wait to see what you would do next. You became my favorite hobby. I remember every single one of your firsts. The first time you drooled. The first time you crawled. The first time you sneezed. The first time you walked. And then, the first time you spoke. I wanted so badly for you to speak, but I wasn't ready for what you would say.

It was a Saturday morning in late November, which for most people means Thanksgiving and the start of Christmas shopping, but for me, it meant must-watch NFL and college football games. I was in the living room, preoccupied with scheduling my daily errands and family time around the best games of the day, when your mother came in with you waddling closely behind. Steve glanced up from his bed near the fireplace, then quickly put his head back down. Business as usual, or so he thought.

"I think she's going to speak," your mother said. "She's been struggling to say something all day."

I looked over at you and surveyed the situation. Your dress showed signs of what you'd had for breakfast, and there was a little snot bubble protruding from your nose. Every time you exhaled, it grew larger, threatening to pop. Frankly, you didn't look like you were a member of a species that could communicate with speech. Grunts and moans maybe, but definitely not speech.

"It's probably indigestion. I don't think she's —" There I was midsentence, and you were about to prove me wrong.

"Puppy," you said.

"Shit," I replied. Steve's head whipped up. He'd heard it too.

"Oh my God. How cute," your mother squealed.

Here's the thing about children: their pronunciation sucks, but people think it's really cute. Me? I heard a bastardization of the English language. Your mother? She heard the most darling thing she'd ever heard in her life. To her, it was like the first time Beethoven's hands touched ivory keys. Your mother saw emerging potential. I didn't. Personally, I think Beethoven probably stunk the first time he tried to play the piano.

"Don't curse in front of her," your mother scolded me. "I don't want her next word to be s-h-i-t."

"I would rather it be shi —"

"Don't."

"Fine. I would rather it be s-h-i-t or d-a-m-n-i-t than p-u-p-p-y."

"Puh-pee," you said again.

"G-o-d d-a-m-n-i-t."

"Adorable. She's absolutely adorable. And what a cute first word."

What a horrible first word.

"I don't think Steve wants us to have another dog," I said to your mother. It had been two days since you'd uttered your first word, and the seed had been firmly planted in your mother's head. She was thinking about how charming our little family would look with the addition of a puppy; I was thinking about the added responsibility and the even greater lack of sleep. I'd grown accustomed to my three hours of slumber, in forty-five-minute spurts.

"You say Steve, but it's pretty clear you're referring to yourself," your mother said.

"Do you blame me? It's tough enough as is with one dog and a child."

"Haven't you always wanted Steve to have a friend?"

I saw right through her veiled attempt to persuade me. I'm not one of those people who falls victim to the "make them think it was their idea" trick. I'm not sure that anyone is. I think that's a concept created purely for television sitcoms. Surely no one would change sides in an argument because they'd been fooled into believing that the opponent's position was initially their idea. It's implausible. I certainly wouldn't. Maybe that makes me stubborn, but "stubborn" is a synonym for "principled."

Your mother's efforts failed. For the next couple of months, she and I tabled the puppy conversation, but it didn't matter, because it was all you would say. Puppy. Puppy. Puppy. You would think that after a couple of months you would've learned a second word—any word—but you didn't. And your pronunciation didn't improve either. Each time you said "puppy," it sounded the same as the first time you'd said it.

Wherever your mother and I took you — to the park, for a drive, to the dry cleaners — that was all that ever came out of your mouth. We'd see a dog very clearly in the twilight years of its life, nearly on its deathbed, and still, you'd call it a puppy.

And any time you said it in public, the people around you, strangers whom we'd never met, would ooh and ahh, then inevitably ask: "So when are you getting her a puppy?" Never, that's when. I didn't actually say that, but I wanted to.

I tried to put a stop to it. I launched a secret campaign to teach you new — but more importantly, different — words. Any time your mother was brunching with her friends or running errands, my plan went into action. I started with something simple: "goldfish." Not simple to say, perhaps, but simple to take care of. My campaign failed. Miserably. No matter what word I tried to teach you, it never worked. Here's a list of the animal words I tried to teach you:

- goldfish
- hamster
- guinea pig
- lizard
- turtle (initially, I wanted something that lived in a bowl or cage)
- lion
- tiger
- bear
- coyote
- black widow
- cheetah

- wolf
- boa constrictor (When you failed to pick up on animals that were easy to take care of, I took a different approach. I tried to get you to say the words for animals that we would never own. Again, I failed. Again, miserably.)
- dodo bird
- T. rex
- brontosaurus (When the dangerous-animals tactic failed, I tried to get you to say the names of extinct animals. None of them worked.)

Finally, I decided to correct you, first with "dog" and then with "doggy." I figured "dog" and "doggy" were both adequately cute, and we already had a dog. I could inform anyone who tried to pressure me into buying you a dog that we had Steve. It didn't work, so then I decided any word would do. I read you children's book after children's book, hoping, begging, pleading, that you would pick up a new word. It was futile. All of it.

Yes, technically you could speak, but still, you would only say one word. And everyone loved it. "Oh, there's this cute little toddler named Annabelle and all she ever says is 'puppy.'"

I could see the writing on the wall, and sure enough, it happened. I was playing with Steve in the back yard, letting him know that he was loved—I feared that the constant "puppy" talk may have made him feel insecure—when your mother joined me and said seven words that made my heart plummet.

"I think we should get a puppy."

"Damn it," I said under my breath.

"What was that?"

"We can't have a puppy."

I gave my speech. Your mother was a champion of due process; she always let me state my case before she ruled against me.

"I mean, what's next, honey? 'B-M-W' or 'B-e-a-m-e-r'? Is this the message that we want to send to our child? If you want something and you can say it cute enough, we'll buy it for you? Mark my words, this puppy is a gateway purchase." Yes, I incorporated the classic "gateway drug" argument into my soliloquy. What can I say? I was desperate. "First, it's a puppy, and next thing you know we're on a street corner somewhere using that very same puppy to beg for change because we went broke from all of the purchases we made trying to appease our adorable daughter. I hope the puppy is still cute when he's living on a diet of fast food and cigarette butts, because we're going to need his good looks to panhandle enough money to put a roof over our heads. First it's a puppy, and then it's the poorhouse.

"And we haven't even discussed who's going to take care of the puppy," I continued. "I don't think that our toddler will be walking it or taking care of its 's-h-i-t'; I can tell you exactly who will bear those burdens. Me! That's who. Yours truly is going to be waking up at five fifteen a.m. on a Saturday because otherwise the puppy is going to poop on the carpet. No, honey, I don't think we should get a puppy. I mean, what's your best reason for why we should?"

"Think of how cute the holiday card will look."

I saw that coming a mile away. "The holiday card? Look, why don't we just rent a puppy for like a day, take the holiday card picture, and then tell everybody we have a puppy? And Steve takes offense to that. He would look great on a holiday card."

"Steve isn't a puppy. I don't think he was ever a puppy. He's just…Steve."

"Annabelle seems to think that Steve is a puppy. I heard her call him a puppy this morning."

"That doesn't count. She calls everything a puppy. He's not a puppy. And why in the world did you name your dog Steve anyway?"

"I'm sorry. Is Steve not an acceptable name for humans?"

"Yes, it is. For humans. Not dogs."

"Well, he's human to me. Would you rather I named him Biscuits or Mittens? How demeaning is that? He deserves better. I respect him too much. He may not be people to you, but he's people to me."

I knew then and there that I had lost. There was only one reason she'd started to criticize Steve's name. She was thinking of names for the puppy that we hadn't yet purchased but almost certainly would.

I took Steve out back just as the sun was setting and had the talk with him.

"I know this hasn't been easy on you, boy," I said to him as I patted his head gently. "I know you've put up with a lot, and God knows, you've sacrificed more than you should have had to. But we lost. I want you to know that I fought hard. I tried to get Annabelle to say something different. I tried to convince the wife that you are all the puppy she'll ever need. But, boy, we are getting the damn puppy."

I'm surprised that Steve didn't run away after that talk. Every time I came home, I expected so see a message spelled out in dog kibble: "Couldn't take it anymore. Had to leave. Love always, Steve. PS: I shit on her side of the bed." But no; like man's true best friend, he stayed by my side.

Kicking and screaming, at least in my mind, I went with you, your mother, and Steve to get a puppy. We drove out to the countryside, to a farm where an elderly couple raised several breeds of dogs. I was ready to leave after only a couple of minutes, but we walked the entire grounds and played with all of the critters they had to offer. Labs. Goldens. Pit bulls. None of the dogs had that, dare I say, "Steve-like" quality. None of them were as perfect, or as intelligent, as Steve, but perhaps that was asking too much. I saw an opportunity to wiggle my way out of this puppy nonsense.

"Honey," I said, "why don't we take a couple of pictures while we're here?" I was thinking about the holiday card.

She wouldn't cede her ground. We walked the grounds again, continuing our search. The puppies were cute, I'll give them that, but nothing seemed to fit.

"See anything you like?" I asked your mother, but I already knew the answer.

"No," she answered.

"Yeah, I don't think Steve's seen anything he likes either."

"I still don't understand why you insisted on bringing him."

"I think it's only fair that we let him have a say. I don't want to bring home a puppy that he hates. Remember the words of Lincoln: 'A doghouse divided against itself cannot stand.'" Truth be told, it didn't matter. Steve was guaranteed to hate whichever puppy we brought home. I was trying to find the puppy he would hate least.

"I could've told you this would happen," I said. "One doesn't simply go out and buy a puppy. It's a careful and tedious process. It could take months, maybe even years."

"That's not how you got Steve. You told me you found him on the side of the road near a hole-in-the-wall burger joint."

"Yes, well, Steve and I are different. We were meant to be together."

"Sometimes I wish that you would speak about our relationship the same way you speak about your relationship with him."

"I don't know what to say. When it's meant to be, it's meant to be."

Alas, it seemed that our efforts were in vain. We'd made our way through the elderly couple's pasture and hadn't connected with any of the puppies. But, silver lining: I snagged a couple of candid shots for the holiday card.

Defeated, your mother abandoned her quest. We headed for the car. I had the car door open when a four-legged terror came racing out of the elderly couple's house. A mixed-breed mutt that looked like it was part Labrador, part pit bull, and all too energetic raced toward us down the long gravel driveway in uncoordinated hops like an inebriated bunny.

Annabelle, you, your mother, and Steve all took cover behind me. Apparently the family had taken a poll and voted me the first line of defense against rabid animals. Fine. I would die first. At least I wouldn't have to watch my loved ones perish. I knelt down and braced for impact. The little monster dove straight for my neck and nearly knocked me on my back. The creature growled for a moment, then bathed me with its tongue.

The elderly couple came trotting down the driveway, apologizing with every step.

"I'm so sorry," the old man said.

"What's this little guy's name?" I asked.

"He doesn't really have one," his wife answered. "We haven't even tried to put him up for sale. All of the dogs we sell here are purebred. He's a mixed breed. A mutt."

Seeing that the little dog was no longer a threat, you came out from my shadow and approached cautiously.

"It's okay," I said. "He won't hurt you."

The little dog looked up at you and cocked his head to the side. It was almost as if he'd never seen a little human before. You both took a moment and sized each other up, then without warning, you crouched over and wrapped your tiny, pudgy arms around him. The little dog responded in kind and started to lick you.

"Puppy," you squealed.

I looked up at your mother and she mouthed, "Well?" to me. I glanced down at you and saw how your eyes had lit up, and every part of me that hadn't wanted a puppy melted away.

"What should we call him?" I asked.

"Rover," you said.

It was the second word you'd ever said, and it stuck. Rover.

So, we got a puppy—and we never recovered. You named him; nobody ever believed that story, but it's true. We brought him home, and I swear even Steve was happy, though he wasn't the kind of person who'd ever admit it. But I looked over at him once when he was staring at Rover, and I saw that my best friend had a look of joy on his face—that or he had gas. It was hard to tell with him sometimes.

Once again, my perfect life got a little more perfect. We'd found our puppy. And as predicted, my sleep suffered. When you add a puppy to the combination of dog and child, the puppy acts like a catalyst. Sleep changes from an activity into a memory. It becomes a carrot on a stick. You're always chasing it, but you never catch it.

Though we'd brought home a puppy, the mystery wasn't solved. Now instead of saying just "puppy" you said "Rover" too. Your mother and I tried to teach you. You'd say "puppy," and she and I would respond, "Rover." But it didn't work. Something was being lost in translation.

"What's going on?" your mother always asked.

But I didn't have an answer. I'd given up trying to solve the puzzle. I was more concerned with the damage that Rover was doing to our household. Steve and I tried our best to teach him the rules of the house, but the little demon—my affectionate nickname for him—seemed incapable of learning even the simplest of commands. Every time I told him not to do something, he did it again, tenfold. "Don't poop in the house," I scolded him one day. Lo and behold, the next day, there'd be even more poop in the house. If I told him not to chew one of my shoes, he'd chew three more. He was incorrigible. Your mother was worried about you; meanwhile, I couldn't afford to take my eyes off Rover, unless I wanted to start wearing only socks everywhere.

The puppy enigma continued for several more weeks until finally we deciphered your code. I was sewing up one corner of the couch that Rover seemed intent on digesting—yes, the puppy's pastimes required that I learn how to sew—when, Annabelle, you stormed into the living room.

"Puppy," you proclaimed.

I didn't want to stop my stitching—the thought of Rover devouring my needle and thread gave me nightmares—so I called for backup.

"Honey, a little help," I said. "I'm stitching."

"Puppy," you called again, this time louder.

"I know. I know. Puppy," I said. I had become accustomed to this common utterance of the word "puppy," but I still had no idea what you wanted. I was not yet fluent in your language. I made sure I had the threaded needle carefully pinched between my thumb and index finger, then I glanced over at you and saw that in your tiny hands there was a picture frame.

Your mother came running into the room. "What's the matter?" she asked. "Is she choking? I'm always worried that she'll be choking."

"No, she's not choking. Can you take the frame from her? I'm afraid she'll break the glass."

Your mother knelt down and kissed you on the head, then gently took the frame from your hands. She stood and looked at the photo under the glass. And then it clicked. "Oh my God," she said.

"What?" I asked.

"She's saying 'puppy,' but she means 'baby.'" Your mother turned the frame toward me and I looked. It was a picture of me as a baby.

"What?"

"Baby."

"S-h-i-t."

Peter, you can thank your sister for your existence.

3

IF I KISS IT,
IT WILL MAKE IT BETTER

Peter, when you were a child, I swear you thought my name was "I want Mommy!" Every time we tried to spend quality time together—that's code for "your mother needed a break"—you would burst into a tantrum and cry for your mother. I felt like the understudy for a Broadway play; I only filled in during the Saturday matinee when your mother went to the nail salon with her friends.

With or without your mother, you cried—a lot. In public. In front of other people. At parties. In the checkout line. At restaurants. At theme parks. At birthday parties. During weddings. At wakes. During funerals. At the doctor. Pretty much anywhere we ever took you, you cried. You even made yourself cry. Once we were in the minivan and you started crying because you'd thrown your beloved stuffed animal, Ellie, a pink elephant, into the back after what looked in the rearview mirror like a heated disagreement from my vantage point, but seconds after you'd thrown Ellie, you decided that you absolutely couldn't live without her. So you cried. I pulled into the nearest gas station and reunited you with her. And then you cried again.

You also fell down a lot. Almost as much as you cried. And forgive me for saying this, but it was malarkey. You were all of two feet tall. If you fell, it couldn't possibly have hurt. Take Daddy, for example. Daddy is six feet tall. If Daddy falls, you will need to rush him to the nearest emergency room, because he will most certainly incur a life-threatening injury. And I know what you're thinking: if Daddy falls in the forest and nobody is around to hear it, does he still say the f-word? Yes, he does. Because falling from six feet hurts a hell of a lot worse than falling from two feet. If Daddy falls from his six-foot-high perch, you won't have to worry about his falling ever again…because Daddy will never be able to stand again. Daddy wouldn't cry if he fell; he would die.

But I get it. There are two things that children cannot live without: chicken nuggets and attention. Your mother limited the amount of chicken nuggets she would allow you—and me—to consume. This led to more crying, but I'll never argue with a person who cries after being denied chicken nuggets; I'd cry over that too.

No matter how many times you fell, or how many times you cried, or how many times you cried and then fell—that was the most likely of scenarios—there was always one person who could make you feel better. News flash: it wasn't me.

Yeah, that person who could always make you feel better—and by "feel better," I mean "stop your crying"—was your mother. This led to much embarrassment for me when we went anywhere together without her. When you cried or fell in public with me, I felt about as helpless as I do when I sing karaoke. Yes, I would love to get up onstage and belt out my favorite songs, but no amount of alcohol or enthusiasm is going to make me sound, or look, like Frank Sinatra.

This helplessness led me to devise an obvious yet simple solution for those times when you screamed — and I do mean screamed — "I want Mommy!" One night, after your mother had fed you, tucked you into bed, and given you a kiss on your forehead — you really were her child — I sowed the seeds for my new device. I sat next to you at your bedside and did my best Isaac Newton impression as I tried to bend the laws of physics.

"Peter," I said.

"Yes, Daddy?"

"I just wanted to wish you a good night."

"Good night, Daddy," you said with a big yawn.

I kissed your head and headed for the door — but wait, I wasn't finished.

"Oh, Peter?"

"Yes, Daddy?"

"Mommy told me that you had a booboo on your finger."

"I fell and hurt it on the playground today." You held your finger out to me. I walked back and sat down on the bed next to you, then examined your finger with scrutinizing care.

"Here, let me kiss it. If I kiss it, it will make it better."

"It will?"

"Of course." I kissed your finger, then left. You were putty in my hands. I felt like something of an evil genius. Muahahaha. I had just changed the universe and parenting forever!

Okay, truth be told, I didn't concoct this solution on my own. It's been around for centuries, but it's not the type of sage wisdom given out by the likes of Dr. Spock—no, Peter, it's not Mr. Spock. That's the alien from *Star Trek*. This is Dr. Spock, and he was a human, as in from the planet Earth. But he was the Mr. Spock of parenting.

I didn't know if it was the right thing to do or if it was horribly wrong and would subsequently result in your needing years and years of therapy, but here's my philosophy on raising children: I didn't know what the hell I was doing. Pretty early on into fatherhood, I gave up on trying to be a "good father" and instead settled for "as long as my children don't grow up and kill anybody, I should be okay."

I could've asked other parents for assistance, but here's the rub on taking advice from other people, parents included: even though I didn't have a clue about what I was doing, I'd have been damned if I'd let anybody else tell me how to raise my children. As far as I'm concerned, you're my children and my responsibility. I'm the one who's signing the check on all of your future decisions. With all due respect to Marcus Aurelius, what you do now does not echo in eternity, it echoes all the way back to my doorstep, and people will judge me because of it. So please don't murder anybody…unless they really deserve it.

Okay, maybe I should have consulted Dr. Spock or some other authority on parenting for some guidance, but I was always comforted by the fact that I had one heck of a copilot. Although I may have been clueless at times when it came to child rearing, your mother was not. She's an amazing human being. I've always known that her efforts would undo any harm I caused.

My plan was perfect, except for one thing: I was something of a germophobe. And by "something of a germophobe," I mean that I lived in utter fear of germs, to the point where the very thought that I was surrounded by tiny, microscopic bacteria was nearly debilitating to me. Don't believe me? I once waited fifteen minutes in a public restroom for someone to open the door because there were no paper towels and I didn't want to touch the door handle. And I'm not one bit ashamed to admit that. The best part of that story? I was in the bathroom, so I didn't have to worry about having to pee while I waited.

I've had nightmares about eating in restaurants where I feared the chefs didn't wash their hands. Personally, I wash my hands before and after I do anything that requires use of my ten digits. And not the cursory wash that most people do. No, I wait patiently for the water to reach a hot temperature and then—and only then—do I let the water wash away the soap.

And let's be perfectly clear on one thing here: my definition of "hot water" is not your definition of "hot water." The hot water that I subject my hands to would cause you third-degree burns. "Scalding" doesn't even begin to describe how hot the water must be for me to feel clean. However, this was all before I met either of you. Because after the addition of children into my life, I had to come to terms with one of life's truths: when you have children, you will never be clean again.

Peter, you're the perfect example of this truth. For most of your childhood, you had a runny nose. Do you know how many times your mother and I took you to the doctor? We had your allergist on speed dial. Our calls to him went something like this:

Ring. Ring.

"Dr. Hamid's office. How may I direct your call?"

"It's Peter's dad."

"There's an opening at three fifteen today."

"Thank you. Does Dr. Hamid want me to pick up his dry cleaning on my way?"

I didn't really pick up his dry cleaning, but I did have a closer relationship with Dr. Hamid than most devout Catholics have with their priests. Why? Again, because your nose never stopped running. Never. Your nose would have made Forrest Gump look like a sprinter.

Here is a list of the objects on which I witnessed you wipe your nose:

- The dog. Which one? Sadly, both.
- Your mother's wedding dress. She should have kept it under lock and key. And if you don't tell her, I won't either. She would murder you.
- My navy blue, special-label Zegna suit—both the pants and the jacket.
- My favorite purple Thomas Pink tie.

- My white Thomas Pink handkerchief (handkerchiefs that nice aren't meant to be used as…well, handkerchiefs).
- The Christmas tree.
- The couch.
- My leather chair.
- Your comforter.
- Annabelle's comforter.
- My comforter.
- The comforter in the guest bedroom, and please don't tell any of our guests. I like to think that we're a hospitable family.
- Your pillow.
- Annabelle's pillow.
- Your mother's pillow.
- My pillow.
- The microwave. (This was impressive to watch. I commend you.)
- The upholstery of every car we have ever owned.
- The neighbor's cat, and it's no wonder that he left us so many presents in our yard.

———————

Even though I'd devised a method to halt your crying, I had backed myself into a corner with regard to my germophobia. The thought of kissing you, especially the part of you that had come into contact with the floor, or any portion of a public restroom or playground, caused me severe anxiety.

Hammer finally met nail at your aunt Sarah's wedding. Kids, I may not have ever told you this, but I really don't like your uncle Ronald…Okay, fine, I've probably mentioned it several hundred times. But I have to give the guy credit; he saved your aunt from dying alone. Until Aunt Sarah met him, well, let's just say that everyone had her pegged as a cat lady. I love my sister, but every night before I go to bed, I pray that one of us was adopted. And I don't really care which one of us it was. I just don't want to be a member of her gene pool. And I especially don't appreciate it when she tells other people that I'm a member of her gene pool.

I kept my opinion of him to myself—meaning, I never told her how I felt, just everyone else in our family. In keeping with the same philosophy I employ on parenting, it's not my job in life to tell other people how to live their lives, even if they are doing everything wrong. No, I much prefer to sit idly by at the table near the bathroom and mock other people from afar. It's not that I'm cheering against them—no, I'm definitely not one for schaden-freude, save for limited exceptions. Regardless, I knew your aunt never would have listened to me even if I had shared my opinion with her. You can lay on the horn all you want, but some people just refuse to move right when they're driving ten miles below the speed limit in the fast lane.

Aunt Sarah and Uncle Ronald both drove slowly in the fast lane—literally and figuratively. They were a match made in heaven, provided that St. Peter occasionally makes a couple of mistakes at the pearly gates and lets the wrong people in—scary thought, but I'm hopeful that's how I'll eventually gain entrance one day.

At the time of Aunt Sarah's wedding, the "If I kiss it, it will make it better" strategy had been working marvelously. Peter, my relationship with you had evolved to the point where I could take you somewhere in public without having to whisper quietly to strangers that you were not my biological son—you were an unbelievably demanding child. Plus, you had finally learned to walk properly and had stopped falling after every third step, and your crying fits were few and far between. Huzzah! Your mother took notice of this change.

"You and Peter seem to be getting along pretty well these days," she said while we were getting dressed before the rehearsal dinner.

"What can I say? Maybe I am a good father after all."

"I've never said you were a bad father."

"Oh. But weren't you thinking it?"

"No, I think you're a great father."

"Well…" This was not the time to enlighten her about my fast-food style of parenting.

I won't bore you with the details of the ceremony, but be happy that you don't have any memory of it. It was an odd amalgamation of a number of faiths, and had representatives from each of these faiths been present to witness this unholy union, Aunt Sarah and Uncle Ronald would have found themselves in the midst of a holy war.

They held the reception in a large white tent at a public park with a man-made lake. I think we were supposed to pretend we were with Emerson and Thoreau on Brook Farm, but I couldn't immerse myself in that fiction. We were less than a mile away from a strip mall. We took our assigned seats, and I prepared myself for the vegan fare soon to come. Knowing that my sister couldn't be happy unless she deprived everyone of their dietary preferences, I had come prepared with granola bars, but not enough. As I read the menu, which included repetitive variations on tofu and weeds, my stomach began to grumble. "Feed me," it said.

"What's the soonest you can leave a wedding without it being considered rude?" I asked your mother.

"We just got here."

"I know, but still, humor me."

She didn't answer but instead shot me a look that told me all I needed to know: minimum time, a couple of hours. Crap damn it.

"Fine," I said, defeated. "Where's the bar? Wait…There is a bar, right?" *She wouldn't dare, would she?*

"Yes, there's a bar."

"What? A wheatgrass bar?"

"No. They have alcohol too."

"I don't believe you. Do they have beer at this bar?"

"Yes."

"It's mean for you to get my hopes up like that."

"They have beer. I promise."

"What's the catch?"

"There isn't a catch."

"C'mon…What's the catch?"

She paused for a moment. "It's gluten free."

"I knew there was a catch!"

"I promise you won't notice the difference."

"I'm sure I'll hate it."

A couple of hours and several courses of plants and imitation meat later, I was checking my wristwatch every two to three minutes, ready to depart at any second. Your mother sensed this and tried to comfort me.

"Let's wait until they cut the cake," she said. "Then we can go."

"Deal," I said. The gluten-free beer had softened my mood. Plus, the mention of a delicious treat had given me a second wind. Finally, there was something at this wedding that I could be thankful for. I left our table, skirted around the drunkards who were dancing to the tribal music Uncle Ronald had personally selected, and found the saddest thing I have ever seen in my life: the cake.

It wasn't a cake so much as a brown, depressed loaf of bread. It looked like what I imagine the surface of Mars looks like. Devoid of any moisture and incapable of supporting life forms of any kind. One of Aunt Sarah's friends joined me, a lanky fellow with wiry glasses, long hair, and a wide-toothed grin. While I privately hoped that someone would deposit the atrocity before me into the nearest Dumpster, he beamed over it with pride. I do not profess to be a master of perception, but I quickly surmised that this gentleman was the maker of the uncakelike substance.

"Doesn't it look great, man?" the lanky gentleman asked.

"Uh-huh," I replied. I retreated back to my seat, where your mother waited alone. "Where are the kids?"

"Dancing. Have they cut the cake yet?"

"Impossible. They'd need a chainsaw to cut that thing. But as soon as they do, let's go. If I stay here any longer, I'm liable to be abducted by the Peace Corps and taken to one of the '-stan' countries."

"If you are, make sure to send me a postcard."

Somehow, through some miracle, the lanky gentleman managed to find a knife sharp enough to cut through the meteorite cake, and at long last, guests started to file out. Finally, we could leave.

"Shall we?" I asked her, and she nodded. I tried to conceal my smile. "I'll find the kids."

I took one step toward the dance floor, a rectangular wooden floor that had been assembled on the grass, and that's when I heard your wail, Peter. I didn't wait for the crowd before me to part; instead, I started mercilessly pushing people out of my way until I found you lying in the middle of the dance floor surrounded by a group of wedding guests.

I saw your tear-filled eyes, and my heart ached, but I knew you were okay. You'd fallen in an area covered with beer, vomit, and remnants of wedding cake. I knelt down beside you, careful to distance myself from the puddle of undigested cake trickling our way. A second passed, and your mother appeared by my side.

"I want Daddy!" you screamed.

"She's right here," I answered, pointing to your mother. "Wait. What?"

"He said he wants you," your mother said, equally shocked and impressed.

"Yes?" I asked.

"Kiss it and make it better," you said, pointing to a tiny scrape on your elbow that was covered in beer and vomit.

Oh boy. Kids, I am an adult. A grown man. I have made many mistakes in my life, many of them attributable to the same flaw: lack of foresight. Had I known that I would be faced with a scrape on your elbow covered in beer and vomit and who knows what else, I would've reconsidered my parenting shortcut.

Aunt Sarah and Uncle Ronald joined the cluster of wedding guests standing over you. The DJ, if you want to call someone who plays tribal music a DJ, cut the music and you, Peter, became the center of attention, a no-no at weddings.

"What happened?" Aunt Sarah asked.

"I'll tell you what happened," I replied, desperately in need of a distraction. "You served these people undercooked plants! Now Peter's gone and slipped in their undigested mulch."

"You can't undercook a plant," she said.

"Exactly! Because it's not meat!"

"Why are you even still here? I'm surprised you didn't leave and go to the nearest drive-through."

I turned to your mother. "We could leave? This whole time, we could leave?"

"C'mon, Peter, let me help you up," Aunt Sarah said.

"No, I want Daddy to kiss it and make it better," you said, pointing to the tiny scrape — emphasis on "tiny."

"Well?" Sarah said. "Go on." She smiled wide. Your request may have been the best wedding present she received.

I thought about fleeing, running for my life and starting a new family across the country. And I could've done it too, but the odds that I would have met someone as patient (i.e., willing to put up with me) as your mother were slim to none. I closed my eyes, bent over, and kissed that which I would not classify as a wound.

I learned a valuable lesson that day. There are no shortcuts in life, and there are no shortcuts in parenting. Okay, I already knew that. I am not a fool, and I suspect that you know that too. No, the lesson I learned was whatever false truth you tell children, they will inevitably believe, remember, and make you regret telling them.

"Can we stop and get a six-pack of gluten-free beer?" I asked your mother on the way home. More importantly, I also learned that I like gluten-free beer. Don't tell anybody. I'm not ashamed to admit when I'm wrong, but I'll be damned if I'll share my being wrong with others.

4

IF YOU PUT A TOOTH UNDER YOUR PILLOW, A MAGICAL FAIRY WILL BRING YOU MONEY

Your mother's parents—notice how I refer to them—have always hated me. You might think, *That can't be true, can it?* Yes, children, it can. Really. Your grandmother once flat-out told me that I wasn't good enough for her daughter. I don't know if it was meant to inspire confidence in me, but it didn't. It did, however, inspire me to break your grandmother's favorite Waterford goblet one Thanksgiving. And then there was your grandfather's favorite tumbler the Christmas right after. Sorry, Mother- and Father-in-Law, I suppose I'm just a bit clumsy.

I knew they would disapprove when I asked your mother to marry me. The realization alone that I considered myself worthy enough for your mother's hand probably took two years off your grandmother's life. Of course I loved your mother, which is why I proposed, but upsetting your grandparents was an added treat. Your mother doesn't know this, but I actually listened in on the phone call when she told her parents that we were getting married. She went to the kitchen to make the call, and I picked up the phone in the bedroom to eavesdrop.

"Mom, guess what?" your mother said. "We're getting married. He asked me to marry him and I said yes!" God bless her, she was so excited.

"He what?!? Oh, honey. No. No. No. No. No. No. No. No. No. No. No. No. No. No. No. No. No." Okay, fine, she didn't really say "no" that many times. It was only five "no"s. But still, five? That's a lot. And it didn't stop there.

"But, Mom, I love him."

"*Him?*" That's how she always referred to me. "*Him.*" If she had ever taken the time to send me a birthday card, I guarantee you it would've been addressed to "*him.*"

And then, as was customary, your grandfather joined the conversation.

"What's happening?" he asked.

"She's going to marry *him.*"

"Jesus. *Him?*"

"Honey," her mother said, her tone softened. "Did we do something to upset you?"

"No, Mother, why would you say that?"

"I don't know. I would just hate to think that you're doing this to get back at us, although I don't know what we possibly could have done. We loved you, gave you everything you ever wanted, paid for your schooling, and…and…and…I don't know."

"If there's something we did, please, tell us!" your grandfather added.

"You didn't do anything. I love him."

"*Him?*" your grandmother asked.

"Yes, *him*. Stop calling him that."

Your mother always stood up for me. And she never spoke ill of her parents to me. Your mother always says, "If you don't have anything nice to say, then don't say anything at all." Yeah, well, here's what is unofficially written on my family crest: "If you don't have anything nice to say, then tell the person to their face." I've amended that and taken a less extreme approach: "If you don't have anything nice to say, then say mean things behind people's backs." In keeping with this mantra, I'll say this: I really don't care for your grandmother or your grandfather. But that's okay, because the feeling is mutual. I put them in my special category of family members whom I love because I have to.

I didn't see a lot of your grandparents when you were growing up. Although I didn't visit them often, you two did. I had an unspoken agreement with them. I wouldn't step foot in their house if they wouldn't step foot in mine. However, there were times when I had to breach this agreement.

Like the time your grandmother was hospitalized with an illness she came down with while visiting "that little third-world country in the Pacific." She was referring to Hawaii when she said that, and I had my doubts regarding the severity of her condition. We visited her in the hospital, and I have to be honest with you, I have never seen a person in the hospital look so healthy. If she'd ditched the hospital gown and put on an evening gown, she could have walked down a red carpet at the Academy Awards.

We stayed in your grandparents' home that weekend. Peter, you were just a baby, and Annabelle, you were in first grade at the time and you were about to lose your first tooth. Every time I glanced over at you, you were wiggling it. You were so excited. You tried to remove the loose tooth by tying one end of floss to it and attaching the other end to a door handle, then slamming the door shut. Despite numerous attempts, it never worked. I was beginning to think that you were going to spend the rest of your life with one loose tooth.

Finally, after one unsettling sneeze, the tooth came flying out, along with your saliva. You looked like something out of a horror movie, covered in snot and blood and missing a tooth. Like any good father who wished to shoo away future unwelcome suitors, I took a picture and saved it. Just remember, I have that photo in my arsenal—it's in a safety-deposit box at my bank and I'll never make you a cosigner on the account.

Despite your Hitchcock-esque look, Annabelle, you didn't cry. The tooth came out and you were thrilled when you put it under your pillow that night. Honestly, I would have given you twenty dollars right there on the spot if you had just thrown the thing away. It was hideous. After you went to sleep, your mother and I had the same conversation we always had when it came to any make-believe children's lore.

"Can't we just tell her that there is no tooth fairy?" I asked. "I don't see the big deal."

"The big deal is that we'll be the only parents who don't give our child money when she loses a tooth. I want our children to have a normal childhood."

"Well, then they should probably spend less time with your parents." Your mother, although very close with her parents, was willing to acknowledge their eccentricities.

"We can't tell her. We have to take the tooth and put money under her pillow."

"Okay, fine. How much do we put?"

"I have an idea," your grandfather said. Your mother and I were having this conversation in private, but I had forgotten that I was behind enemy lines, where free speech and the right to privacy did not exist.

"About?" I asked with narrowed eyes. There was a brief period in my life where I was young and impressionable, and this naivety led me to try to impress your mother's parents. But I had since learned from this mistake, and now I had settled into a different strategy: if they wanted a dumb son-in-law, then a dumb son-in-law they would have. Because they treated me like an idiot, I became an idiot—now that I've written it down, yes, it was immature.

"The tooth fairy," your grandfather answered.

"Oh, we're just going to put some Monopoly money under her pillow and tell her it's from the Dominican Republic. That way she'll think it's special."

"Is he…?" your grandfather asked, looking to your mother.

"Think about it," I said. "It could be a good opportunity for Annabelle to learn about other cultures and international business."

"No, he's not serious," your mother answered. "But we can handle it, Daddy."

"Okay, I don't want to meddle," he said.

"You're not," your mother said. Yes, he was and he did. That's all he wanted! Why couldn't she see that? Well, far be it from me to burst her bubble.

Your grandfather left us alone, for the time being, and your mother immediately turned to me. "You don't really want to give her Monopoly money, do you?" she asked.

"Honey, I think your parents' disdain for me is beginning to rub off on you. Of course we're not going to give her Monopoly money. I just don't like it when your dad tries to interfere in our parenting."

Now, kids, your grandparents weren't overtly horrible people; they just chipped away at you slowly until you went crazy and divorced their daughter—at least that's what I thought their plan was, but I wouldn't let them succeed. However, I wasn't dealing with amateurs. They knew which buttons to push.

Annabelle, you went to bed that night in one of the many bedrooms in your grandparents' home with your tooth placed carefully beneath your silk pillowcase. Your mother and I were staying in a room down the hall, and after some discussion, we decided that we would wake up before you in the morning and place a nice, crisp five-dollar bill under your pillow. We figured the tooth fairy paid a premium for the first tooth that you lost.

We awoke the next morning eager to surprise you on this momentous occasion. After sneaking into your room, I carefully lifted your head and started to place the five-dollar bill under your pillow, but to my horror, your tooth was already gone and it had been replaced with a silver coin.

"What is that?" I asked your mother, a little too loudly.

You woke, turned over, and checked under your pillow. I envied the way you children could go from a moment of complete slumber to wide awake without five cups of coffee in between. You held the coin in your hands and smiled, revealing the gap in your teeth. Anger would come later; at the time, I was just happy to see you so happy.

"What the crap! Grandpa strikes again!" I exclaimed. I said anger would come later; I didn't say much later. Your mother and I were back in our bedroom rehashing the impromptu visit from the tooth fairy. "What kind of coin was that anyway?"

"A 1926 Buffalo nickel issued in San Francisco in extra-fine condition," your grandfather answered. "That's the best condition for a circulated coin. It's from my personal collection." He was standing in the doorway of our bedroom. It was impossible to have a private conversation in that house. Seriously, there must have been some secret passages I wasn't aware of. "I know you two wanted to give her something special from you," he continued, "but it's what your grandmother would have wanted."

"What do you mean 'would have wanted'? She's not dead, is she?" I asked, trying my hardest not to sound hopeful.

"Oh, did I use the past tense? Sorry, no. I spoke to her this morning and she's feeling much better." For the record, I know I said that your grandmother was suffering from some illness, but come to think of it, I think she was in the hospital for "an elective procedure" (i.e., plastic surgery).

"Daddy, could we have a moment please?" your mother asked.

"Oh dear, I'm sorry," your grandfather said. "I hope I haven't upset you." And with that terse apology, he left us in peace, for the time being.

"So, let me ask you this," I said. "How much does a 1926 Buffalo nickel issued in San Francisco in extra-fine condition even cost?"

"I have no idea," your mother said.

"Something tells me it's a hell of a lot more than five dollars, even when the five-dollar bill is in mint condition. Honey, I know you love your parents, but there's a reason that the general populace doesn't give their children rare coins when they lose their teeth. If word got out that the tooth fairy was handing out expensive coins, then nobody in this world would have any teeth. I for one would rather rip my own teeth out than go to work on Monday."

Kids, the word you're looking for is "numismatics." And yes, I had to Google it. You grandfather was obsessed with it. Apparently earning lots of money wasn't enough for him; he had to collect it too.

Well, two can play at that game.

The Wednesday after we returned home, Annabelle, you took your Buffalo nickel to school for show-and-tell. All of the children in your class were impressed by the gift you received from the tooth fairy. Needless to say, the other parents hated me. I tried to explain that it hadn't been my fault, that your grandfather was to blame for usurping me, but they wouldn't let me defend myself. "Get control of your tooth fairy," one father told me. "What's next? You going to put a Bugatti under her pillow?"

For several weeks, you were the star of your class. I was happy for you, but at the same time, I couldn't move past the bitterness I felt after being shown up by your grandfather, and I was afraid that the next time the tooth fairy visited you, you would be disappointed by the offering you received. Unfortunately, I couldn't afford to trade rare currency for teeth. Yes, apparently, two could not play at that game, because that game required a steeper ante than I was willing to pay. After much thought, I decided upon an alternative option. They say necessity is the mother of invention; well, necessity is also the mother of most felonies, misdemeanors, and even a few citations.

I'll ask you not to repeat what happens in the rest of the story as, well, it's not strictly legal. And by "not strictly legal," I mean it is most certainly, definitely, and unequivocally illegal. If asked questions regarding these events, I would be forced to take the nickel. That's a really cool way I learned to say "Fifth Amendment." Thank you, Michael Connelly.

I decided that if I couldn't afford to assume the life of a wealthy numismatist to pay for your teeth, I could fake it. It started with a blank piece of white printer paper. I was working on something at the office when a paper got jammed in my printer. After several grueling minutes and numerous curses, I managed to dislodge the paper from deep within the printer. I held the crumpled eight-and-a-half-by-eleven sheet in my hand. It felt almost like currency to the touch.

While holding that piece of paper between my thumb and forefinger, I realized that I didn't have to purchase rare money—I could make it. The deed started the same way any criminal act commences: with a lie. I told myself that I wouldn't actually go through with it, that I would just see if it was possible. But once I started, there was no turning back. I just so desperately wanted to witness again that moment of joy I had seen on your face when you found the Buffalo nickel.

That night I did several sketchy Internet searches on the ins and outs of how to counterfeit money, and I made sure to delete my browser history when I finished. All of my research led me to one dissatisfying conclusion: I didn't have the means to counterfeit money. I had enough information to rob Fort Knox—I had seen *Goldfinger* numerous times—but not the paper, machinery, or plates needed to pull off this feat. I hadn't learned much about counterfeiting money, but I had learned enough to know that I was in over my head.

But I wasn't deterred. After all, I wasn't trying to fool the United States Treasury Department, just my seven-year-old daughter. I set up shop in the garage with my computer, my HP Deskjet printer, and several reams of paper. Between the money I spent on supplies—color ink cartridges and paper—and the hours I spent alone in the garage, I could have bought you a rare bill, but I was determined to make it myself. After much research, I settled on a 1928E blue-seal silver-certificate one-dollar bill. There's nothing particularly unique about it, except that it's rare, and in 1928 bills were reduced to their current relatively diminutive size. Also, these particular bills, all the ones from 1928 to 1934 in fact, have a nickname: "funnybacks." The nickname comes from the unique design on the back of the bill, which is noticeably different from the present design. And I thought the moniker was rather fitting, considering that I was making funny money.

After going through most of my paper in an effort to create a passable fake, I discovered that although I could create a bill with the same size and look as a funnyback, I couldn't create one with the same feel as a one-dollar bill. I did several blind tests, and each time I was easily able to determine which bill was fake. The paper just wasn't good enough. I had to use the real thing. I was halfway there—I had the design; I just needed the right paper.

I scoured all of the office supply stores near our home, but there was no paper that could pass for currency. Finally, I realized that I was looking in the wrong places. I had the perfect paper with me the whole time. I felt foolish looking all over town when all I needed was one of the bills in my wallet. I took a one-dollar bill and soaked it in a degreasing liquid. Then, using a toothbrush, I slowly scrubbed all of the ink off it, careful not to cause a tear. Next, I used your mother's hair dryer to dry the bill. After all of that, I had a blank note. At long last, using my ink-jet, I printed out the design

I had created for the 1928E blue-seal silver-certificate one-dollar bill. Voilà! I had made my first counterfeit dollar.

I kept the fake bill in my wallet until I would need it. I figured the exposure to other currency would help give the bill the appearance of being real. For the next several weeks, every time I drove past a police cruiser, a nervous chill went down my spine. I knew that there was no way that the cops had any idea what I was up to in my free time, but I was convinced they would be able to see the guilt on my face. I was no longer a suburban dad. I was a criminal, a threat to the establishment of justice and the rule of law.

At last, the day came for me to part ways with my masterpiece. Another ill-fated sneeze, and you lost another tooth. This time I was ready. You went to bed that night, and I snuck into your room and placed my manufactured bill under your pillow. The next morning, you mother and I awoke to your squeals of joy. She and I were still in bed, and you raced down the hallway and flew into our bedroom.

"Look what the tooth fairy brought me!" Annabelle exclaimed. "A dollar bill."

"Here, let me see," I said.

You took one giant leap and landed on our bed, then crawled up until you were between your mother and me.

"This isn't just any dollar bill," I said. "Look at the year on it. What does it say?"

"Nineteen twenty-eight," Annabelle said.

"And check out the back. Here, take a look at this dollar and compare." I grabbed a dollar bill from my wallet on the nightstand and handed it to you. "Pretty cool, huh?"

"Very cool," your mother answered.

Oh boy.

"Sure is some tooth fairy we have," your mother said. We were in the kitchen, making breakfast. The coffee couldn't brew fast enough. I considered bringing her in on my crime, but I didn't want to make her an accessory after the fact. Plus, I couldn't be sure that she would understand why I'd done it. Heck, I wasn't even sure why I'd done it. I just kind of…did it. But I knew one thing: my tooth fairy couldn't compete with your grandfather's. Here's a list of the reasons that I determined the tooth fairy could no longer distribute rare coins under your pillow:

- I'm not made of money, and rare money at that.

More than anything, my pride was to blame. It defeated me. I suppose I could have given you normal currency as your tooth fairy money — you certainly wouldn't have noticed the difference — but I couldn't stomach the idea of your grandfather's offering trumping my contribution. I had to match the rarity of his coin — at least I thought I had to.

And I was thrilled after my counterfeit money worked. You took your new bill to school, and no one was the wiser about it. Sure, it didn't look perfect, but your teacher and the other kids were impressed — even more impressed than when they saw your Buffalo nickel. Naturally, the other parents hated me again, but this time around, I could stomach it. I had provided for my daughter in the same manner as her grandparents had.

Yes, life was good. That is, until I came home one Thursday expecting everything to be normal, but it wasn't. I entered through the back door, placed my briefcase down, then headed to the kitchen to see what your mother was making for dinner, as I always do. Annabelle, you and your mother were waiting for me. Call it intuition, but I could tell that something was wrong. There was a sense of excitement in the air, and it scared me.

"What's everyone in such a good mood about?" I asked.

"My father just called," your mother said. "My mom's feeling better and they want us to come visit for the weekend."

"Grandpa wants to see the dollar the tooth fairy brought," Annabelle said.

Crap.

"Annabelle, sweetie," I said, "why don't you go pack for your trip? I need to speak to your mother for a moment." You scurried off to your room, and I turned to your mother. "This trip…"

"Yes?" your mother asked.

"It may not be such a good idea."

"Why wouldn't it be a good idea? My parents love seeing the kids. And you know my father; he can't wait to see that bill. He loves old money." Kids, he loves new money too — he just loves money, more than he loves people.

"So you're definitely going this weekend?"

"Yes."

"This weekend."

"Yes, this weekend."

"It can't wait?"

"My mother really wants to spend some time with the kids."

"Oh." I had to do something. If your grandfather got even a whiff of that bill, he would know it was fake and my life would be ruined. Kids, as the saying goes, drastic times call for drastic measures. "Well, I'm coming too."

"You never come with us. You want to come?"

"What do you mean? I always go to your parents' house."

"You do not. You always have to work the weekends when the kids and I go."

"What? Am I not invited or something? You don't want me to go?"

"I should probably call and ask."

"Really?"

"No, of course not. My parents won't mind."

"Good. Then I'm coming." I headed for the bedroom to start packing for what could turn out to be the most horrific weekend of my married life, but I turned back to your mother. "Still…"

"Don't worry. I'll call."

———————————

I was worried. Sure, my counterfeit bill had worked on my seven-year-old daughter, but it most certainly would not fool her grandfather. In order to avoid embarrassment, I had to become the man your mother's parents had always feared me to be. A deviant. I had to steal from your grandfather. I needed to find the exact same bill in his collection and replace it with the one the tooth fairy had given Annabelle.

We arrived at your grandparents' late Friday night. I made sure of that by taking numerous detours along the way to their house. By the time we pulled into the driveway, you two and your grandparents were already asleep. Your mother and I carried you into the house and tucked you into bed.

I waited until your mother fell asleep, and then I quietly snuck into your grandfather's study, where he kept his rare coin collection. His private collection was rather extensive, and I looked at bill after bill in his binders — literally, pages and pages of rare coins and bills — studying each item with his magnifying glass, but it wasn't there. To my dismay — and horror — he didn't have a 1928E blue-seal one-dollar bill in his collection. No wonder he was so anxious to see Annabelle's.

The next morning I wasn't prepared to face your grandparents. This was going to be the moment they had waited for my entire marriage. Your grandparents, your mother, and I were in the living room, enjoying coffee and croissants, when you, Annabelle, charged in. It would have been nice of you to sleep in that morning. I would have been able to finish my croissant.

"Good morning, sweetie," your mother said.

"So, let me see this bill," your grandfather said.

Annabelle, you ran back to your bedroom and quickly returned with the bill. You handed it to your grandfather, and he put on his reading glasses and studied it carefully. I held my breath as I waited to hear his reaction.

"Well? How did the tooth fairy do?" your grandmother asked.

"Impressive. I've never seen one in this good condition. You should be very proud, Annabelle."

I couldn't believe it. How? I didn't know, but somehow it had worked. My fake bill had worked. I took a big bite of my croissant, then washed it down with coffee. I didn't have to worry about your grandparents' team of attorneys.

And then something truly amazing happened, something that had never happened to me before. Your grandfather stood up out of his chair, walked over to me, and placed his hand on my shoulder. I didn't know what to think. Maybe I had made him proud. Maybe I was a master counterfeiter after all.

———————————

I could call myself your father again, because I was able to provide for you. I had lived up to your grandparents' expectations — for once. Seriously, that may have been the only time. I went back to the bedroom, still elated by what had happened, and your mother joined me. But I wasn't meant for a life of crime. As happy as I was that my bill had tricked your grandfather, I couldn't live with my secret any longer. I had to come clean. I had to tell your mother what I had done.

"Is it okay if I shower before you?" she asked.

"Yeah, sure," I said. "Honey, I need to tell you something. This may shock you, but I—"

"You counterfeited our daughter's tooth fairy money."

"Shhh! Honey, keep your voice down! The fuzz might be listening in."

"My parents?"

"No. Not them. Although I wouldn't be surprised if they bugged our room, but I meant the fuzz. You know, the men in bobby hats."

"The police?"

"Don't even say that word! If you say it, then they'll appear. Like Beetlejuice."

"They will not appear."

"Will too. They're probably already here." I went to the window and looked out. All looked normal on the residential street. I closed the blinds just to be safe. "And how did you know that I…made some funny money?"

"You weren't exactly sly about it."

"Reasonable minds can differ on that. C'mon, really, how did you know?"

"The laundry."

"The laundry?"

"Yes, I put two and two together. Lately, your undershirts have had ink stains all over them. Then you show up with a 1928E silver-certificate one-dollar bill?"

I took a step closer to her. "Honey…Are you a cop?"

"What? No."

"FBI?"

"No."

"Secret Service?"

"No, no, no. None of that."

"You would tell me, right? If you were?"

"Yes, right after I arrested you."

"Am I under arrest?"

"No."

"Oh thank God. So, that's it? Ink stains on undershirts?"

"That and my father has been collecting rare bills and coins all my life. I know how to spot a fake. Gold, coins, bills, Rolexes, I can spot a fake a mile away."

"Apparently your father can't."

"No, he definitely can, which is why I replaced your bill with the real thing before Annabelle took it in for show-and-tell and brought it here."

"You replaced it?"

"Yes."

"Why?"

"To save Annabelle the embarrassment and you the stress. You think I'm going to let my daughter bring counterfeit money to show-and-tell? She would never live that down. The other parents would have had a field day. Plus, I knew you would tell me eventually. You've been tossing and turning in your sleep ever since the tooth fairy visited her."

"Oh…I guess it was a bit much for me to bear. Thanks. How much did that bill set us back?"

"Believe me, you don't want to know." She stepped closer to me and gently touched my face. "You don't need to worry about impressing our daughter. She'll be happy with anything the tooth fairy or you give her. And so will I. You know that, right?"

"I do. I guess your parents just got in my head."

"Well, get them out of your head. And no more breaking the law, okay?"

"Okay."

"Good. So, can I take my shower now?"

"Sure." She headed to the bathroom, but I stopped her. "Wait. As long as I'm confessing, there's something I need to tell you about your engagement ring."

"What? No…You wouldn't. You didn't."

"Just kidding."

———————

Your mother was right. Annabelle, the next week you found a rock in our yard that was shaped just like a Christmas tree. You took it to show-and-tell, and the other children in your class loved it, even more than the Buffalo nickel and the bill your mother purchased. And then it hit me: I committed a felony trying to please you when I could have just gone into the front yard and found an oddly shaped rock.

It was a sobering realization. And the other parents still hated me. A few accused me of carving out that rock. There was no way I could please them, but that didn't matter because you were happy. That's all that mattered to me.

5

THERE IS A BUNNY WHO BRINGS YOU PRESENTS ON THE DAY JESUS ROSE FROM THE DEAD

Annabelle, Easter Sunday when you were ten years old was the day that I first knew you were my daughter. Before that day, I was absolutely convinced that your mother had cheated on me because you were way too beautiful to be my descendant. For that reason, your birth was truly a bittersweet moment for me — also, I was convinced that I would die penniless after raising a girl. I suppose I could have paid for a DNA test, but I had to start saving for your wedding.

We were scheduled to attend the Fairchilds' fourth annual Easter egg hunt, and that morning your mother and I had the same fight we had every Easter. She wanted me to dress like I had been assaulted by a group of kindergartners with a pack of highlighters, and I wanted to wear all black in protest of the Fairchilds.

Children, let me tell you something about Prescott and Gwenyth Fairchild. They suck. Yes, they pay their taxes, attend church every Sunday, and most importantly host an Easter egg hunt so that I don't have to, but seriously, they suck. You know those pictures of families that come with new picture frames? That's the Fairchilds.

They're too perfect to be real. It's all an act. They pretend to be supportive friends, but they're not.

Gwenyth Fairchild is one of your mother's closest friends. And you would think that would make her a good person, because generally speaking, your mother is a great judge of character, but in this instance, that isn't the case. Why? Because Prescott and Gwenyth are the king and queen of one-upmanship. In Gwenyth's mind, she's Batman and your mother is Robin. Your mother will always be the underappreciated, overworked sidekick who never gets her own spinoff series. It's nananananana, Batman. Not Robin. Any time your mother and I acquired something in life, they had to go out and get something better.

Don't believe me? Check this out: Your mother married me. Gwenyth married Prescott—he's more attractive than I am and makes more money than I do. No, I'm not ashamed to admit that, but I will kill any man, woman, or child who says that I'm not funnier—some things we don't joke about. Unconvinced? I'm just getting started. Your mother and I bought our first luxury sedan; the very next week, Gwenyth and Prescott bought two. Your mother and I bought a house; Gwenyth and Prescott bought a bigger house—an estate really. Your mother started doing yoga; Gwenyth started doing hot yoga. I ran (i.e., walked) a 5K; Prescott ran a marathon two months later—I'm still not sure how he trained that quickly. Your mother and I adopted a dog, Rover—they don't acknowledge Steve's existence. Gwenyth and Prescott purchased an AKC-registered, pedigreed dog and a cat. Gwenyth would have gotten two dogs, but I think that would have made Prescott jealous—he couldn't handle two other creatures following her every command.

A brief detour. Their cat, Annapurna, is my favorite creature on this planet because she's the only creature on this planet that detests Prescott and Gwenyth with more passion than I do. Every time I go to the Fairchild estate, I bring her treats. Prescott and Gwenyth swear she's the only cat in this world that can't purr, but it isn't true. She always purrs for me. They thought she went missing for a week, but in truth, I brought her home with us to keep me company while you kids were away at camp. I helped the Fairchilds put up signs around their neighborhood to try to find her. There was even a reward, which I planned on collecting. Your mother wasn't amused, but she did enjoy having another female in the house.

And finally, most impressive of all among these efforts in one-upmanship: we had you two children, then—and frankly, I don't know how she pulled it off—Gwenyth had the triplets.

I would have bet my life that we had her beat when we had you two because Gwenyth is the single most selfish person on this or any other planet. The only thing she hates more than not being able to spend money on herself is spending the money that she would otherwise spend on herself on someone else, even her own children, and especially Prescott.

Naturally, it irked me every time the Fairchilds one-upped your mother and me—save for when they adopted Annapurna, of course. But then she had the triplets, and something truly amazing dawned upon me. I owned the Fairchilds. I'd been a bit daft not to come to this conclusion sooner—I guess I'd been too bogged down in the competition to see the truth emerging—but yeah, I owned them. The Fairchilds were my bitch. I could have convinced them to buy anything I wanted them to.

A wise man once told me that if you know a person's insecurities, you can predict their every move. That wise man was my cousin's husband, and it's a shame that he lives far away, because he's one of the few people in my family whom I actually enjoy spending time with—and not surprisingly, he's not a blood relative. This maxim allowed me to reign over the Fairchilds.

Annabelle, I heard you scoff as you read that, but are ya ready to be proud of your dear ol' dad?

I present to you my life's crowning achievement—besides you two…obviously. No, but seriously, this is probably my life's crowning achievement; don't be offended. Here is a list of the things I manipulated the Fairchilds into buying:

- Time-share in Cabo San Lucas. Your mother and I went there one year and then every year after that we stayed at the Fairchilds' time-share because they "couldn't possibly use the space." Why they bought into a six-thousand-square-foot beachfront property with maid quarters I'll never understand, but I didn't protest.

- A sixty-inch plasma television. I bought a fifty-eight-inch plasma television and Prescott went out and bought the sixty-inch the next day. I returned the fifty-eight-inch the day after and told him that it was a lemon and thereafter "never got around to buying another one." Do you know how many football games I watched on Prescott's sixty-inch TV?

- The 911 Turbo Porsche. This one was especially difficult to pull off because there was no way in hell that I was going to buy a brand-new Porsche. I had to make the guy at the dealership my accomplice. He was hesitant at first, but I finally made him an offer that he couldn't refuse. I said, "I bet you that I have a friend so insecure that if he thinks I walked in here and bought a brand-new Porsche, he'll come in the next day and buy one too." I was right, and the guy gave me a discount on the next car I bought—I also told him that Prescott would pay closer to the sticker price than any customer he'd had within the last year, which he did. So I "bought" the Porsche, then "traded it in" days later for a family SUV. Mission accomplished. It wasn't hard to guilt Prescott into letting me take his fully loaded Porsche for a spin every once in a while. And hell no, I didn't feel bad for him. He got a freaking Porsche out of it! If anything, Prescott should have thanked me, because I can guarantee you this: without me, there is no way that Gwenyth would have ever let him buy a sports car.

- The speedboat. After the Porsche incident, I started making friends at all of the local dealerships in town, and so help me God, if somebody would have let me borrow a plane, I promise you that we would have been flying private on all our joint family vacations.

And before you tell me what a horrible family friend I am, here's a list of all of the cool stuff you two got to play with at the Fairchilds' house because of your crazy, manipulative father:

- The epic two-story tree house. Ask any contractor and they'll tell you, "Measure twice, cut once." Okay, that's all fine and good, but here's my philosophy: hire some neighborhood kid to build a half-assed tree house and then watch as your wife's best friend's husband struggles to build one of the best tree houses in the world because "He did it. Why can't you?"

- The go-karts. Peter, do you remember when I told you that I went to a junkyard and bought a crappy go-kart that didn't work and then "Uncle Prescott" went out and bought two new go-karts? I know what you're thinking: "Yes, Dad, I do, but what ever happened to the crappy go-kart?" Yeah, well, I went to a junkyard, but I never bought a go-kart. I went inside and spoke to the owner for a while then used the bathroom and left. I just needed you to tell Prescott that I went to a junkyard. So thank you. Yes, you were a pawn…a pawn who got to ride in a brand-new stinkin' go-kart.

- The four-wheelers. The junkyard. Again.

- The dirt bikes. The junkyard. By that point, the owner thought I was crazy. I made the mistake of telling him why I was visiting him so often and then I had to give him a hundred bucks to keep him quiet. Remember that. Your father was the one who was really taken advantage of in all of this.

Another benefit to my manipulating the Fairchilds, though not one that I particularly intended, was that our family pictures started to look a lot more awesome. Your mother was pleased.

Sadly, not all of my cunning schemes were a success. Here's a list of my failed attempts:

- Cookies from Gwenyth. I tried to get Gwenyth to bake me cookies, but I should have known better as there are few things she loathes more than empty carbohydrates. Kids, her blood sugar isn't just low; her blood doesn't have sugar. Instead, she made some type of kale monstrosity that I had to eat. On a positive note, I forced down a couple of those cookies before my first colonoscopy and the doctor said he was impressed—it's really difficult to find a silver lining when somebody's sticking something up your butt, but with Gwenyth's help, I managed to. Prescott didn't see the humor in that one.

- The Atkins Diet. I thought it would be funny to tell Gwenyth that your mother and I were on the Atkins Diet. We weren't. It was fun seeing Prescott suffer as he watched me inhale slice after slice of thin-crust pepperoni pizza with extra sauce. The plan worked beautifully until Gwenyth started asking your mother about it; then guess who had to go on the Atkins Diet? Yours truly. I lost ten pounds.

- The juice cleanse. I convinced Gwenyth that my michelada—that's a Bloody Mary with beer instead of vodka—was tomato kale juice. Your mother found out and I had to endure ten straight days of juice. The worst part was you kids didn't have to endure it with me. Twenty minutes into the cleanse, I thought I might die. By day ten, I was frail. Weak. And your mother could tell. She took me to an all-you-can-eat barbecue joint, where I consumed ten days' worth of meat. I lost twenty-seven pounds in ten days on the cleanse and then nearly ate that same amount at the buffet.

At some point, I realized that there was no way I would ever convince your mother not to spend time with her best friend, so for my own mental well-being, I decided to embrace the constant one-upmanship. There are some people in this world who cannot find happiness unless they measure themselves against others. I freed myself from that constraint with the comfort of a Porsche, go-karts, and a time-share in Cabo San Lucas.

Annabelle, had there been any doubt that you were my biological child, the events that unfolded at the Fairchilds' fourth annual Easter egg hunt quashed it. It was no coincidence that the Fairchilds were hosting the Easter egg hunt; I was actually the impetus for that. One of my diabolical plans backfired. Foreseeing that I would have to attend at least ten straight years of Easter egg hunts—which is enough to make a single man consider having a vasectomy—I decided to host an Easter egg hunt myself. It was a kamikaze mission. I applied one of my philosophies on life: If you do something poorly, no one will ever ask you to do that something again. I made the mistake of calculating the tip quickly in front of your mother on one of our first dates. Every time we go out with large groups of people, guess who gets stuck with everybody's credit cards? I fell in the yard once and hit my head, then tried to convince her I forgot math…She didn't buy it. I wanted to host a lackluster Easter egg hunt in the hopes that I would never have to host one again.

But I went a little overboard. I hosted quite possibly the world's worst Easter egg hunt. People still give me grief over it. Your mother offered to help, but I told her that it was *my gift to her*. That I would *do all of the work*. She regrets trusting me.

How did I ruin Easter? Well, for starters, I hid the eggs in one of two places: in the open where every child could see them, thus resulting in numerous disputes as to ownership, or in impossible-to-reach places—atop trees, the roof, the highest shelves in the garage—thus resulting in numerous disputes over whether parents could assist children with the hunt.

I also provided a couple of unsolicited hints to children: "I think there might be an egg in the fridge, and whoever finds it gets another hint if they bring me a beer."

Johnny Sampson's mother's discovery of a beer bottle in her son's Easter basket was probably all the damage I needed to ensure my plan prevailed, but I didn't stop there. I also fixed the piñata. It was a pastel-colored piñata molded in the shape of an egg that looked like it had come from the dinosaur that ate all of the other dinosaurs—at least it was festive. I told everyone that I bought it for twenty bucks from some random college kids selling piñatas on the side of the road, but that was a lie. I made it myself, and it was indestructible. Most piñatas are made with papier-mâché, using old newspaper or some form of cardboard. They're easy to destroy. A grown adult can take one out with only a few swings of a Wiffle bat.

Not this one. It was made from synthetic rubber. It would've taken Babe Ruth nine innings to destroy this thing. The Babe would've had a better chance of launching the damn thing into outer space and landing it on the moon than breaking it open. The rubber egg was chock full of candy that no one would ever see.

I had to bite down on my cheeks to keep from laughing as I watched child after child smack the piñata with no result. It wasn't long before I could taste the blood in my mouth. Nobody stood a chance. I'd made sure to charge the camcorder the night before.

By the end of the party, I heard a constant refrain from every parent there: "You are never allowed to host a party again."

Your mother led the chorus. "Never again," she said to me after everyone had left.

"Honey, don't say that," I said. "It's hurtful. You know how much I love planning parties. It's not my fault those college kids sold me a trick piñata."

My cover story didn't last long. A couple of hours after the party, your mother found me in the garage devouring Easter candy and watching the piñata reel. I couldn't help but chuckle as I watched Prescott swing and swing and swing with no result. I like to think he was imagining Gwenyth's face every time he squared up.

"You planned this," she said.

"Just what are you accusing me of?"

"You planned this whole catastrophe, didn't you?"

"Yeah, I planned this. I purposefully hid the eggs in hard-to-find places or out in the open where everybody could see them. I'm sorry I didn't realize there were rules governing where to hide and not to hide Easter eggs. And as for the piñata, well…" I was dead to rights. "It was pretty ingenious, right?"

We laughed all night watching the videos of the parents trying to break open that piñata. I can't tell you how many times your mother and I watched that video over the years. Every time she was upset about something—usually involving one of the parents who was present—it always cheered her up. They did eventually bust it open of course. One of the fathers had to use his house keys and a pocketknife while another father held it down.

I'm lucky your mother didn't divorce me after that, but that's one of the reasons I fell in love with her in the first place. No matter how upset she is, she can always laugh about something. She has a great sense of humor. I mean, she'd have to, right? Otherwise how else would she be able to put up with me? Plus, I absolved her of any of the blame by telling the other parents she had nothing to do with the party preparation. Her reputation was still intact; mine wasn't. Even so, after she saw how much time and planning went into organizing a bad Easter party, she had no interest in hosting a good one. My plan may have been exposed, but she was willing to concede that the end result—that we would never be hosting a holiday party again—was a blessing in disguise. It's a lot easier to bring a casserole to someone's house than it is to host the Fairchilds. True story: Gwenyth didn't even know what a casserole was before she met me. You see, she doesn't eat casseroles; she eats quiche. The only time I've seen her eat mayonnaise was on a chicken salad sandwich with alfalfa sprouts. She's the only person I know who could walk into a barbecue restaurant and emerge without a single speck of sauce on any of her garments. Remember, she doesn't wear clothes; she wears "garments." As much as I despise the woman, she fascinates me. To paraphrase my only fictional hero, she belongs in a museum. She's Marie Antoinette, but after the guillotine; there is no head on those shoulders.

My epic failure led to Prescott and Gwenyth's becoming the regular hosts of the Easter egg hunt. They decided to one-up me and show everyone the proper way to host an Easter party. Realistically, they should have been hosting the damn thing from the get-go. There's something to be said about the fact that they had three children in the same grade. If you ask me they should have had to pay a tax for any event hosted by another family, but I didn't make a habit of complaining because Prescott and Gwenyth were subsidizing my lavish lifestyle. I was already on the payroll. Honestly, I probably cost them more money than their three kids combined.

Having lost my annual battle with your mother regarding my choice of wardrobe for the Easter party, we arrived at Fairchild manor, where I suffered the yearly round of criticism about the worst Easter party—nay, just worst party—ever thrown. "Bring any piñatas?" "Don't let him hide the eggs. We'll never find them again!" "Hey, kids, I hid an egg in the fridge. When you find it, can you bring me a beer?"

Your mother joined in the fun too. She sang a constant refrain of "We won't be hosting any parties any time soon." I took the yearly ribbing like a champ and joined the other parents in laughing at my own expense.

Ten minutes into the party, the egg hunt commenced. Children raced across the lawn tightly gripping their baskets as they searched for pastel-colored eggs.

"How long until somebody finds the golden egg?" I asked your mother. The Fairchilds' egg hunt featured a golden egg hidden among the others, and whoever found this special egg received one hundred dollars from the Easter Bunny, a.k.a. Prescott "Money-bags" Fairchild. Personally, I think it was just another way in which the Fairchilds tried to show me up.

"Ten minutes and you're ready to go?" your mother asked. "That's a record." She knew me well.

"I'll go check out the spread." I may have dreaded coming to this party every year, but on the plus side, the Easter cookies were bountiful—though not made by Gwenyth; she had her caterer on speed dial. It was the best of times; it was the worst of times.

The caterer was something of a legend because Gwenyth had ridiculous standards. Whatever is beyond perfectionist, well, that's her. I'm pretty sure that the caterer developed carpal tunnel syndrome or early onset arthritis while laboring over the delicious treats she made for Gwenyth's parties. The cookies that year were almost too beautiful to consume; each one was carefully crafted with strict attention to detail—the egg-shaped ones resembled Fabergé eggs, and the bunny-shaped ones had a scary sense of realism.

Deep into the egg hunt, still no one had found the prized golden egg, and I was struggling. Here's a list of beverages that you can drink when you eat cookies:

- milk
- lemonade
- punch
- Capri Sun

Here's what I drank with the cookies I consumed that day:

- beer

In need of moral support, I found your mother standing near a group of parents whom I didn't want to engage in small talk with (that describes nearly all of the parents at the party).

"Honey, could you come over here for a second please?" I asked. I stood at a safe distance from her and the parents so that I wouldn't be sucked into their conversation.

"Just a second, babe."

"Your aunt Claudette is on the phone. From Paris." As you read this, I know what you're thinking: *Wait, we have an Aunt Claudette? And she lives in Paris?*

No, you don't. That's a code I invented and your mother agreed to go along with. Here's how it works: when I say "Aunt Claudette," that tells her I'm having a problem. From there, the city Aunt Claudette is calling from identifies the level of the problem.

"Dad, that's genius."

Thank you, children. I know.

There is a twenty-seven-point scale to determine how bad the problem is.

Okay, so that was my initial plan, but your mother isn't that patient. There's a three-point scale: London means "I need you, but it can wait a while," Madrid means "Come over as soon as reasonably possible," and Paris means "Everything is FUBAR"—fucked up beyond all recognition—"so call the chopper and let's get out of this poppy field. Radio in the airstrike. Lives are at stake. Bill Clinton is seeking a third term and he's already begun interviewing interns. I might die. Pick out my best suit, but close the casket."

Your mother utilized the Aunt Claudette code several times, but she always used London. Naturally, I used Paris and only Paris. The twenty-seven-point scale would have been overkill.

After a moment, your mother joined me. "Paris, really?" she asked.

"Honey, smell my breath, does it smell like diabetes?"

"How many cookies did you eat?"

"You know that time your brother came to visit and you made cookies and I didn't want him to have any because I secretly hate him?"

"I know you hate him. He knows you hate him. My parents know you hate him."

"Whatever. That many. That. Many. I think I need to go to the hospital. I'm going to give birth soon."

"Honey, go to the bathroom and stick your finger down your throat."

"What? Why? I'm not running for prom queen."

"I'm going back to my conversation. You should come talk to them too."

"Wait, can I borrow your purse?"

"You are not throwing up in my purse."

"It's not to throw up in. I want to put some cookies in it for later."

"Good lord," she laughed. "Go into the house and just throw up."

"Okay. Where do you think is best? Master bedroom? Gwenyth's jewelry box?"

Your mother shook her head at my suggestions, and I went inside to use the guest bathroom. I stood over the toilet trying to use the power of my mind to throw up. It didn't work. After much hesitation, I stuck my finger down my throat and tried to press my uvula. Yes, I know that word. Impressive, right? Nothing.

Begrudgingly, I joined your mother and the Fairchilds. Gwenyth was going on and on about something I didn't care about. It would probably make this story a hell of a lot better if I could remember what she was talking about, but for the life of me, I haven't a clue. For the sake of the story, let's just pretend she was talking about the merits of washing with coconut-oil-based products. That sounds like her.

"Has anybody found the golden egg yet?" I asked.

"Not yet," Prescott answered.

"Want to bet on who finds it first?"

Gwenyth scoffed. "Well, that does not seem like something we should be doing on Easter Sunday, now, does it?"

"No, definitely not," Prescott said. He was a valiant lapdog; I'll give him that. "Honey, why don't we go check on the children?"

They scurried off, no doubt offended. And that was the longest conversation I've ever had with either of them…I wish that were true.

"Are you okay?" your mother asked. "Did you…?"

"No. I tried, but I couldn't. Looks like we're having this baby after all."

She rolled her eyes at me, but I know she was laughing on the inside. Luckily, I didn't have to wait much longer for the egg hunt to end. Across the manicured lawn, one of the Fairchild triplets—and I'm not sure which because I cannot now, nor have I ever been able to, tell them apart—cried out with joy.

"I found the golden egg! I found the egg!"

Thereafter a trumpet sounded, and the hunt was over. Honestly, it was like we were living an episode of *Downton Abbey*. I've never seen an episode of that show, but if it involves a bunch of snooty British people wearing uncomfortable clothes and looking down on people of a lower social class, then yes, that's exactly what it was like.

"This marks the third year in a row that a Fairchild has found the egg," Gwenyth said, beaming with pride.

"Look! Another egg! He's found another egg!" another child exclaimed.

"What? That can't be!" Gwenyth said. "There's only supposed to be one golden egg!"

"I found one too!" another child cried, different from the first.

The parents looked around, stunned, as child after child presented their eggs. Trophies. One hundred dollars a pop. Never in my life had I seen Gwenyth a whiter shade of pale — a chore that her doctors had for years been trying to accomplish with Far Eastern medicine unapproved by the FDA. The Easter Bunny had delivered gilded eggs for everyone.

How could this happen? The parents looked around at each other, clueless. We'd been coming to this party for the past four years, and each of those years there had been only one golden egg. Three of those years, a Fairchild had found the egg, which made perfect sense because Prescott and Gwenyth undoubtedly aided their children with tips on where to hunt. The one year a Fairchild didn't find the egg, I had given the triplets a couple of unsolicited tips of my own. When a child finally found the egg, the triplets were on the other side of the lawn. Coincidence? I think not. And the child who found it? She wasn't invited back the next year. Granted, she and her parents moved halfway across the country, but that's how you tell a story, kids. You leave out salient details and imply foul play. Just ask any lawyer.

The parents exchanged more looks, and eyes slowly started to fall on yours truly. Rightfully so. After all, I'd thrown the worst Easter egg hunt ever. In their minds, it was exactly the kind of gaffe I would commit. Normally, I would've relished the opportunity to proclaim my innocence, because I absolutely was innocent. Really, I was! I wish I had come up with something so brilliant, especially because it meant spending more of Prescott's money. I would have defended myself; however, I was dealing with some gastrointestinal difficulties.

"You don't look so good," your mother said to me.

"I don't feel so good."

"Please tell me you're not suffering from a guilty conscience."

"It wasn't me. I swear."

"You promise?"

I didn't have to exonerate myself any further because right then the culprit admitted her own guilt.

"Look, everyone, I found five golden eggs! Five! Can you believe it?" the last child proclaimed.

I should have recognized the voice right away, but given the ongoing war in my stomach, I was a little preoccupied. I turned and saw the guilty party. It was you, Annabelle. You were smiling wide, beaming with pride, and in your pink basket, there were five golden eggs.

"Aunt Claudette. Par—" I didn't get the last word out. I lurched forward, my eyes closed, and I puked. And puked. I voided my stomach, my bowels wrenching, my eyes burning. The sound was horrifying, but I didn't care. And when I thought there was nothing left inside of me—no solid, no food condensed to paste form, no liquid whatsoever—I puked more, dry-heaving. Your mother would later tell me that it was one of the most horrific things she had ever witnessed. That if given the option between puking in the manner in which I did and childbirth, she would choose giving birth.

When I was done, I wiped the tears from my eyes and saw that in front of me one of the Fairchild triplets stood, crying, covered in my vomit.

"Well, on a positive note, now you won't have trouble telling this one apart," I said.

"Prescott!" Gwenyth cried. She scurried forward and started dabbing at her son with her handkerchief. "Prescott!"

"I am so sorry," your mother said as she knelt down to help Gwenyth.

It's always an awkward moment when your child does something horrible in public that you're secretly proud of. Peter, you once asked me why a woman in the grocery store had a mustache, within earshot of said woman. That was the day I realized that you were my child. To take the heat off you, I followed up with "Son, it's not nice to say truthful things to people." Your mother subsequently scolded both of us, but a week later we saw that same woman in line at the grocery store sans facial hair. You're welcome, lady. We could have started our own salon for women. I even thought of a tagline for it: "The truth hurts, but our skin peels don't."

Annabelle, I hope you learned a valuable lesson that day. If you're going to pull off a heist, it helps to have a distraction. Fortunately, you didn't have to plan a distraction. I was there to aid and abet your crime—unknowingly, of course. Also, maybe next time find two golden eggs, not five, okay? We never spoke about it afterward, and Prescott paid up, but everybody knew you were the culprit. I was proud of you. That was the day I knew you were mine.

6 IF YOU EAT TOO MUCH CANDY, YOUR TEETH WILL FALL OUT

There is no person in this world that I hate more than James Perkus. If Hitler had a son with the devil, then that child would find itself the second-most contemptible person in the world after James Perkus. What? You thought that I was going to say that the child would be James Perkus? No, James is worse. Much worse. The very mention of the name "James Perkus" causes my stomach to flip. If James Perkus were on fire, I wouldn't cross the street to put him out. I don't understand that expression; it should be amended as such: if James Perkus were on fire, it would be because I lit him on fire. There. Done. Simple and to the point. I despise the kid so much that I took time out of my busy schedule to go to Home Depot and purchase kerosene and matches. Finito.

Every superhero needs an archnemesis, and that audacious thirteen-year-old boy was mine. In case that wasn't clear, yes, I am a superhero—although the only cape I wear is terry cloth, and I only don it when I'm getting out of the shower. We were Superman and that rich, crazy bald guy. Spider-Man and that rich, eccentric green guy. James Bond and that rich, fat gold guy. Why are all of the villains so rich? Given the income gap between hero and villain — Batman excluded — I think I might prefer to be evil. Who says crime doesn't pay? Clearly, it pays, and it pays well. It's the getting caught part that doesn't pay.

Although my disdain for Perkus was a constant theme running throughout your childhoods, I'll bet that neither of you knows the genesis of my feud with him. It all started the year I decided to go on strike in my role as your father.

To be fair, that could have been any number of years, because I went on strike a lot during your childhoods — being a parent is difficult and whoever said it was a full-time job was wrong, because it's more like an indentured servitude — but it happened the year that I went on strike for Halloween.

Again, there was more than one time that I went on strike for Halloween. But can you blame me? Annabelle. Peter. Have I told you how much I love your mother and you? Well, I was lying. During Halloween at least. Somehow your mother had the idea that we should dress up in group costumes as a family. Wait, not somehow; she thought it would be "cute." I can't tell you the number of times I have suffered under the pretense that something would be "cute." The group costumes were dreadful enough for me, with your mother choosing my costume each year, but it was even worse when you two were old enough to start dictating costume choices.

Here's a list of some of the costumes I was forced to wear for these festivities:

- Frog when Annabelle was a princess. Peter was the prince. Your mother was the queen of the kingdom.

- Toad when Annabelle was Peach. Peter was Mario. Your mother was Yoshi.
- Velma when Annabelle was Shaggy. Peter was Scooby. Your mother was Daphne. Nobody liked Fred.
- Grouchy when Annabelle was Snow White. Peter was Sleepy. Your mother was Happy.

After years of being tortured on Halloween by you three, finally I'd had it. I told your mother, "This year I'm staying home. And there's nothing you can do about it. The end."

Okay, we all know that didn't happen. Here's what really happened. I told your mother, "I'm filing for divorce if your children make me dress up in another demeaning costume. I'll be at Motel 6 if anybody needs me, and I'm not leaving the light on."

In truth, I was sick. Not sick enough to warrant hospitalization, although the diseases you brought home with you from school were quite often pandemic, but still sick enough that I was able to evade some of my Halloween duties.

"You're still going to dress up, aren't you?" your mother asked me. Reminiscent of a beached whale, I was lying on the couch enjoying the warmth of two blankets. I was in and out of consciousness, comforted to sleep by the quiet lull of the humidifier and *SportsCenter*.

"The doctor said it would probably be best if I remained in comfortable clothes," I answered.

"I was there with you. He didn't say that. He didn't say anything close to that."

"I was hoping you weren't paying attention."

"You're the love of my life. Of course I was paying attention."

"Okay, what unwarranted punishment have you and the children chosen for me this year?"

"Well…This year, Annabelle wants to do… *The Wizard of Oz*."

"Let me guess. She's Dorothy."

"Yes."

"You're that hot witch."

"Glinda the Good Witch of the North. Yes."

"Peter is…the Scarecrow?"

"Yes."

"And I'm…the bad witch? Oh Jesus, she's going to drop a house on me, isn't she?" I reached for the Robitussin and took a swig.

"That's the Wicked Witch of the East, and no."

"What then? Not that annoying little dog, I hope? Steve will never look me in the eye again if you make me dress up as that pissant dog."

"Not Toto either."

"What then?" And then it hit me. What's the worst, most humiliating character from that movie? "God no…Not the Cowardly Lion."

"We need you in the costume for the family album, honey. You put it on, take the picture, wear it when the trick-or-treaters come by, and then you're done. You never have to wear it in public."

The family album. I used to wish that the house would burn down if only so that the family album would be destroyed with it, but how naïve I had been to wish such a thing, because even if the house were on fire and in danger of burning down, your mother would save the family album first, even before poor Steve, who, let's be honest, would be on a catamaran in the Atlantic once the first spark flickered — that dog's survival skills are second to none. And if by some miracle the family album were destroyed in a fire, your mother would just replace it with a new one, and worst of all, she would probably make me relive every single humiliating picture in the damn thing. The book was simultaneously a treasured piece of our family's history and a record of my past embarrassments. But it wouldn't matter now, since the arrival of social media.

"Fine. I'll wear the costume," I said. I didn't have the strength to fight.

"And the makeup."

"Makeup? Lions don't wear makeup."

"This one does."

"Worst. Lion. Ever."

———————————

Fifteen minutes before trick-or-treating officially commenced, I was sitting in full costume and makeup, begging for death, not because of my cold, but because of my festive garb.

Your mother rounded you both up and headed for the door. Of course, she made for a beautiful Glinda the Good Witch, and I think she really enjoyed having that wand in her hand as she barked out orders.

"There's candy in the bowl," she said, the wand moving to the tempo of her speech. "It's fifteen minutes until trick-or-treating starts. Only give a few pieces of candy per child, otherwise you'll run out."

"We won't run out. Look how much candy there is." The bowl was filled to the brim, and there were a couple more bags on the bar in the kitchen.

"I still don't know what I'm going to tell people when they ask what happened to our Cowardly Lion."

"You could tell them he was too cowardly to come," Annabelle said.

"No, not that," I said. "Tell them he was experiencing post-traumatic stress syndrome after serving several tours of duty during previous Halloweens."

"I'll just tell them you're sick," your mother said. "Now, don't eat any of the candy. It's for the children, not for you. You don't need candy."

"Relax. I'm not going to eat any of the candy."

With Rover following along as the Tin Man, you left me. I don't know how you managed to get that dog to wear anything other than a collar. I couldn't even keep him from digging up our neighbors' yards when I took him for a walk. So, it was just Steve and me, with a bowl full of candy and a fridge full of beer. By "full of beer," I mean that I had one beer hidden in the crisper. It was the last place your mother would ever look for my secret stash.

I settled back in on the couch and covered myself with blankets. Having finished his dinner and in need of a comfortable space for a nap, Steve walked into the living room and came to a dead stop when he saw me. I tried to make eye contact with him, but he looked away.

"It's bad enough that I have to wear this costume, but you're not going to talk to me?"

If the tables had been turned and I had been the dog and Steve my owner-companion, I'm fairly certain he would have taken me to the vet and had me euthanized that night. He left me alone in the living room and went upstairs. I think he was a little miffed that I too had a tail now.

You children weren't gone for more than five minutes before my willpower weakened and I started devouring the candy, but give me a break, okay? I was sick. It was a blessing that my health hadn't deteriorated to the point where I'd completely lost my appetite. Then it would have been serious. My lame justifications aside, despite the silly costume—you'd really outdone yourself that year—and my best friend, Steve, abandoning me, it was going to be the greatest Halloween ever because I got to stay home and eat candy.

The phone rang, disturbing my bliss. It was your mother. I hid under the blankets for a moment, paralyzed by fear. How could she possibly know? Was there a nanny cam hidden somewhere in the house? She would do that, wouldn't she? My mother was right about her. Finally, on the last ring before the answering machine picked up, I reached my hand out from Fort Blanket and answered.

"Hello?"

"Gwenyth called and invited us to trick-or-treat in her neighborhood, so we're going to head over there. I just wanted to let you know."

"Okay. Have fun. Love you."

"Love you too."

Phew. She knew nothing. I resumed munching on candy from the safety and comfort of Fort Blanket.

I couldn't blame her for wanting to go to Gwenyth's neighborhood. It was the type of neighborhood where the residents started handing out two-dollar bills and dollar coins when they ran out of candy. To start the night, they gave out full-size candy bars. Your mother and I ran out of Halloween candy one year, and I started giving away her bowel-regulating yogurt and assorted fruits. Three children called 911 on us that night.

The trick-or-treaters started coming to the door, and I operated like a well-oiled machine. See a child, give them candy. See a child, give them candy. Over and over again. I gave out a few pieces of candy per child and then had one for myself as well. The treats were disappearing quickly, and I had to tap into the reserve candy, but despite your mother's warning, we definitely weren't going to run out. Personally, I think she was still scarred from our previous experience when we had to explain the benefits of bowel-regulating yogurt to the local sheriff.

Though I had wanted to stay home, I'd been reacquainted with the difficulty of manning the door on Halloween. The doorbell rang. And rang. And rang. And rang. And just when I thought it couldn't ring anymore, it rang seventeen more times. I was beginning to wonder if maybe sugar might be an addictive substance.

Still, handing out candy was far more favorable than parading around Gwenyth's neighborhood dressed as the Cowardly Lion. I'd reached my boiling point on wearing embarrassing Halloween costumes in public. There I was, in my house, watching football, alone with two friends whom I hadn't seen in a long time: peace and quiet. Not Steve. He was still upstairs.

I had almost dozed off when the doorbell rang yet again—it was becoming increasingly difficult to nap while watching football. It was a couple of older kids who were dressed as zombies with tattered clothes and an unrealistic amount of fake blood. I could tell that it'd been a while since any of them had watched an animated feature. I don't know that there's an official age limit on trick-or-treating, but there definitely should be. I gave them each a few pieces of candy and then indulged in one myself.

"You shouldn't eat that candy. That's for us." Perkus!

"I'm sorry," I said. "I must have misunderstood you. Did you just say the candy, which I purchased with my hard-earned money, was yours? No, no, no. I own this candy, and when you come to my door in your costume, I opt to give some of it to you as a treat and not a trick. It's 'trick or treat,' not 'give me candy'!" I shifted my tail for effect. I still wasn't in love with the costume, but I could get used to having a tail.

"Give me more candy, Cowardly Lion."

"Not with that attitude, I won't. Not until you say the magic words."

"Fine. Trick or treat."

"Trick." I slammed the door.

Now, look, I know what you're going to say: *"Dad, is it your mission in life to embarrass us?"* And the answer is, "Yes." I take extreme delight in doing things that embarrass you. I'm surprised that you even have to ask that question.

Rid of the children raised by wolves, I settled back into the couch and began watching the game again. The fourth quarter was just starting. Hello, old friend, peace. Can I get you anything, quiet?

Your mother called and told me she was on her way back, then asked if I wanted any frozen yogurt. I love that woman, but I was chock full of candy.

"Are you sure you don't want any yogurt?" she asked.

"Honey, no. Thank you. I'm just not feeling well enough for yogurt."

"You didn't eat the candy, did you?"

"What? No." *Yes.*

"Okay, see you soon."

Crap. I leapt off the couch and ran to check my reflection in the hall mirror. My face was covered in chocolate. It was one thing to lie to your mother about my candy consumption; it was another to get caught lying to her about my candy consumption.

I was heading to the bathroom to clean my face (i.e., erase the evidence of the crime I'd committed—eating the candy that I, an adult, had paid for) when the doorbell rang one last time.

Ah yes, probably somebody's children trying to hit the same house twice. You see, I may have evaded my duties so that I could stay home, watch football, and feast on the candy bowl, but I had integrity. And I wasn't going to let a child get more than one go at our candy bowl. We weren't giving candy away for free...Well, we were, but everybody got one handout, not two. I was ready to give these kids a piece of my mind, but when I opened the door there was nobody there.

"Hello?"

No answer.

I moved out onto the porch and looked around, but still I didn't see anybody.

"Annabelle? Peter?"

I stepped out into the lawn and looked around some more. Now, kids, I don't believe in ghosts, ghouls, zombies, vampires, werewolves, or any of that paranormal stuff. I'm not saying it's not possible that such creatures exist, but that was a trap, and yes, that's exactly what I'm saying. They don't exist. I'm more afraid of the guy who cuts me off in the carpool line than I am of any of the aforementioned undead characters, because the guy who cuts me off when picking up his six-year-old is a veritable sociopath with no sense of right or wrong and is likely to commit murder one day.

"There's still some candy left if you want it." I took another step forward, and that's when the door slammed. Crap. Another reason I loathed this costume. No pockets. I was locked out.

"We'll take that candy."

I recognized the voice before I turned around. James. Freakin'. Perkus.

"I thought I told you to go home," I said.

"I did, and I came back. With friends."

From the bushes, under the porch, everywhere I could see, children emerged in support of their psychotic leader, armed with water balloons and eggs. Somehow I'd found my way onto the pages of classic literature, and unfortunately for me, it was *Lord of the Flies* and not *Pollyanna*.

Faced with imminent death—well, not death per se—I was forced to go to the nuclear option.

"If you and your friends don't go home now," I said, "I will be forced to call your parents."

"Oh no! My parents," he cackled maniacally. "Guess what, old man? I'm an orphan. I don't have any parents."

I have to give him credit, that sounded pretty badass, but it wasn't true. His mother was a podiatrist and his father an accountant. I'd never met them, but from what I'd heard, they were pretty nice people. It's a shame they'd given birth to the Antichrist.

"What do you want? Candy? Well, I'm fresh out."

"No, not candy. Revenge."

We stared each other down. It was me against him. And his army of little minions whose parents I wished I could call. Never underestimate the power of a man who's not afraid to snitch.

The stare-off continued for a good ten seconds, and I knew the first person to budge would be the loser, but I didn't care. Kids, if you ever find yourself in a fight to the death, check your pride at the door. When you emerge victorious, you can tell the story of how you won the stare-off and weren't the first to run for help. At that moment, I just wanted to live to tell the tale.

So I did exactly what the Cowardly Lion would have done. I ran. Like hell. But everywhere I turned I was pelted with eggs, rocks, toilet paper, Silly String, water balloons—or at least I hope it was water in those balloons—and whatever other objects those children found to throw at me. I have to give those little miscreants credit. The unintended shrapnel from their weapons of mass destruction all but blinded me, and thanks to the Cowardly Lion's makeup, it became nearly impossible to remove it. Every time I used my...paw—damn it—to try to remove eggshell or Silly String, it only made the mess on my face worse.

They chased me around the yard in circles for what seemed like forever until I had no choice but to head for higher ground. I was losing vision and steam. I ran straight for the big oak tree in the middle of our yard, took a giant leap, and grabbed one of the lower-hanging tree branches. I kicked my feet up and bear-hugged it, then worked my way around until I was on top of it—there was no way in hell, after all of that candy, that I would have been able to do a pull-up. I continued to climb higher and higher, until the angry children's throws could no longer reach me.

"You have to come down sometime," Perkus taunted me.

"No, I don't. My wife will be home soon."

They waited below me for a full twenty minutes before giving in. Their throws unable to reach me, and incapable of climbing the tree themselves, they gave up, announcing victory as they departed. Internally, I thanked your mother for begging me to trim the lower branches on the oak tree so that you children wouldn't be tempted to climb it yourselves. Your mother's worrywart nature had saved me, though unintentionally.

"This isn't over," Perkus said as he led his band of hooligans away from our house.

You're damn right this isn't over, I thought to myself. I wish I'd yelled that aloud, but I wasn't in a position to be doling out threats. I waited atop my perch in that tree, coughing and sneezing. Being stuck in nature wasn't helping my cold, and I couldn't see a thing. Not only was the lion a coward, but he was blind too. Just when I was starting to consider shinnying down the tree, I heard your mother's minivan pull into the driveway. I mean, how long does it take to get froyo anyway?

She parked, and the three of you headed for the front door. I considered staying in the tree and making a life for myself there rather than facing your mother and the inevitable barrage of questions, but it had been a good while since I'd had any cough medicine and I missed Fort Blanket.

"Honey," I called. She looked up, shocked to see me atop the tree.

"What in the h-e-l-l are you doing up in that tree?" your mother asked.

"Mom, I'm old enough to spell," Annabelle said. "Actually, I think I'm a better speller than you or Dad." You had just reached that age where you began to question your parents' intelligence. Oh how I miss that phase—yes, that's sarcasm, and I look forward to the day when your children go through that phase too.

"I know, sweetie, but if I don't at least pretend to be a good parent, child services will take you away." Then she turned to look at me. "Get down from there. Now."

"I can't," I said.

"Why not?"

"I can't see. I got…something in my eye. Can you get the ladder and help me down?"

"I can climb the tree and save Daddy," Peter said.

"I appreciate that, son, but I don't think you can carry me." Translation: Your costume was perfect for you, Scarecrow. That was a stupid idea. Still, I'll never forget that you offered. "Honey, can you get the ladder from the garage to get me down?"

"We don't have the ladder, remember? We loaned it to Prescott and Gwenyth."

"Jesus. Well, finally we know whose fault it is that I'm stuck up here." I started the campaign that this wasn't my fault. And technically I was right; it wasn't.

"I guess I'm going to have to call the fire department," your mother said.

"No, that's humiliating. Don't you dare do that."

"Okay, well then, I'll call Prescott and Gwenyth."

"Crap." The lesser of two evils. "Call the fire department."

Your mother pulled out her cell phone and dialed. "Yes, I'm calling because I have a cat stuck in a tree."

"Oh, you would, wouldn't you?" I growled. After all, I was a lion.

————————

After ruining my azaleas and your mother's rosebushes with their fire truck, the firefighters finally got me down from the tree. Everyone in the neighborhood came by to watch. In retrospect, I wish that we had just asked for help from one of the neighbors, but I did feel safe being guided down the ladder by the chief himself. When I got to the bottom, they covered me in one of those brown blankets that you see in every movie and TV show. They might as well stitch "victim" on those things. By that point, your mother had noticed the evidence of the assault upon me by Perkus and his misfits as well as all of the candy wrappers in the kitchen trash can. Had I not been trapped in the tree, I would've taken the trash out.

Still, she felt the need to question me: "Why is your mouth covered in chocolate?" she asked. In our household, you were innocent until proven guilty, but only because she wanted to catch you in a lie. But I was too smart for that.

"Because I ate all of the candy and I won't apologize for it. Those children were monsters. They don't deserve Halloween candy. And for the record, I wouldn't have had to eat candy if the children weren't always eating my cookies."

"Mommy makes those cookies for us," Annabelle said.

"Yeah!" Peter chimed in.

"Fine," I said.

"I am never letting you stay home alone on Halloween again," your mother said.

It was that day that I decided I was going to kill James Perkus.

Fine. I wasn't actually going to kill Perkus. I just wanted to scar him emotionally, which in some sense is a lot worse than killing him because it was sure to cost him a lot of money in therapy and ruin every relationship that he would ever have in his life.

It was painful waiting a full year until the next Halloween, when I could finally take my revenge, but when it came around, I was ready.

The Saturday before Halloween, we were having breakfast together as a family. I so enjoyed those moments when we could have a real breakfast together, but never more so than when I was about to hatch a plan for revenge—I hatched plans for revenge pretty often, and Saturday morning breakfast always seemed like the appropriate venue for such an occasion.

After several painful minutes of listening to you all drone on about school drama, the topic of Halloween costumes finally came up and I pounced: "Let's all pick amazing costumes," I said. "This year, I want to be Al Capone."

"Who's that?" Annabelle asked.

"He was a famous gangster. He would kill you if you looked at him funny."

"Why would he kill someone for looking at him funny?" asked Peter. "Why wouldn't he just laugh?"

"Not that kind of funny," I said. "Weird funny."

"That doesn't make sense," Annabelle said. "Why would he do that?"

"Look, that's irrelevant. That point is that he was awesome and people feared him. I want to be a hero. I want to be awesome. I want to be the star. I'm tired of being the lowly sidekick in your Halloween costumes. Make Daddy a star. For once, just once, let me be the hero. Please! So I can kill Perkus and save the princess."

"Wait. Is Mom dressing up as a princess?" Annabelle asked.

"No, not a real princess. A metaphorical princess. Look, it doesn't matter. Just pick the coolest, most awesome hero you can think of and I'll be that."

Annabelle, sweetie, you are my only daughter and my firstborn child, but when you told me what I was going to be for Halloween that year, a little part of me died. And I don't think I'm ever going to get that part back. It's gone. Forever.

Frodo. Effing. Baggins.

It is with the utmost scorn that I now curse Peter Jackson and J. R. R. Tolkien. How they managed to create a book and movie franchise with a four-foot-three—give or take—hero with hairy feet and no physical skills whatsoever is beyond me. They lied to the world. Annabelle, you loved those books, and being your father, clearly it was my fault that you did. I should have raised you better. That year, I was Frodo. Your mother, God bless her, was nice enough to be Samwise Gamgee, who I take it is like Frodo in all respects except that he carries a lot of food. As such, cookies (in place of scones) were an integral part of her costume. This only added insult to the injury that you had wreaked upon me.

Annabelle, you were Arwen, a beautiful elf who kicks a lot of butt, and your friends filled out the rest of the much-more-awe-some-than-Frodo group: the elf with the bow and arrow, the rude little dwarf with the axe, the human with the sword, the wizard with the tree branch, and the other human with the sword. Yes, I know their names, but it makes it way more fun if I pretend that I don't because I know how much it upsets you.

By Halloween night, when I donned my Frodo garb, I was pretty downtrodden, but at the same time, I didn't really care. I suppose that's what happens to a person when he's made to suffer to the point where his soul is broken and all that remains is the shell of the man that once was. I begged you to choose *Game of Thrones*, even though I'd never seen it, but I knew that everybody died, which was the exact message I was trying to send Perkus.

Your mother threw a little party before we went trick-or-treat-ing. All of your friends gathered at our house. Normally, I would have been vehemently opposed to having this many children under my roof, but I made an exception. While your mother was busy in the kitchen finishing her special Halloween treats — pumpkin cookies and ghost brownies — I wrangled all of the invitees together in the living room.

"Okay, kids, I've gathered you here for one reason, and one reason only," I said. "Tonight, we wreak havoc on the criminal known as James Perkus. Now, does anybody know what his Halloween costume is?"

"He's being Wolverine for Halloween," the human with the sword said.

"Wait. The animal? Like the mascot for the University of Michigan?"

"No, the Marvel character," the human with the sword said. "You know, Wolverine?"

"Is that the one who's in the wheelchair?" I asked.

"No," the elf with the bow and arrow said, rolling his eyes.

"The one with the eye thing?" I asked.

"No, it's the one who has powers of regeneration," Annabelle said. "If he gets hurt or something, the wound heals automatically. He can't be killed."

"Wow," I said. Now, why couldn't I have been that?

"And he has adamantium claws that come out of his hands," the elf with the bow and arrow said. "His whole skeleton is made from adamantium. It's the strongest metal in the world!"

"No," I said, correcting him. "That's titanium, or steel, or tungsten. Or something like that."

"It's adamantium!" the elf with the bow and arrow said.

"Okay, I'm pretty sure that adamantium, or whatever it is, isn't even real," I said. "I'm pretty sure Perkus's adamantium claws are made from plastic because his mother probably bought his costume from Target just like the rest of your parents."

"Actually, his mother makes his costume," the wizard with the tree branch said.

"My God," I responded. "We are dealing with a monster. We must find Perkus, and we must kill him."

"Perkus must be destroyed," Annabelle said.

"Yes! That's the spirit," I replied. "But where is he?"

"Palisades Park," the other human with the sword answered. "That's where he and the older kids hang out."

"Palisades Park?" I asked. "Wait, can we walk there, or do we need to drive?"

"One does not simply walk into Palisades Park," the other human with the sword said. "It is riddled with fire and ash and dust. The poisonous fumes alone could kill you."

"What?" I asked.

"We have to drive and there's a lot of trash on Halloween," the other human with the sword explained.

"Okay, that's fine," I said. "I'll make sure to find the address before we leave."

"You do not know the way?" Annabelle asked.

"What? I just said that. No, I do not know the way."

"I will help you bear this burden, Frodo Baggins," the wizard with the tree branch said. "As long as it is yours to bear."

"If by my life or death I can protect you, I will," said the human with the sword. "You have my sword."

"And you have my bow," the elf with the bow said.

"And my axe," the dwarf with the axe said.

"If this is the will of the council, then Gondor will see it done," the other human with the sword said.

"Great. This is really great," I said. "I might take you up on that offer to use your weapons. I was really upset when my costume didn't come with one, except for this puny dagger."

"What am I missing in there?" your mother called out from the kitchen. "I hope you kids are having fun! Treats will be ready in a minute!"

"Nothing, honey, we'll be ready to leave soon," I answered. "Now, where were we, kids?"

"We shall call ourselves the Fellowship of the Ring," Annabelle said.

"Right. I don't agree with that, but if it makes you kids happy."

"Dad, you're doing such a good job of Frodo," Annabelle whispered to me.

"Well, thanks, sweetie," I said. "I wasn't enthused about this costume choice initially, but I'm glad to have so much help. Peter, we're going to need your help too."

That year, Peter, you were unwilling to be a part of the ragtag group of hobbits, elves, dwarves, etc. Instead, you chose to join your friends with their *Star Wars*–themed costumes, because "*Star Wars* is so much cooler than *Lord of the Rings*, Dad." Peter, my second child, you ought not to spend your limited time on this planet splitting hairs. They're both nerdy and, by default, not cool. You know what's cool? Rock stars. Not hobbits or Jedis.

And for the record, I despise George Lucas almost as much as Peter Jackson and J. R. R. Tolkien. However, I hate him less because he popularized the swords with the lasers, and pretty much all of his characters except for those two robots had weapons—yes, I know they're called droids. This is a man who had the foresight to realize that all Halloween costumes need to be cool, and yes, by "cool," I do mean that the package for the costume should read, "Deadly weapon included."

Across the living room, Peter and his *Star Wars* friends were busy playing Nintendo—I don't care if it was PlayStation or Xbox; when I say "Nintendo," you know what I mean. It's just like how people use "Kleenex" when they mean "tissue," or "Coke" when they mean "soda," although that last one may only apply in the southern United States. Regardless, Peter and his friends were playing their Sega game. You really want to yell at me right now, don't you?

"Peter, what do you say?" I asked. "You and your friends want to join in on this epic battle with Perkus? We really could use your help."

"Are we your only hope?" asked the bearded kid with the blue laser sword.

"I mean, I have the dwarf, the wizard, the humans, and the elves over here. So no."

"Say I am your only hope and I will help you."

Damn these entitled kids.

"Fine. You are my only hope, bearded kid with the blue laser sword."

"I will help you."

"Okay. Good. Leave your flashlight on the couch there and go use the bathroom before we go," I said. "What about you, Peter?"

"Help you, I will," Peter said. You were dressed as some green gremlin with long ears and sparse hair. I take it that this was an important character in *Star Wars*. I suppose in the *Star Wars* universe there is a direct correlation between power and ugliness.

"Peter, your mother and I spend a lot of money educating you. Speak like a human."

"Speak like this, Yoda does."

"Okay, you're dead to me." No, obviously I didn't say that to you at the time. You were only a child, and I would never say that. But that's why I wrote this book, so I can tell you now. I could have lived like a Saudi Arabian prince with the money I've spent on your education. When you speak like somebody knocked you on the head, it upsets me. Greatly.

"Okay, fine. You should go use the bathroom too."

"Pee, I did, fifteen minutes ago."

"Yeah, well, if you have to pee after we leave, one mad troll I'll be."

"Hobbit!" Annabelle said, correcting me.

"Whatever. All right, everybody grab your flashlight swords and weapons. We're going after Perkus—as soon as we finish the cookies and punch, of course."

"To the *Millennium Falcon*," the bearded kid with the blue laser sword said.

"It's a minivan," I said.

We made our way to Palisades Park with me driving the mini-van — oh, I'm sorry, the "*Millennium Falcon*" — and your mother following behind in the...not *Millennium Falcon*? Sorry, I don't know the name of any of the other *Star Wars* vehicles. Oh, wait. Wasn't there a Death Star or something? Whatever.

We arrived and there were numerous trick-or-treaters and parents celebrating the holiday. As a diversion, I sent your mother to find out more about the local costume contest and hayride, and then we all set off to exact my revenge.

We found Perkus and his band of heroes skateboarding on the benches near the soccer field. The grassy field was reminiscent of a Civil War battlefield, and I felt like a general, ready to lead my troops. Huzzah!

Together, our *Lord of the Rings* and *Star Wars* legion lined up side by side, ready to march on the enemy. Perkus and his gang took notice. They stopped whatever shenanigans they were up to and faced us. There was nothing but the distant sound of cheerful families in the background.

I watched as Perkus's eyes moved over our group until they finally stopped when they spotted me. Of course he remembered me from the prior year, and he knew why we were there.

"You!" he yelled.

"If you want him, come and claim him," Annabelle said.

Annabelle, I think that was the first time in your life you actually stood up for me. Usually, it was "Dad, you're embarrassing me!" or "Dad, not now," or "Dad, can't this wait until we get home?" or "Dad, my friends are watching!" or "Dad, I told you not to come here!" or "Dad, put a shirt on!" or "Dad, go watch TV in your bedroom!"…I could go on and on and on and on and on…Well, you get the point. Anyway, I was truly touched. For once, you weren't ashamed to be seen with me in public.

Perkus and his mutants (so…come to find out that his friends were actually dressed as mutants that day because whatever they were dressed as — the one-eyed thing and the blue monster — yeah, well, they're actually mutants, but I didn't mean it that way) charged toward our brigade.

"Dad, you're on your own," Annabelle said as she retreated from our position. "My costume took me a long time to get together, and I don't want those meatheads ruining it." Well, now, there was the Annabelle I knew and loved. Your public affection for me did not last long.

But that's okay, because your friends were there to help. Just when I thought all hope was lost and that I would be fighting Perkus and his mutants alone, they came to my rescue.

"For Frodo," the human with the sword said. And we charged.

The battle lasted for a good while, with most of the kids essentially pretending to hit one another. I think the general message — that we were there for blood and to murder Perkus — was lost on everyone except Perkus and me. I chased him all around the park until the battle started to turn in their favor. I suppose that was always going to happen considering the mutants had superior weapons — I'm sorry, but we were fighting against kids whose mothers made their costumes. How do you compete with that?

"Make for the *Millennium Falcon*!" the human with the other sword shouted.

I stopped chasing Perkus, and we ran for our lives toward the minivan. Those troll feet you made me wear didn't help my cause. My chances of survival would have increased exponentially had I been allowed to wear sneakers.

In the end, the battle was like the movie *Platoon*. If you haven't seen it, I suggest you watch it. There's a bunch of great actors in it and it was directed by someone who would never direct a Disney movie: Oliver Stone. It was about the Vietnam War. I don't know what you kids learned about the Vietnam War in school, but here's my summary of it: a lot of really messed-up stuff happened in the jungles of Vietnam, and any time somebody said "Get to the chopper," you ran like hell, and if you didn't make it, a tiger would eat you. Look it up. That's accurate.

The battle at Palisades Park that day was exactly like the Vietnam War; there were even tigers. No, seriously, there must have been some tiger movie that had come out that year, because there were a few kids dressed up like tigers. Either that or those kids just really liked tigers. I don't know, but the point is we battled with Perkus until the bitter end. We gave it all we had, and when we didn't have any more, we ran to your mother in the hopes that she would rescue us.

Perkus was right on my tail, and unbeknownst to him, I had him right where I wanted. It was just him and me. You see, I had a surprise weapon in my costume. Something I called the Egg Launcher 3000. No, it didn't launch three thousand eggs. I wish. It held six eggs and was small enough for me to easily conceal at my lower back. While you children ran to the minivan, I turned and faced my nemesis. I pulled the Egg Launcher 3000 out and pointed it directly at him.

"Well, well, well, Perkus," I said. "Say hello to my little friend." Okay, so yeah, I was trying to channel a combination of MacGyver and Scarface—by the way, that would make an awesome movie or one-hour TV series.

I cocked the Egg Launcher 3000 and that's when it happened. My worst nightmare. I took one step forward, and my not-so-youthful body betrayed me.

My knee gave out.

I fell to the ground writhing in pain, the Egg Launcher 3000 lying by my side. Perkus's laugh in that moment will haunt me until my dying day. I turned over on my side and saw a hand snatch the Egg Launcher 3000 out of view, and I prepared for the worst. I looked up, expecting to see Perkus standing over me with my weapon, but instead I saw someone else: your mother.

"C'mon, Mr. Frodo," your mother said. "I can't kill James Perkus for you, but I can carry you to the *Millennium Falcon*."

"Why won't you just leave me to die?" I asked, doing my best Lieutenant Dan impression.

"Because you have a wife and two children who love you. Also, after trick-or-treating, you and I have to go through the candy before the children eat it and make sure some psychopath didn't put a razor blade in any of the candy apples."

"Okay, fine. But can I eat all of my favorite candies before the kids have a chance to?"

"Yes. You've earned it, Mr. Frodo."

Your mother lifted me up to my feet and aided me as I limped to the minivan. Meanwhile, Perkus and his mutants retreated in fear. I think they knew your mother wasn't afraid to pull the trigger. And, Annabelle, you know that ring you gave me to hold? The thing you said was the most powerful ring in the world? Yeah, it didn't do anything for me, and I lost it somewhere in the park.

Yeah, so, I didn't murder James Perkus. Sadly enough, we ended up trick-or-treating and having a pretty good night, and, Annabelle, it was a good thing you didn't join in the fight because you won first prize in the costume contest. Nevertheless, I felt vindicated. I stood and faced my nemesis and lived to tell the tale—with your mother's help, of course. It's not important that you defeat your enemies; sometimes just standing up to them is all that matters.

7

YOU CAN BE ANYTHING
YOU WANT TO BE

Your cousin Derek is the little engine that couldn't, shouldn't, and never will. Why? Well, you might assume it's because Aunt Sarah and Uncle Ronald, two people who couldn't find a grain of sand in the desert, raised him. Although they're certainly at fault, that's not it. It's because Derek was dropped on his head as a baby. I realize that's a clichéd expression often used in a joking manner to describe someone with a dearth of intelligence. (See how I used a big-person word to describe another's shortcomings? As a general rule, you'll want to avoid doing that in your lives. It'll only make people hate you.) But seriously. Kids, Derek really was dropped on his head as a baby. I know, because I'm the one who dropped him.

It happened in February 2008. Annabelle, what major sporting event happens every year around that time?

Peter? Care to take a guess?

I'm waiting.

Yawn. I'm looking at my watch. Tick. Tock. Tick. Tock. I wonder if I should order Chinese or Indian for dinner. Chinese is good because you can get egg rolls, but Indian is good because they have naan.

Sigh. It's the Super Bowl. By the way, I ordered Indian. I really love naan. It might be my favorite bread right before pita. No, wait. I like brioche more than pita. Torta is good too. Look, I know neither one of you cares for football, so I tried to liven up the football talk by interspersing it with a little culinary discourse.

It's probably not helping. The Super Bowl that year wasn't just any Super Bowl, it was Super Bowl XLII. Don't Google it. That's forty-two. The Patriots entered that game with a perfect 18-0 record, set to make NFL history by becoming only the second team ever to go undefeated. The Giants, well, they limped into the playoffs and nobody was giving them a chance.

I was dying to watch it, but I couldn't. Instead, I was headed to Anita Batheja's seventh-birthday party — thanks, Annabelle. Kids, I'm not remotely xenophobic, but I hold this truth to be self-evident: if you're an immigrant from a foreign land trying to make new friends in the United States, it's a beyond terrible idea to throw your daughter's birthday party on Super Bowl Sunday. There's not a more sacred day in this country.

"What about Christmas, Dad? Or July Fourth?"

As Dr. Seuss once wrote, "I meant what I said and I said what I meant." The Super Bowl is the most important American holiday.

I didn't go to Anita Batheja's birthday party willingly. Twenty minutes before it was time to leave for the party, your mother found me in the bedroom holding an open bottle of Drano. Now, I'm not saying I was going to poison myself in order to miss the birthday party, but I could've watched the game from my hospital bed. And that's what I tried to do. Here's a list of the things I ingested before your mother found me with the Drano:

- Leftover sushi.
- Raw rib eye.
- Expired yogurt.
- Crayons.
- Play-Doh.
- Legos. (I forgot that children's toys are nontoxic. Sorry, when I grew up, we played with mercury…Okay, that's not true, but I guarantee you that something in my old toy chest would've killed you if you'd eaten it.)
- Dog food.
- Cactus. (I really thought the cactus would at least cause some internal hemorrhaging, but nada.)
- Pinecone. (I know what you're thinking, and yes. Hurts just as much on the way out.)
- Kale. (Apparently I'd built up a tolerance to kale. I blame Gwenyth.)

This series of failures led me to the nuclear option, but give me some credit. I took the time to read the label on the back of the bottle and it led me to wonder whether the lawyers who drafted the disclaimer had exaggerated the negative consequences resulting from its consumption. My guess was that there was probably a little leeway in how badly it would hurt me to consume it. Then again, I'd seen Drano clear out some pretty miserable situations. Usually observed after Indian food night—I liked my food extra spicy and still do.

"What're you doing with the Drano?" your mother asked.

"The toilet's clogged."

"What do you mean? We didn't have Indian for dinner last night." Welcome to married life, kids. Live together long enough and there will be almost no secrets between you.

"I…Honey, I want to use my 'Get Out of Parenting Free' card.'" Okay, I debated for a long time whether I should reveal this little tidbit, but it's time to fess up. Yeah, we—your mother and I, not just me; I want that on the record, Your Honors—appropriated the "Get Out of Jail Free" card from Monopoly and applied it to parenting. Once per year, we each received one "Get Out of Parenting Free" card. No questions asked, she or I could, at a moment's notice, use our card. There were some obvious exceptions to this: family gatherings, your birthdays, and parent-teacher conferences, to name a few.

"You used your card last weekend when the kids and I went to the movies with the Fairchilds," your mother said.

"Dad, stop the story! When was that Super Bowl thing again?"

C'mon, Peter, you can't go back and reread?

"Just tell me."

Fine. It was February 3.

"Then how come you'd already used your free pass?"

I'll tell you how come, but it should be obvious. Between your mother's parents and the Fairchilds, I never stood a chance of making it more than a month before I used my card. Since we'd instituted the system, my card had never lasted longer than the second weekend in January. As for your mother, well, she only ever used the pass for things she wasn't really invited to anyway, like go-karting and laser tag. She really loves you kids. That's not to say I don't. I just don't really like the rest of the world.

"Wait, I used my pass?" I asked your mother.

"Yes, and we went to the movies without you."

"What'd you see again?"

"*The Golden Compass.*"

"Oh, well, that doesn't count. I read the book. You can't expect me to go see a movie when I've read the book."

"You did not."

"Did too!"

"Prove it. You show me some shred of evidence that you read the book and you can stay home and watch the Super Bowl."

"Easy peasy. It's a British-American novel written by Philip Pullman about a girl named Lyra Belacqua and her daemon, Pantalaimon, who go on an adventure to rescue Lyra's kidnapped friend Roger. It's actually the first book in a trilogy, and I plan on reading the next two as well."

You again, Peter?

"*Dad, there is no way that happened. You didn't read that book.*"

Oh, but, Peter, I did. I foresaw this happening, so I sat down and read the book just so that I could get a second "Get Out of Parenting Free" card and use it to watch the Super Bowl…

Okay, fine, I didn't. That's not what happened. "Easy peasy" should've been a dead giveaway. I don't think I've ever uttered those words. Here's what really happened:

"So, wait, it really is based on a novel?" I asked your mother. "Because that was just a guess on my part." And while we're on the topic, I'm a little shocked that something called *The Golden Compass* isn't about a beleaguered ship captain. We need more books about beleaguered ship captains.

"Yes, it is. And we, as in you and the children and me, are going to this party."

"About that…Just to be clear, does 'we' have to include me? Maybe you and the children can go? I'll stay home and take care of the clogged toilet."

"When we decided to have children, we knew there would be sacrifices. This is one of those sacrifices. The other fathers are going to support their children, and you need to be there to support your daughter."

"Who?"

"Your daughter, Annabelle, who you love more than anything in this world."

"I know who. I was just hoping that this was a nightmare from which I would suddenly wake. And yes, of course I love the children."

"It troubles me a little bit that when you say that, it sounds like you're trying to convince yourself."

"Baby," I cooed. Cooing had never worked on your mother before, but I was desperate. "I knew when we had the kids—"

"Peter and Annabelle."

"Right. Peter and Annabelle, that there would be sacrifices. Sacrifices like lost sleep, free time, and money. I mean, yes, it did occur to me that maybe I'd drive a less expensive car, I wouldn't get to go on as many vacations, or I'd have fewer suits."

"You drive a more expensive car, we go on more vacations, and you have more suits now than you ever did before."

"True, but I would give all of that up for the kids." Kids, if you do not want to be quickly disinherited, then stay away from my Italian suits.

"I'm glad you feel that way. Now get ready, because we're leaving in fifteen minutes."

"Another day of my life spent with Gwenyth and Prescott."

"Gwenyth isn't coming. She's feeling ill."

"That's such a load."

"No, really. She's ill. Hasn't eaten anything."

"She never eats anything. If she starts eating, then we should be worried. And how come she's always 'ill' and not 'sick'? Wait. Does it cost more money to be ill? That must be it." Though I would never choose to spend time with Gwenyth, I would've enjoyed seeing her in a Chuck E. Cheese's.

"Fifteen minutes. Get ready."

———————————

Children, I'm not the type of person who believes in love at first sight, or whose heart skips a beat watching Montagues pursue

Capulets—in fact, I'm surprised that I'm even capable of making that reference. When I saw your mother for the first time, I thought she was gorgeous, but I didn't think I was staring at the future mother of my children. That's not me. However, I became a believer in love at first sight after I met Pradeep Batheja for the first time.

There I was at his daughter's birthday party, leading everyone in a chorus of "The Sun Will Come Out Tomorrow" from my favorite musical, *Annie*...Just checking to see if you were paying attention. No, of course that didn't happen. Here's the truth: there I was sulking in the corner of Chuck E. Cheese's, because not only was I about to miss one of the greatest moments in sports history, but I'd also lost five dollars trying to free a blue dragon from the claw machine, when Dr. Batheja approached.

I was pouting. I was upset. I didn't want to talk to anyone, especially not him, but my heart skipped a beat when I heard his first words to me.

"There's a mini-keg in the ball pit," he said.

I am not an emotional man, but when one has children, and one raises those children, there are moments during that experience when even the strongest of men is reduced to tears. For me, this was almost one of those rare moments.

Never have more beautiful words ever been spoken. Dr. Batheja's soft utterance with his slight Indian accent was like a choir of angels proclaiming the birth of Jesus. Hark, the herald angels sing, glory to the newborn king. Hark, the herald angels sing, Dr.

Batheja hid a mini-keg in the ball pit of Chuck E. Cheese's on Super Bowl Sunday.

"Come again?" I said.

"I believe you heard what I said."

I looked him dead in the eye. "Let me get this straight. You snuck a mini-keg into a Chuck E. Cheese's on your daughter's birthday and hid it in the ball pit? How in the—?"

"I gave it to my daughter for her birthday. It was hidden in one of her presents."

"And what's in that box now?"

"An inflatable pool raft."

"You're a genius."

"Want a beer?"

Part of my job as your parent was to make friends with other parents, no matter how annoying, socially awkward, or contemptible they were. It's one of these so-called sacrifices I made. Having said that, I can honestly say, Annabelle, if you didn't become and stay best friends with Anita Batheja, I might have disowned you.

I was on my third beer when I finally decided that Chuck E. Cheese's might not be such a horrible place for a child's birthday party. Alcohol has a funny way of making even the most difficult of moments in life tolerable. (Don't quote me on that or everyone will think your father's an alcoholic.)

Even Prescott was in on the fun, but you know what they say: when the heinous, overbearing, and maniacal wife—I mean cat—is away, the underappreciated, submissive, and overworked husband—I mean mouse—will play.

Sure I was missing the Super Bowl, but I figured that the Patriots were probably up by a million points and going to win handily. I could always wait to watch the highlights when we got home.

Wrong. The game was close. Real close. Like "maybe one of the best Super Bowls in NFL history" close, only I didn't know it until the Chuck E. Cheese's worker manning the ticket counter alerted me to the drama unfolding in the game. I had gone to the counter to trade my Skee-Ball winnings for a bouncy ball.

"How do you know the game is close?" I asked the Chuck E. Cheese's worker. I'm sure that Chuck E. Cheese's is a lovely place to work, especially if you enjoy the company of screaming children, the smell of stale pizza, and the sound of arcade games, but he looked almost as pitiful as I did—and the poor guy didn't have access to beer.

"We have a TV," the worker said. "The Giants look like they might make a comeback, which is awesome because I'm a huge—"

"Tommy's in trouble? Oh my God, he needs me. Where's this TV?"

"In the break room."

"How many tickets do I need to win the TV?"

"No can do. If I traded the TV for tickets, I would definitely get fired."

"Then can I go watch in the break room?"

"It's employees only."

"Fine. We'll play by your rules. I'd like to apply for a job here. At Chuck E. Cheese's."

"No way."

"Yes way."

"Let me get my manager." The worker left through a door behind the counter, and your mother joined me. I was careful not to breathe on her because I didn't want her to smell the beer on my breath.

"You've been spending a lot of time in that ball pit," she said with narrowed eyes.

"I'm just trying to do exactly what you said. Socialize with the other parents."

"Uh-huh."

"You don't believe me?"

"This is coming from the same man who once said that the ball pit at a McDonald's PlayPlace was more toxic than Chernobyl?"

"That's different. We're not at McDonald's. We're at Chuck E. Cheese's. You can't just compare ball pits." Kids, ball pits are disgusting. Stay out of them.

"Huh." She knew I was up to something, but she didn't know what.

The worker returned with his manager before your mother could probe me any further. "This is him," the worker said, pointing to me.

"Hi, I hear you want to apply for a job at Chuck E. Cheese's," the manager said, extending his hand for me to shake. Kids, if you ever have an important job interview, I recommend that you don't drink three beers before it—or any beers for that matter. But if you do, remember to give a firm handshake, make eye contact, and believe in yourself.

"Wait, what?" your mother asked.

"They have a TV in the break room," I explained.

"Yeah, he's not interested in the job," your mother said. "He just wants to watch the Super Bowl."

"Are you sure?" the manager asked. "We do have a few openings."

"Thank you, but no," she said. "We'll leave you alone now."

Your mother dragged me away from them, which I appreciated because it would have been foolhardy to waste all of my tickets on a bouncy ball. I could save for something better, like a stuffed animal or a glow-in-the-dark Frisbee.

I returned to the ball pit, where Pradeep and most of the other fathers were making good headway on the mini-keg. Sure, it looked a little sketchy, but the screaming children begging their mothers for more tokens made for a nice distraction.

"We need to call an audible, and fast," I said.

"What's the matter?" Pradeep asked.

"The Giants are keeping it close. Too close."

"But Brady…He's the greatest—"

"Quarterback in NFL history. I know, Pradeep, I know." Did I not tell you that I loved this man? Turns out, he was a huge Tom Brady fan too. "We have to do something. Tommy needs us."

"If I leave this party, my wife will kill me."

"I'm sorry to hear that. My wife doesn't care about little things like that. She's truly an amazing person and partner. I am lucky to have her in my life."

Look, kids, let's just say that's what I said, because if your mother ever reads this book, I could be in big trouble if I write what I actually said.

"Your wife sounds like a very understanding woman," Pradeep said. "I wish that I too had married a wife as understanding as yours." Okay, so yeah, you get the drift, but for the record his wife, Priya, is pretty awesome too. "What do we do? Is there a television we can watch?"

"Negatory. The television situation has been compromised. I tried to infiltrate the enemy's ranks but was unsuccessful. There's no way to follow the game out here in the open. We're going to have to do an evac to a safe location."

One of the other fathers who'd been listening in joined our conversation. Usually, this would've annoyed me, but unlike most people who join other people's private conversations, he brought useful insight. "What about the men's room?" he asked. "No women allowed, and we can bribe the children who come in there with tokens to keep them quiet."

"What's your name, soldier?" I asked.

"Bill." It might've been Frank. I don't recall.

"That's good thinking, Bill," I said. "Men's room it is. Pradeep, how do we get the mini-keg out of here?"

"I don't know. I figured someone would have discovered it by now. Never thought I would make it this far."

"My God, man," I said. "No exit strategy? Are you sure you weren't born in this country? That's the most American thing I've ever heard."

"Even if we do get it out of there, do you guys even have a TV?" Bill asked. "I mean, what use is the mini-keg without a TV?"

I was ready to court-martial Bill, or Frank, or whatever his name was, but luckily for him, I was distracted by an addition to our three-man group.

"What're you guys doing over here?" Prescott asked.

"What? Nothing," I said.

"Whatever, chief. Anyway, I just got off the phone with Gwenyth. She thinks the Giants are going to win. The Patriots just scored and took the lead, but they left too much time on the clock. The Giants are driving down the field. If they score a touchdown, it's over."

Oh, for God's sake! Gwenyth was watching the Super Bowl? Although I was incredibly jealous and unbelievably peeved that she had somehow opted out of coming to this birthday—there's no way she was ill—I respected that she was at least watching the game. Her priorities were in the right order, for once.

"What do you mean they're driving down the field?" asked Pradeep. "Why would the Patriots leave so much time on the clock? Why wouldn't they run the ball and burn time? What's Belichick thinking? I don't understand!"

"At ease, Pradeep," I said. I placed my hand on his shoulder and squeezed. I was nervous too, but there was no time to sit and worry. "It's time to call in some reinforcements." I motioned for the other fathers nearby to join us. "Men, let's huddle up." The other guys moved in close and we formed a circle. "Okay, fellas, this is the most important day of the year, and I for one am not going to spend it out here at a little girl's birthday party watching other people's children play Skee-Ball. No offense, Pradeep."

"None taken."

"On three we break and head for the men's room. We'll be safe there. And remember, nobody here tells his wife anything, *capisce*?" The men nodded in agreement. "Prescott, that was really meant for you, because our wives hang out a lot. Okay?"

"I won't say anything to Gwenyth," he answered. Eh, she would beat it out of him.

"Anybody asks, there's a sick kid in there, okay?"

The troops nodded in agreement.

"What about the beer?" Bill asked. "We're just gonna leave it behind?"

"Not all men make it home to their mothers, Bill. I'm sorry." I studied the faces looking back at me. Minus Pradeep, these weren't the men that I'd have chosen to go into battle with, but when you're being held hostage at a little girl's birthday party, you're not given the luxury of choosing your men at arms. "Let's do this. One, two, three, break!"

We were ten grown men huddled together in the boys' restroom at Chuck E. Cheese's. Turns out it said "boys" and not "men." It's a wonder that Chris Hansen guy didn't walk in there with a throng of sheriff's deputies. There was no doubt that your mother was going to be angry with me for orchestrating this impromptu mission—the only question was how shallow a grave she was going to bury me in—but she'd be even angrier if I were legally prohibited from going within fifty feet of your elementary school. That would mean no more chauffeuring you two to and from school—oh, how I would miss that carpool line—and no more attending school functions. I would've enjoyed having a valid excuse—at least in the eyes of the law, not your mother—to skip the school's talent show, but was it really worth registering as a sex offender? I'll be honest. Some years, yes.

Somehow, we all managed to exit the party unnoticed and regroup in our current safe haven, though it wouldn't be long before our absence was noticed. We were running low on tokens—the bribes worked, but word had spread quickly, and every boy at the party was coming in to use the facilities and get his share of the action. I'd never met such opportunistic children. Our plan was working, except I hadn't found anybody to update us on the game. I scrolled through my contacts, calling everyone I could think of, but nobody answered and I couldn't blame them. For obvious reasons, the one person I knew who would answer, Gwenyth, wasn't an option.

"You guys think that this is why women always go to the bathroom together?" Bill asked. "So they can talk about sports in private?

Maybe we should open a sports bar and call it the Boys' Room…" It turned out that Bill guy had only ever had one good idea in his life.

"Can't you think of anybody that will pick up?" Pradeep asked.

"I'm trying." I started to go through my contacts again. There was one name I had skipped the first time around. One person who I knew would answer, but I really didn't want to call him. "I know somebody, but he's a pain in the ass."

"Do it," Pradeep said. "For Tommy."

I took a deep breath and called.

"Who is it?" asked Pradeep.

"My brother-in-law Ronald. Aside from the fact that he treats my sister well, is an amazing father, and would do anything for my sister or their son, he is an utter disappointment. I just wish she'd married someone I could have a beer with, not someone who only wants to talk about the mating habits of the Irrawaddy dolphin."

"Hello?" Ronald answered. Thankfully he picked up after I said "dolphin," otherwise I would've been subjected to a thirty-minute lecture, and the troops would've mutinied. "Don't tell me you're calling to cancel on watching Derek next weekend. Sarah and I asked you months ago if you would do it."

"Relax, Ronald. I'm not calling to cancel. Are you watching the Super Bowl?"

"That's today?"

Jesus. "Yeah, that's today. Can you turn it on and tell me what's happening? Please."

"Hold on, let me go find the bunny ears."

"Bunny ears?"

"You know, the antenna for the TV."

"Make sure you wake up the hamster that powers your house and tell him to get started on the wheel. We're going to need a light jog from him—at a minimum."

"What?"

Fortunately, I received another call, because after hearing about the bunny ears, I knew we were looking at another twenty minutes until Ronald finally set up his TV.

"Nothing. Ronald, I have to go. There's another call coming through. Forget the bunny ears. Bye." I hung up and answered the other call. "Hello?"

"Hey, man, you called?" It was Dennis Kantor, my college roommate and one of the groomsmen at my wedding. I knew he'd be watching the Super Bowl, unlike Uncle Ronald. Why couldn't he have married my sister? He was a responsible and conscientious human being—after all, he had called me back, during the Super Bowl no less.

"Dennis! Thank God! What's going on in the game?"

"What do you mean what's going on in the game? You're not watching?"

"Afraid not."

"What? Why not?"

"Long story, but here's the short version: give me the play-by-play."

"Put him on speaker," one of the fathers near me said. I did, and we all huddled around my phone.

"Well," Dennis said. "Let's see…Madge just went into the kitchen to get me a beer."

"In the game, not the kitchen."

"Sorry, bud. I've had a couple."

"Evidently."

"Okay, so the Giants have the ball at their own forty-four. It's second and five. Minute twenty left in the game. Wait, scratch that. Now it's third down, five. Incomplete pass. Minute fifteen."

The door to the restroom opened, and we all held our breaths, then breathed a collective sigh of relief when we saw it was one of the other fathers — I think his name was Jack.

"This is where you guys are," Jack said. "The women sent me to find you so they could sing 'Happy Birthday' and cut the cake. We figured you were watching the game, but we didn't know where."

"What's going on over there?" asked Dennis. "How about you give me the play-by-play?"

"We're not watching the game," I said to Jack. "We're listening to it." I motioned to the phone in my hand.

"Right," Jack said. "Well, you better finish listening quickly because the children are circling. They want cake. And they want it now."

"Oh my God!" Dennis shouted, nearly busting out the speakers on my phone. "It was amazing!"

"What was amazing?" I asked, shouting back.

"The play!"

"What play?" I asked.

"Madge, did you see that?"

There was barking in response—from Dennis's dog, not Madge. The other fathers and I, Jack included, huddled even closer together, to the point where we were now touching shoulders.

"Take the dog outside, Dennis," Madge yelled.

"What happened?" I asked.

"He's chewing on my damn slippers again," said Dennis. "Tore a piece out of one of 'em. I don't know what I'm going to do about that damn dog."

"Forget the slippers," I said. "I'll buy you a new pair. Tell me about the play."

"Fine!" Madge shouted. "I'll take him outside."

The barking grew louder, and this time it wasn't just the dog. Madge barked—or howled. I'm not sure which, but it sounded like she was in pain. She must've put up one hell of a fight for those slippers.

"God almighty," Dennis said. "Now he went and bit Madge while she was trying to take him out."

"Forget Madge. I'll buy you a new one of her too," I said. "Tell me about the game."

"Oh yeah. It was the most amazing play I've ever seen. Peyton's little brother went back to pass and almost got sacked. I thought for sure they'd whistle him down, but somehow he broke free and threw the ball down the field to a receiver who used his helmet to catch the ball. Best catch I've seen. Ever. They've already replayed it like a hundred times."

Well, shit.

Turns out, that catch, by a relatively unknown receiver by the name of David Tyree, might have been the greatest catch in Super Bowl, if not NFL, history. And where was I when it happened? Hiding in the bathroom at Chuck E. Cheese's.

It's not important what happened after that. Suffice it to say, I am no longer allowed at Chuck E. Cheese's, the Patriots lost, and your mother gave one of the least inspirational speeches in the history of postgame speeches.

As promised, I watched Derek the weekend after, and Pradeep came over to hang out and mourn the outcome of the Super Bowl with me—and also prove to your mother that the Bathejas and I were still on speaking terms.

By then, we'd both had a chance to watch highlights from the game, and Tyree's catch was something to marvel at. He leapt into the air and caught the ball by pinning it against his helmet. As he fell to the ground, the Patriots' defender Rodney Harrison tried to wrestle the ball away, but the refs ruled that Tyree maintained possession.

I still can't believe he caught the ball—it defied the laws of physics. But he caught it. Fair and square. It was truly a thing of beauty—the very definition of clutch.

For reasons that are still a mystery to me, Pradeep and I decided to reenact that play. We decided to use—and let me just warn you, this sounds a lot worse than it was—your baby cousin Derek as a football. Look, I couldn't find anything else more football shaped, and, well, two birds, one stone. Watch the kid, play football. By the way, it's partially your fault I couldn't find anything more appropriate to use. We didn't own a football because you kids spurned sports during your childhood.

I played the role of Tyree while Pradeep acted as Patriots safety Rodney Harrison. I pinned your cousin against my head just as Tyree had pinned the football against his helmet, and I was trying to keep Pradeep at bay, when splat! I fumbled your cousin Derek.

My initial reaction was to fall to the ground and cover up the fumble (i.e., your cousin) — that's football 101 — but I didn't act on that instinct. Instead, I stared helplessly at Derek during what was one of the longest silences of my life. Then Pradeep said something that until my dying day I will never forget.

"I'll get the shovel."

We couldn't contain our laughter and pretty soon your cousin Derek joined in. I picked him up, and Pradeep did a thorough medical examination of him. There wasn't a scratch on him. I was worried I may have seriously injured the kid, but Pradeep, a pediatric surgeon, assured me that Derek was fine.

Still, I never forgot about that drop. The very next weekend, when your cousin ran into the glass door leading to the porch, I thought about that drop. When he failed his driving test three times before he finally passed on the fourth attempt, I thought about that drop. And when he misspelled his name on his SATs and had to retake the whole damn test…Well, you get the point.

Kids, you can't be anything you want to in life. I love your cousin Derek as if he were my own child—my own child who was kidnapped by two fruitcakes and raised according to the laws of a different universe, one with sprites and forest nymphs—but the kid's not going to be designing rockets any time soon—unless it's for North Korea.

But it doesn't matter. Derek may not be the smartest kid in the world, but he understands something that not everyone in this world does. Peter, when you were eight years old, there was a group of neighborhood bullies that used to pick on you. And there was one time when they went a little too far. It wasn't a fair fight. Those little bullies were a couple of years older than Derek and you. You were out playing in our front yard, and I hadn't heard your voice for a while, so I sent Derek to check on you. When he didn't come back right away, I went outside to check on him. I got there just in time to see Derek wreak havoc.

Derek charged those bullies like a child possessed. You were in the middle of the group about to get your butt whooped, and your little cousin came to your rescue. He didn't use jujitsu, karate, judo, or krav maga. Derek used something a lot more primal than that: you hurt one of mine, I kill all of yours. Legs churning and arms flailing, Derek kicked, punched, slapped, chewed, bit, spat, and clawed those older kids until every last one of them had wet britches, and tears streaming down their faces.

It reminded me of a quote by William Shakespeare: "Love all, trust a few, do wrong to none." Far be it from me to criticize one of the greatest writers ever to have lived, but I think ol' Billy had it a little wrong and I would amend it thusly: "Love all, trust a few, do wrong to none, unless 'none' hurts one of yours, then you kick his butt." Those kids never picked on you again, let alone made eye contact with you, because they feared your cousin.

Derek may not understand rocket science, but he knows right, he knows wrong, and he damn well knows what to do when he sees wrong. I learned something that day: revenge is a dish best served by your cousin—because that crazy kid isn't afraid to give everybody two helpings of his fists. Keep him close, love him dearly, trust him absolutely, and remember that when you're in trouble, you should always call me, but sometimes it might be a good idea to call Derek first.

The world needs more people like your cousin. The world needs more people who don't have to think about what to do when they see somebody doing something wrong.

And by the way, we're lucky that I wasn't looking after him during the rise of Odell Beckham Jr., otherwise my little football may have gotten seriously injured.

8

THERE IS A JOLLY FAT MAN WHO BRINGS YOU PRESENTS (ASSEMBLY REQUIRED)

I'm about to tell you something so shocking—so hard to believe—that I hope you are literally sitting down when you read it. I'm waiting. C'mon, Annabelle, sit down. Okay, ready? Oh, wait, before I tell you, remember how we lost the remote for the television like ten years ago and I accused your mother and you of taking it from me and hiding it because you never want to watch football and I always want to watch football? Well, it turns out that…I love Christmas!

See how I turned that around on you and told you the shocking thing? Also, I haven't found the remote because one cannot find that which was stolen from him and not merely stuck between two couch cushions. For the record, I wasn't the only person who wanted to watch football. Steve wanted to watch football too, but I suppose you didn't care about his feelings.

Anyway, I love Christmas.

It goes without saying that I like the food. So. Many. Cookies. And as for the dress, your mother is content as long as I wear clothes without stains, and this is actually the one instance where, unlike Halloween, I humiliate you with what I wear. Generally speaking, your public embarrassment has no bearing on what I decide to wear—if anything, my own comfort and a desire to spread Christmas cheer does—but nevertheless, your anxiety is an added benefit, a stocking stuffer, if you will. And I am very proud of my candy cane sweater.

I even love the music, and in that regard, I am a traditionalist. I like the classics, but I make an exception for some of the selections from the soundtrack to *Home Alone*—John Williams is an amazing composer—and Mariah Carey. I don't care to listen to every artist's Christmas ballads; however, I can tolerate the existence of such recordings because who can blame them? I read *About a Boy* (I saw the movie too; surprisingly good). You write one popular Christmas song and then you don't have to work for the rest of your life. That's an offer more tempting than forbidden fruit.

"Sure, Dad, but what's the catch?"

There's no catch. I'm offended you would even say that. I legitimately love something, and you automatically assume that there have to be strings attached? The nerve! There's no catch. That's it. Look, I may seem to you like the second coming of the Grinch or Ebenezer Scrooge—without the third act where both characters redeem themselves, the Grinch for his grand larceny and Scrooge for being a Republican—but cannot I, despite my antagonistic tendencies, love something unconditionally? Must I always be characterized as a villain?

By the way, I'm going to find that remote. I don't care if we already replaced the TV it accompanied. Don't for a moment think that I stopped looking for it. I don't care if you shipped it to Abu Dhabi along with Nermal; I'm going to find the darn thing and when I do, the catch is that I hate Santa Claus! Yeah, okay, so I did it again.

Time for a little fatherly advice. Hold on; give me a moment while I put on my Mr. Rogers sweater. Okay, here goes. If you ever wake up in the middle of the night and there's a large man with a sack standing in front of your fireplace, realize this: he's not there to bring you presents; he's there to steal your presents. There is no such selfless figure. Aim for the chest and fire in rapid succession.

You want the truth, the whole truth, and nothing but the truth? I wanted to tell you there was no Santa Claus from the get-go, but your mother wouldn't let me. Annabelle, my first words to you were, "There is no Santa Claus." Okay, maybe not the first words, but almost the first words. I used to whisper it to you every year starting the day after Halloween and ending on Christmas morning. I was so proud when you were the first child in third grade to figure it out. Do you know how many calls I received from concerned parents after you spoiled the fun for all of the other kids right in the middle of the class Christmas party? But it was worth it. I had to mute the phone so they wouldn't hear me laughing.

"Dad, if you hate Santa so much, why don't you just tell him that?"

I know you're trolling me, you…trolls—love that use of the word by the way—and I answer you thusly: Oh, but I did. Yes, I did.

"Wait…You did? But how? He isn't even real!"

Do your little dance now, sugar plum fairy! Yes, I even love *The Nutcracker*, I mean it's Tchaikovsky, for God's sake.

"Hold on! Tell us about the time you told Santa that you hated him."

All right, fine. It was the year that we had an unexpected houseguest for the holidays, at least unexpected to me. The rest of you already knew about him, but as usual, I was left in the dark. It was a frosty morning in December, and your mother had left your POs on my bedside table so that I would know what to get you for Christmas—yes, I refer to your Christmas lists as "purchase orders."

I was on my way to make my usual complaints regarding Santa Claus when I saw him…well, *it* really. Your mother was in the kitchen baking—ah, Christmas, 'tis the season for baked goods. I opened my mouth to speak but stopped. He was sitting on the bar in the kitchen, just staring at me with those creepy, beady little eyes. He wore a red hat over his pointy ears.

"What is that?" I asked your mother.

She'd been humming a festive Christmas tune to herself. "That's Wayne Peppermint."

"I'm going to need more than that. What is he?"

"He's an elf. And his name is Wayne Peppermint."

"Have the kids been hanging out near the airport when I'm not around?"

"What? No. Why?"

"How else do you explain the stripper name?"

"Peter wanted to name him Wayne, and Annabelle wanted to name him Peppermint. We compromised."

"I really hope they're not telling everyone at school that some-one named Wayne Peppermint lives here now. And I'm still a little unclear on what he's doing here. Is he paying rent?" Fingers crossed.

"He's the Elf on the Shelf. I told you about this. I gave you the book and asked you to read it. Everyone is doing it nowadays."

"Doctors used mercury for over a century to treat various dis-eases like typhoid fever. That didn't make it right. If everyone is doing it, everyone is probably wrong."

"You seriously don't remember? We had a conversation about it."

"It's not a conversation unless both people are speaking."

"You definitely spoke."

"Hold on. Let's just back up a bit. Was I sleeping when we talked about it?"

"No."

"Was there football on?"

"No."

"Were there sports of any kind on TV, including, but not limited to, sports highlights?"

"No."

"Was I hungry?"

"No."

"Had I just eaten a large meal?"

"No."

"Was it within five days of the release of a new movie starring either Al Pacino or Robert De Niro but not one with either chil-dren or Barbra Streisand?"

"No."

"Okay. I apologize. I forgot. So catch me up on this Wayne guy."

"He's an elf who reports everything that happens here to Santa Claus."

"Wow. So Santa hired another worker to do his job for him? What ever happened to 'he's makin' a list and checkin' it twice'? Son of a gun doesn't make the toys and now he's outsourced this too? Those poor elves." Turns out J. K. Rowling addressed the issue of elves' rights in those wizard books — *Harry Potter and the Insert Magical Crap Here*. And more power to her, she's good people. I've got nothing against Rowling, but I'm not going to read those books — if I want to know more about things that don't exist I can call Aunt Sarah and Uncle Ronald.

"Well, the kids love it," your mother said.

I stared at the demon elf sitting on the bar, uncertain how I felt about him. I needed time to digest the news of this addition to our household. For the moment, I had bigger fish to fry. I don't get that idiom, by the way. Does it take a long time to fry fish or something?

"And I hope you didn't come in here for cookies, because they're not ready yet. I have to let them set before I frost them."

Kids, there is only one reason to wait to eat cookies, and that is when they are going to be frosted.

"No, I didn't come in here for that. I came in here to—"

"Bitch about Santa Claus. I know."

"What do you mean *you know*?"

"Every year we send out holiday cards, decorate the house, buy a noble fir, string Christmas lights and ornaments on it, and hang the stockings. Annabelle and Peter write their Christmas lists, I bake wonderful holiday treats, and you bitch about Santa Claus. It's one of our family traditions."

"I'm confused. Does that mean you're going to let me bitch about him? Or not?"

"Go ahead."

"I love you."

"I love you too."

"Okay, threshold question: is this the year that we can tell the children that there is no Santa Claus?"

"No."

"Follow-up question: is this the year that we can tell Annabelle that there is no Santa Claus, you know, because she's older?"

"No."

"Okay. I hate Santa Claus. First off, let me just say that I really don't enjoy that this massive lie about Santa puts me in such an awkward ethical position. I don't want to lie to my children. How will they ever trust me if I lie to them?"

"I suppose you're not counting all the times you've changed the clocks in the house so that we could sleep in?"

"Well, I..."

"Yeah, I wouldn't open that can of worms. You lie to the children all of the time."

"Fair point. Statement rescinded. Moving on, here's the problem with Santa. I work hard for my money, spend it on the kids—who I love, of course, but really I do it because law and society require me to—and then give all of the credit to some other guy? Not *share* the credit with Santa Claus. *Give* all of the credit to Santa Claus.

Were Santa Claus a real person, he would arguably be the most altruistic person in the world, save for a few endorsement deals and all of the times he's sold his likeness for movies. But Santa Claus, the imaginary man, is a barnacle that everybody treats like a whale. He does none of the work yet gets all of the credit."

"Do you want green or red frosting this year?"

"Red. And another thing. Hold on. Maybe I'm crazy for saying this, but can you do blue?"

"I can do blue, but I'll do red or green too because they're more festive."

"Works for me. Now where was I?"

"Another thing."

"Oh right. This is supposed to be a holiday to celebrate the birth of the Messiah, but let me tell you who really died for the people's sins: me. From hard, backbreaking labor. Because in addition to buying presents, I also build the presents. And let's just call it like it is. My life expectancy has been shortened for the happiness of our children. Granted, if we hadn't had children to begin with, I definitely would have died young because of all of the fun I would have been having. I suppose there's a natural give-and-take there."

"You're making a mountain out of a molehill. No, that's not even a molehill. You're making something out of nothing."

"No, I'm not. Generally speaking, children are incredibly ungrateful people, probably the most ungrateful people in all of society. We feed them, clothe them, and house them. And every Christmas, I spend weeks searching for their presents, only to have them amend their list at the last minute, and when I can't find what they want online I spend hours driving around town, going from store to store, waiting in obscenely long checkout lines, until I find the perfect gifts. Despite all of that effort, they never say a word of thanks to you or me. Then, when they do give thanks, it's, 'Thank you, Santa Claus.' The worst part? He's not even a necessary cog in the process. He doesn't make the toys or wrap the presents; the elves do. He doesn't feed the elves; Mrs. Claus does. He doesn't lug the presents to the children; the reindeer do. And apparently, now he doesn't even spy on the children to see whether they've been naughty or nice; his little friend Wayne..."

"Peppermint."

"Thank you. Wayne Peppermint does. All Santa does — literally, all he does — is get out of the sleigh, magically squeeze his fat ass down a chimney, and place the presents under the tree. He should have been fired years ago. When the economy went down the tube, Mrs. Claus should have given him his pink slip. She should have told him to go squeeze his fat ass into a suit and apply for a new job. Santa Claus is just a figurehead, like that colonel from Kentucky Fried Chicken. I'm over here making the chicken and biscuits, while everyone says 'Colonel this' and 'Colonel that.' Well, screw that. I'm tired of exposing myself to grease fires and kneading the dough while getting none of the colonel's respect. I want to be a colonel too, damn it!"

"Why don't you tell him that?"

"That's the whole point. I can't. Because he doesn't exist!"

"There's a Santa Claus at the mall. Annabelle and Peter are writing their letters to him. I suggest you do the same. We're going next weekend. That gives you a whole week."

"I don't want to go to the mall during the holidays and wait in line for three hours to see a person who's impersonating an imaginary man whose very essence makes me more frustrated than a blind man at a magic show."

"We need a picture with Santa Claus for the family album. So it's either you dress up as your mortal enemy and take a picture with the kids, or we go to the mall and get it taken care of in three hours. And maybe we'll get one of those fourteen-hundred-calorie coffees."

"Fine." I started marching toward the living room.

"Where are you going?"

"I'm going to write my letter to Santa."

I had a week to write my letter to Claus. It had been a while since I'd had to complete a writing assignment, but I employed the same tactic that I'd used during my college days. It had worked then, and it was sure to work again. My approach was to spend six days not writing the letter and then write the letter on the seventh day. Then when writing on the seventh day, I would curse myself for not having written the letter during the previous six days. So yeah, I hadn't really changed (i.e., learned anything) since college, except that now I had the self-awareness to realize that what I was doing was foolhardy. Nevertheless, it's hard to argue with a strategy that resulted in my receiving a four-year degree. I guess that's the problem with success—sometimes a couple of wrong turns will get you there.

In the meantime, I got acquainted with my friend Wayne Peppermint. Yes, that's right, I said "friend." I was getting used to having ol' Wayne around the house. Okay, not initially. Initially, he scared the living crap out of me. I didn't realize that your mother and I were supposed to move the little guy to various locations, which I gather was intended to trick you into succumbing to the belief that he was real and spying on you from numerous vantage points within our domicile.

Though it went against my gut instinct, I indulged in the fantasy of the Elf on the Shelf. Why? Because while you two may not have listened to (i.e., respected) my guidelines (i.e., orders), you certainly weren't going to disobey Claus and his first mate. Yes, that's right. If Claus was the skipper, then Wayne was Gilligan. And although Gilligan may have been a mindless little foot soldier, he was a mouthpiece for a greater man.

At some point since my meeting Wayne, I'd decided that if Claus was going to take all of the credit for my presents, I was going to employ the help of his agent. I became a snake charmer and Wayne was my *pungi*—to be clear, yes, I did just analogize you to snakes, cobras no less. I used Wayne to do my bidding. Here's a list (Santa's not the only one with lists) of the ways in which Wayne Peppermint furthered my agenda:

- He made sure that you didn't take my spot on the couch when I wanted a warm winter's nap.
- He prevented you from changing the channel when I went to get food from the kitchen.
- He stopped you from eating my cookies (arguably the most important of all).
- He got you to clean your rooms and the playroom after my only asking one time (a record).
- He "encouraged" you to eat your vegetables.
- He "encouraged" you to eat my vegetables.
- He made certain you brushed your teeth before heading off to sleep.
- He reinforced the importance of making your bed each morning.

With Wayne Peppermint's help, I had our little group running like the von Trapp family singers—a well-oiled machine. How do you solve a problem like Maria? James Bond would say, a Walther PPK. MacGyver, duct tape. Indiana Jones, a whip. Me? I would employ Wayne Peppermint, that's how! Under his supervision, our household was more rigorous than basic training in the Marine Corps. OORAH! Wayne and I could have had the two of you cleaning all of the baseboards with worn-down toothbrushes. You were like Cinderella without the fairy godmother. I didn't have to wait until the clock struck midnight and your carriage turned into a pumpkin—there was no carriage. There was no ball. There was no prince. There was no glass slipper. Just an evil stepmother.

Sadly, the power of the Elf on the Shelf did not work on everyone. I had Pradeep over to "help me with my letter" that week, which of course was code for "watch football and basketball," and although I told him that I had enlisted Wayne Peppermint to surveil my last pale ale in the fridge, when I returned from the bathroom I saw Pradeep taking a long swig of it.

"What?" he asked. "I'm Hindu. I don't answer to your Santa Claus."

"A loophole."

Oh well, I guess Wayne Peppermint wasn't all-powerful after all.

By day seven, as predicted, I was in trouble. God may have rested on the seventh day, but I didn't have that luxury, as I'd spent the previous six days watching Christmas movie marathons, eating cookies, sipping eggnog, and hanging out with my new best friend, Wayne. After a serious brainstorming session—one filled with a lot of Christmas cheer (i.e., bourbon)—I finally decided that I needed inspiration. And when I say "inspiration," I don't mean I needed to go walk around in nature and watch water trickle down a brook. No, when I say "inspiration," I mean that I needed to plagiarize from other sources. It'd been a number of years since I'd written a letter to Santa Claus. I required help, from professionals, so I went to the two people I knew best who actually wrote letters to the man in the red hat: you two. It was like having the answer key. And guess what? I still have the letters you wrote that year. Annabelle, this was your letter:

Dear Mr. Claus,

Last year I asked you for a new dollhouse and sweaters for Rover and Steve to wear while I walk them in the park. The dollhouse was very pretty, but now I need a new guest dollhouse so that my dolls will have a place for their friends to stay. I will also need more dolls so that my dolls have friends to stay in the new guesthouse. I would also like pink bows for Rover and Steve. You never brought me a sweater for Steve last year. Just for Rover. Did one of the elves forget to pack it? Maybe you delivered it to the wrong house? Please check on that.

I would also like to ask for world peace and good-will toward all people.

Merry Christmas,
Annabelle

And, Peter, here's your letter:

> Dear Santa Claus,
>
> I hope you had a good year. How was your Thanksgiving? I had a good Thanksgiving. I had a lot of turkey and stuffing.
>
> This year for Christmas I would like as many Star Wars Legos as you can fit down the chimney. I really would like the Millennium Falcon and anything else with Han Solo or Master Yoda. I do not like Jar Jar Binks. Do not bring anything with Jar Jar Binks. Also I would like Chewbacca collars for Steve and Rover. My sister Annabelle wants to put bows on them but I think that would look horrible.
>
> After you park your sleigh, you need to know that the alarm code is 13578 and try not to wake up Rover because he will bark.
>
> I will leave you some cookies. Don't tell my dad.
>
> Merry Christmas,
> Peter

Sadly, your letters weren't as helpful as I'd hoped—I should have known better than to take advice from two people who adored Santa. And, Peter, I didn't realize I was raising a little Benedict Arnold. After reading your letter, I feared for the safety of our family. But don't worry. I made sure to change the alarm code, and guess who I didn't share the new code with?

As for the cookies…Really? For shame, Peter. For shame. I know we always leave cookies out for Santa, but to go out and advertise them like that? It hurts.

Alas, without your help, I somehow managed to write my letter:

> Dear Santa Claus,
> You suck.
>
> Very truly yours,
> Annabelle and Peter's Father

Thoughts? I thought it was pretty good myself. Yup. I was ready to face Kris Kringle. It was time to brave the Russian winter and head to the mall during Christmas.

We made it, and with only three parking lot confrontations—a merry Christmas indeed. Standing in line for Santa Claus, I felt an unusual sense of camaraderie as I saw all of the children clutching their letters. I had my fourteen-hundred-calorie coffee in one hand and my letter in the other. Yeah, I was ready.

But heroes often face challenges on their road to glory. For me that challenge was the lady in line behind us. She did something that I absolutely abhor. She spoke to me.

Look, lady, just because by some random twist of fate—which I don't believe in—we found ourselves in the exact same place at the exact same time, do not take that as an opportunity to address me. Sadly, children, I was born with a warm and friendly disposition, which often betrays what I'm really thinking, which is, *Do not disturb*. If you children one day decide to buy me a present with your own money (i.e., not the credit cards that I pay for every month), a T-shirt with "Patient Zero" on it is all I want. I hope that the shirt, along with a manufactured cough, will keep the socially inept at bay.

"Did your daughter write that letter?" the lady asked.

"No, I did."

"Oh…"

Awkward.

"Yeah, I just had a lot of things that I had to get off my chest. You know, because I really don't like Santa Claus. I mean, when you think about it, he might actually be the most horrible person who has ever lived."

This was a tactic I used when people spoke to me in public. This epiphany found me later in life: the people who talk to you in public when you clearly don't want them to are incapable of picking up on social cues, and thus the "short responses" tactic, a tried and true approach for most people, will never work on them. If you offer short responses and couple that with an unwelcoming tone, then you're the bad guy, even though you didn't want them to initiate the conversation.

However, there is one approach that does work: awkwardness. People with this lack of social awareness are like cheap metal detectors — they may be incapable of finding anything beneath the surface, but they'll go off when they're near a two-ton car made from corrugated metal. Awkwardness is that car. So, instead of deliberately not making eye contact or providing curt responses, I implemented the "I'm going to make things so awkward that you won't want to speak with me ever again" method. Or "leave me the hell alone" for short.

"Between you and me," I said, "I went into credit card debt last year and ended up paying more in interest than I did for my children's presents. We almost had to take out a third mortgage, and sure, we had to put the dog down a couple of years earlier than we wanted to, but I guess that's the price you pay for a holiday completely run by corporate greed. So yeah, I wrote the letter. I just had to speak my mind. And I have one wish. Can you guess what it is?"

"Oh dear…"

"I want Santa Claus to die."

Mission accomplished. The lady left me alone, and I waited in line without further intrusion until it was finally our turn to see Santa.

"C'mon, let's go," your mother said. "I wonder if I can get someone to take a picture with my camera."

"Doesn't the photographer take one?" I asked.

"Yeah, but I want one with mine too."

We hadn't even seen the photographer yet and already your mother distrusted him. It was like a sixth sense. Your mother always had the uncanny ability to know who was good or bad at taking pictures. Luckily for her, I had the uncanny ability to find people to help.

"I'm sure she won't mind," I said, pointing to the lady behind us. She didn't respond, but I gave her the camera and joined you two and your mother next to Santa.

"Ho, ho, ho," Santa bellowed. "Merry Christmas!" You two squealed, and I swallowed the bile that had quickly climbed its way up my esophagus. Here he was. Your American Express black card. "I hope you brought me some letters so I know what to get you for Christmas!"

"I brought you a letter, Santa," I said.

"Aren't you a bit old to be writing letters?"

"Here. Read it anyway."

We handed him our letters and he read them while we positioned ourselves for the family picture. He breezed through your letters—not caring what you had asked for because he wouldn't be the one buying your presents (just making sure that dead horse is beaten to a pulp)—but he read mine with care. And his expression, which before had been one of annoying merriment, quickly transformed to one of confusion, before it eventually settled on discomfort.

Our family beamed with smiles; Santa, on the other hand, well, he was still trying to wrap his head around the letter that I'd penned. I don't think his cheeks had ever been that rosy.

"Okay, everybody smile wide," your mother said.

A couple of quick clicks of a button, and we were finished. We headed toward the exit, and I turned around to wave good-bye to Claus. When I looked back, I saw that his eyes were fixed on me.

"Merry Christmas!" I said. "Ho, ho, ho!"

———————————

Okay, so yeah. I didn't really give Santa the "you suck" letter. Here's the letter I gave Santa:

Dear Santa Claus,

When I was eight years old, I asked my mother for a BB gun, but she told me that I couldn't have it because I would hurt myself. She didn't think that I was mature enough to own a weapon at such a young age even though all of my friends' parents were buying them BB guns. I imagine that's exactly how Native Americans must feel every day of their lives. You're entitled to something, but it's taken away from you without any type of explanation or warning, and then instead of getting that something that you deserve, you get something far worse. For Native Americans, it was alcoholism, cholera, and the worst territories strung across North America. For me, it was an embarrassing costume that my aunt got me. I awoke on Christmas morning and was heartbroken. Christmas was ruined.

Or so I thought…I noticed a gift behind the tree. Could it be…? I opened the package and there it was! A Red Ryder BB gun! Just like the ones my friends were getting for Christmas. You saved the day, Santa! My hero. I took it outside and tried it out. And, just like my mother had warned, I almost shot my eye out.

Seriously? Are you that stupid, Santa? That's the plot to *A Christmas Story*. That never happened to me, or to anyone for that matter—except that it's a pretty ubiquitous story, but that's beside the point.

Much like that story, you aren't real. You don't exist. You didn't save the day in that story. Ralphie's father did. He was the real hero. The man who worked twelve hours a day down at the plant just so he could make his son's Christmas special. You took that from him. And every year you take that from me and parents all around the world. I hope you're proud of yourself, you damn pilgrim.

Merry Christmas,
Annabelle and Peter's Father

PS: If you don't smile for this picture, they will make us take it again. I don't want to spend any more time in this godforsaken mall than I have to, so you better smile the first time.
PPS: If you come to my house and eat my cookies, I will beat them out of you. Chip by chip.

———————————

We returned home and I settled in for a long winter's nap—another of my traditions during the holidays. There I was, stretched out in my chair with a mug of cocoa and a plate of cookies on my side table. A classic Christmas movie was playing on the television, and

I had a death grip on the remote because I lived in a house with people I couldn't trust.

"Okay. What'd you do with him?" your mother asked, barging in and disturbing my perfect slumber.

"What?" I yawned and stretched out my arms, then enjoyed a bite of cookie.

"The Elf on the Shelf. I can't find him anywhere. He's gone missing."

And with that, I was wide wake. I swallowed the cookie and washed it down with a quick sip of cocoa. My life before Wayne Peppermint flashed before my eyes—it was a world where rambunctious children didn't obey even the simplest of commands. I needed that elf back, and I needed him back fast.

Our search began. Your mother and I checked every part of the house, high and low, and even the front and back yards. I tried to employ the help of our canine companions, but they wouldn't budge from their naps. They'd become too domesticated; the allure of hunting no longer appealed to them.

I checked every shelf in the house just in case he had decided to return to his natural habitat, but nada. He was gone, which left me to posit several theories about his disappearance.

"I'll tell you exactly what happened to him," I said. "He witnessed a crime, somebody tried to give him some hush money, and he wouldn't take it. So he got whacked."

And:

"Maybe one of the dogs ate him. That explains why they wouldn't help us. One of them already knows where he is—in the culprit's digestive tract."

And finally:

"Maybe he fell down a well. Remember when everyone used to fall down wells? Why doesn't that happen anymore?"

Your mother graciously listened to my tinfoil theories, but she wasn't buying them. After a couple of hours, we decided to take a break in the kitchen, and I got the uneasy feeling that I might be the one charged with Wayne's kidnapping.

"Look, honey," I said, "if it were Santa who was dead…I'm sorry. That's premature. If it were Santa who was missing, then yes, that would have been me. I confess. But Wayne Peppermint? I was starting to enjoy having him around to protect the house. Not for any of that Christmas-tradition stuff, because we all know that is a bunch of poppycock, but he was pretty good at surveillance. Ironically, the only person who could tell us who kidnapped him is…Well, it's him. Wayne, we need you now more than ever."

"You like the Elf on the Shelf?"

Ah criminy. I should've just confessed to the kidnapping. I'd piqued your mother's curiosity, and accordingly, I had to explain to your mother how I'd used Wayne to coerce you children into doing chores and staying away from my cookies. Mea culpa. Still, that didn't bring Wayne back from the bottom of the well.

I took my lashes and then decided to retire to my place of quiet reflection—the only place on this Earth where you dare not disturb me: my bathroom. I was standing in front of the toilet, debating which magazine I would comb through while I rested on my throne, when I saw a pair of feet staring back at me.

"I found him," I said. "Honey, bring in the sidewalk chalk. There's a body."

"Where is he?" your mother asked. I heard her enter our bedroom and come toward the bathroom. "Is it safe to come in there?"

"Yes, it's safe. I haven't started yet, thank you very much."

She joined me in the master bath. "Where is he?"

"Somebody tried to send him to the South Pole." I pointed down at the toilet bowl, where Wayne's little feet were just visible beneath the water. "They flushed him. Headfirst. The poor guy never stood a chance."

We didn't need Hercule Poirot to tell us what happened. It was evident from your behavior over the next several hours that the two of you had joined forces to murder Wayne Peppermint. I don't know which one of you distracted him while the other put the chloroform-soaked rag over his mouth, but it didn't matter. You were both guilty. It was *Murder on the Orient Express*. You both did it.

Also, after I confessed to your mother about how I'd used Wayne for my own selfish reasons, she solved Wayne's murder and blamed me, not you. As she put it: "You may not have been the one who put him in the bowl, but you pushed the flusher."

I apologized, profusely, and Miss Marple told me to invite you down for cookies and cocoa so I could mend things. You two skulked into the dining room and joined us at the table. You barely nibbled at my cookies, and that's when I decided it was time for me to come clean about all of this nonsense.

"Let me tell you something your mother won't tell you," I said. Your mother looked at me with a raised eyebrow—just the one—and if she'd been sitting next to me, I'm sure she would have grabbed my wrist and squeezed until I didn't have a pulse, which was her way of saying, "Shut up." But I didn't care. I had to tell you the truth. "The Elf on the Shelf isn't real."

"What do you mean?" Annabelle asked.

"He isn't real," I said. Your mother raised her second eyebrow, and I sensed I was about to be the next one flushed to the South Pole. "What I'm saying is that he doesn't work for Santa Claus."

"If he doesn't work for Santa Claus, then who does he work for?" Peter asked.

"Vladimir Putin," I answered.

"Who's that?" Peter asked.

"He's the leader of Russia. And Wayne Peppermint is something of a double agent for him. You may think he works for Santa, but he actually works for Mother Russia. I caught him talking on the phone in Russian."

"Dad, you don't speak Russian, do you?" Annabelle asked.

"Well, I've seen all of the James Bond films. Plus, I've read almost every Tom Clancy book. The early ones at least. Not the crap that came out that he didn't write. The point is, I know some Russian. And he wasn't just spying on you kids, but he was spying on all of us. Our family and America."

I reached down beneath my chair and removed a Ziploc bag with "Exhibit A" written on it in Sharpie. I placed it on the table, and your eyes widened. Inside was the body of Wayne Peppermint.

"Now, kids, we know what you did, and it's okay. I wish you'd given him a better send-off than a goldfish, but—"

"What do you mean?" Annabelle asked.

"Just that...," I stuttered. "He can't swim. Because he's not a fish. Regardless, you did your country a service in getting rid of Wayne."

"Are we at war with Russia?" Peter asked.

"Not exactly," I said, "but America's relationship with Russia is complicated."

"Complicated?" Annabelle inquired.

"Yeah, kind of like Bert and Ernie."

"Are we Ernie or are they Ernie?" Peter asked.

"America is definitely Ernie," your mother said, helping me out. "Don't worry."

"Let's give Wayne a better send-off," I said.

"Like what?" your mother asked.

"We still have that baby pool, right?"

———————————

There we were, in the back yard, around the baby pool, with Steve and Rover, watching as Wayne's little elf body rested on a burning bed made from Popsicle sticks and dry leaves. A Viking funeral for my first lieutenant, who, in the end, turned out to be a Russian spy.

I was sad to lose him, but it turned out to be a useful opportunity to teach you more about Vikings.

It was hard watching his body turn to ashes, but I'd learned a lot from the experience. Namely, that people should really have two elves on their shelf: one for their children to murder and the other to report that behavior to Santa.

"It's what he would have wanted," I said.

"How do you know?" your mother asked.

"Wayne and I were close. Real close. I didn't know he was a double agent, but still, I counted him as a friend. Good night, sweet comrade."

9

THE DOG WENT TO LIVE ON A FARM WITH YOUR GOLDFISH WHERE THEY'LL HAVE MORE ROOM TO RUN AROUND

I hate losing things. It drives me crazy. When I was younger, I never forgot where I left anything. I always remembered. And with ease. One of the hardest parts of aging was saying good-bye to my short-term memory. If I could have one superpower, it would be to remember where I left anything at any given time. All I would have to do is think of something that I had lost, and then bam! I would remember where I left it. But there would be one major problem with this power. I would have to remember what I had lost first—sometimes that isn't so easy.

No, I haven't lost my mind. Obviously, if I could only have one superpower, I would choose flying over having a super memory. Still, it would be a close sixth place. Yeah…It would definitely be far from my first choice. So really, if I could have one superpower, my first choice would be flying, and my second would be which-ever power could solve whatever predicament was ailing me at the moment that I decided I needed a superpower. Am I doing it right?

A super memory might help for inanimate objects, but what would happen if, say, I lost something that was living and breathing and also my children's favorite person in the world? And what if this person, if you will, was technically a canine that always protected me when the neighborhood cats gave me the stink eye, and that always barked at the mailman whenever he bent any of my packages? What if initially I didn't want this canine to be a part of our household, but after he had joined, I came to love him just as much as another canine by the name of Steve? What if this canine was not lost per se so much as he ran away on a day when I just happened to take a personal day at work while my wife and my elder child were out of town on a fifth-grade field trip and my younger child needed to be picked up by three o'clock, otherwise he would demand that the principal call the police? And what if this canine whom I — well, we — lost was named … Rover?

Before this gets ugly, by "we," I mean Steve and me. I'm not the only one to blame here. And let me go ahead and level a preemptive strike, because by "lost" I do not mean lost. Rather I mean that he ran away. And it totally ruined my personal day, but I'm sure that's immaterial to you both.

That's right, I had the day off, and it started as perfectly as any day could. I slept in. That's a phrase that takes on new meaning as you grow older and sleep becomes like a pot of gold at the end of the rainbow. Unattainable. The stuff of legend. Once you have children, it will be many years before you ever have the opportunity to sleep in again. And then, by the time those children are of an age where they want to sleep in and accordingly you can actually rest because they won't wake you at some ungodly early hour, you no longer have the ability to sleep in. Waking up at dawn has become so ingrained in you that your body has forgotten how to sleep in. Kind of like how my hands have forgotten how to touch my toes.

I literally had only two things I had to do that day: drop you off at school, Peter, and then pick you up. Showering was optional, although advised. I opted to take one.

I spent that day as if it were my last day on Earth. After sleeping in, at the late hour of six thirty a.m., I dropped Peter off at school and then returned home—still sporting my bathrobe over my pajamas (athletic shorts and an old T-shirt)—where I prepared my breakfast: black coffee and vanilla ice cream. You know what's better than breakfast for dinner? Dessert for breakfast. I felt very European—don't French people eat dessert for breakfast like all the time? Oh, they don't? Then explain éclairs.

Exactly.

After lazing about the house for a couple of hours and catching up on decades of morning television, I called my favorite Italian restaurant, which started taking lunch orders at 10:30 a.m. I showed restraint and waited until 10:31 a.m. to place my order for delivery. People who have a serious problem call exactly at 10:30 a.m. By waiting that extra minute, I proved that I had self-restraint.

After devouring my chicken parm sandwich, I did what any man who lives in fear of being judged by his fellow man—especially his spouse—would do. I placed all remnants of the meal I had just consumed in the trash can in front of the house two doors down. And it wasn't just my fear of persecution that led me to use another man's trash; it was the privately held belief, or hope, that using somebody else's trash would somehow mean that the calories I consumed wouldn't be attached to my body. If only science were cool like that.

I was about to settle in for a long winter's nap when it dawned on me that I should probably make sure that the only other two occupants of our house that day—Steve and Rover—had everything they needed. I could have gone straight to slumber, but I'm glad I didn't, otherwise this story may have ended much differently. I don't know what exactly made me check—I'm not one for coincidences—but I did, and that's when I noticed. There was a member of our household missing. He was nowhere to be found. I searched high. I searched low. I couldn't find him anywhere. Rover was gone.

This was bad. Real bad. If I didn't find Rover by carpool time, I would have to answer a lot of questions. Children have the uncanny ability to ask difficult questions when you least want them to. Usually it starts with a simple question, and then, after delivery of an unsatisfactory answer to that simple question—that part is inevitable—the conversation evolves into the child asking a series of whys while the adult provides more unsatisfactory answers, until finally the adult is forced to lie, or say, "I don't know," and then lie. I foresaw this happening, and I couldn't think of a viable reason for Rover's absence that wouldn't implicate me in his disappearance, although I was completely innocent. I swear!

Needless to say, I needed help. So I did what any self-respecting man with two children and a wife would do. I called my mother.

"Mom, I need your help. Rover ran away."

There's something you have to understand about your grandmother. I wasn't calling her to vent. Emotional support was not going to help me find Rover. No, I was calling Grammy because she was the modern equivalent to Dr. Dolittle. Yes, that is the children's book that Eddie Murphy ruined in a different medium, although it probably wasn't his fault. *Beverly Hills Cop* was awesome, but *Dr. Dolittle* was a horrible movie. And no, I never actually saw the film version of *Dr. Dolittle*, but let's be serious for a moment. Some films you don't have to watch to critique. Sometimes the trailer is enough. Actually, sometimes the movie poster is enough. Maybe even the title in a couple of instances.

Enough about 'enry 'iggins; the point is your grandmother knew animals. She couldn't speak to them, but she could understand them.

"Where's Steve?" she asked.

"He's here. Helping me look." We were in the front yard, and Steve was sitting next to me, leashed. To that point he hadn't really helped me so much as observed while I searched for Rover. Nevertheless, I brought him with me, because do you know what's worse than losing one dog? Losing two.

"He will find him."

"Who are you? The Oracle at Delphi? What do you mean 'he will find him'?"

"Steve. Is he on his leash?"

"Of course he's on his leash. I'm a responsible pet owner…present disaster excluded, of course." I felt like any workplace that had a sign that read "X number of days since last accident." That sign was so unfair. Until this day, we hadn't ever had a "workplace" accident! We'd been flawless.

"Take him off the leash."

I reached over and unhooked the leash from Steve's collar. I waited for a moment, but he didn't budge.

"It didn't work," I said. "He's just sitting here."

"Well, did you ask him?"

"Ask him?"

"Yes, you have to ask him. Nicely."

I placed the cell phone down at my side and knelt in front of Steve. "Look, fella, I know you haven't always been Rover's biggest fan, but he could really use your help right now. And so I could I. So if you could help me find him, well, I…I'd really—"

Before I could finish that thought, Steve took off—faster than I'd ever seen him run before.

"Oh my…," I said. I put the cell phone back to my ear. "Mom, you were right. It worked! He's running."

"Go after him!"

"Oh. Right."

For many years now, Steve had been something of a glorified house cat. He was moody, kept to himself, and never really bothered anybody unless he wanted something—whether that was food, a bathroom break, or a belly rub. He may have grown jaded by family life, or perhaps this was all just a part of his getting older. It's tough to say. But that day, Steve came alive. He was a dog again. A bloodhound. A hunter. A predator. He was the forlorn royal who'd strayed off the path but had come back to reclaim his crown, his birthright. The prodigal son had returned, and I—clad in my bathrobe and pajamas—tried my best to keep up with him.

Unfortunately for me, neither Nike nor Under Armour made bedroom slippers—but seriously, they should, right? And last time I checked, marathoners don't eat ice cream and chicken parm sandwiches before a big race. It was challenging, but I was determined. There was only one thought going through my head, besides *Find Rover*, and that was, *Let him be alive. Please let him be alive.*

I don't know how long we ran. And I don't know how I managed to keep up with Steve. There were several times when he turned a corner and I completely lost sight of him. Eventually, we came to a two-lane highway a few miles from the house, and I turned onto it and stopped. I couldn't see Steve. Now I'd lost two dogs.

"Steve!" I yelled. "Steve!"

Several seconds passed, and then I heard him barking. I scanned the area until I finally spotted him on the other side of the road in a ditch. Oh no. I made eye contact with him and he barked some more. I looked up and down the highway, then bolted across both lanes.

When I reached the ditch, I saw Rover lying on his side and breathing heavily. I'd known this dog since he was a pup, and not once had I ever seen him like this. I knew something was wrong. I had to get him to the vet, and fast. I took off my bathrobe and wrapped it around Rover, then picked him up in my arms.

Steve and I were in the waiting room at the vet's office, surrounded by all types of animals, but mostly dogs and cats. When I had first seen Rover's body in the ditch, I feared that a car may have hit him, but I checked him over and over again and there wasn't a scratch on him. I started carrying him back home, which was no easy feat — the mutt must've weighed seventy pounds. Thankfully one of our neighbors saw me and stopped. I must have been a curious sight. I was holding one dog in my arms while the other barked at me repeatedly, begging me to move faster. The neighbor graciously drove the three of us to the vet's office.

I sat staring blankly at the floor tiles in front of me. Meanwhile, a loyal Steve stood at attention watching the door through which Rover had disappeared what seemed like hours ago. He wouldn't take his eyes off it. For the first few years that we had Rover, Steve had completely ignored his existence. Rover would playfully attack Steve, but Steve never accepted this invitation to play. Naturally Steve's tacit rejection only made Rover want to play with him more. He was the pesky younger brother whom Steve didn't want to be seen with in public. I had always suspected that Steve really loved Rover, but until that day, I didn't know how much. Sure enough, he loved him. After all, they were brothers.

The same was true for me. A vet's office is a noisy place. There's a lot of barking, even more meowing, and the occasional squeal. I didn't hear any of it. My mind was lost; I was thinking about Rover. I'll be the first to admit, I didn't initially want another dog, but after we brought him home — and he nearly destroyed it — I fell in love with the little guy. Sure, he'd cost me several thousand dollars in property damage, but he never failed to put a smile on my face. He was a puppy who never grew up into a dog.

I glanced up at the door and saw a mother and her child walk by with their pooch. Oh no. Peter! I had forgotten that I had to pick you up. I reached for my cell phone and dialed Grammy's number. She picked up on the first ring.

"I need a favor," I said. "I don't know if I'm going to be able to pick up Peter today."

"We're already on our way."

"Dad too?"

"He's driving. Like a bat out of hell."

Grammy had always been a strict believer in obeying all traffic laws. I had spoken to her several times when she was in the car while Grandpa was driving, and I had never once heard her say that he was driving above the speed limit without her quickly thereafter telling him to slow down — until then. Kids, it's easily a three-hour drive from Grammy and Grandpa's house to our home. That day they made it in half the time.

"Carpool starts at three o'clock sharp. Are you sure you can —"

"We'll be there."

"Thanks." I hung up and resumed my staring contest with the floor.

I was not prepared then, and I don't think I would be prepared now, to speak with you about death. I didn't know what to say, and I still don't. The problem is that I don't have any answers that will comfort you. I don't know where you go when you die. I don't even know that you go anywhere. I can tell you what some believe on faith; I can tell you what I've read in books; I can tell you what your mother told me to tell you; I can tell you what my mother told me.

That's right, I once went to Grammy seeking answers on this topic. It happened after my first real experience with death, when I was old enough to understand what it meant. I had a distant relative who'd passed away. I've forgotten exactly how we were related, and I had only met him a couple of times, but I'll never forget Grammy telling me about his death. It was an accident. Something that never should have happened but did. It was tragic. Truly tragic. Sometimes I think that's the only word we have to describe death, and even it doesn't fully encompass the sorrow we feel when a person dies.

I went to the funeral and the reception that followed with her. There was something that stuck with me during that experience. It was a comment I heard said over and over again that I didn't quite understand: "I hope he didn't suffer." What does that even mean? I didn't know. After making small talk with all of the relatives, we left and went home. A couple of hours passed, and I couldn't get that comment out of my head, so I went to Grammy. I was still wearing my suit from the funeral, and Grammy was in the living room reading a book, as she often was. I shuffled in quietly and stood next to her until she looked up from her page.

"Mom, I wanted to ask you something," I said.

"Oh, sit down, dear. I'm always here for you. You know, this reminds me of the time that your aunt Patricia and I—"

"Seriously? How could this remind you of something? I haven't said anything. Mom, I haven't even asked the question yet and you've already gone off on a tangent. What if I was here to tell you that I had been diagnosed with an inoperable brain tumor and I had only thirty days to live? Can you imagine? With what little precious time I had left on Earth, I would have to spend twenty minutes of it listening to you go on about Aunt Patricia." What can I say, kids? I was a temperamental youth…who hasn't aged a day. Emotionally, that is.

"Oh my God. Have you been diagnosed with an inoperable brain tumor? Thirty days? Is that all we—"

"No, that wasn't the point."

"I want to talk to your doctor."

"Mom, I'm not dying. The point is I have a question, and you should relish this moment. I'm coming here to ask you and not Dad."

"Honey, your father doesn't like answering questions."

"I'm aware. I was trying to make it seem as if I had a choice in the matter so that you would feel special, but clearly I underestimated how well you know your husband."

"Thank you. Now, what's your question?"

"Okay." I took a breath. I still don't enjoy broaching sensitive topics with people. "Mom…where do babies come from?"

"Oh, dear…"

"Relax, I'm kidding." Some things never change. I've always used humor to defuse difficult situations. "Mom"—I breathed in deeply—"why do people care whether or not people suffer when they die? That's all I hear. Did she suffer? Did he suffer? Was it quick? Was it painful? Did she know it was coming? Did he go in his sleep? I don't understand it. I mean, who cares if someone suffered? They're dead. Without life. Gone. Forever. I just don't get it."

"Baby," she said, "one day you will understand." Then she went back to reading her book.

"That's it?" She didn't budge. Just kept reading. "I came here for parenting, and you, my parent, refuse to parent me? Well…I think I want my money back. Or, if not, can I put myself up for adoption? You think if I put on a diaper and lie down in a basket, a group of nuns would find me and raise me?" Kids, if you ever talk to me like that, it'll be the last words you ever say. My household was complicated. We lived with my father.

Truth is, I could've ranted for hours like that and she wouldn't have heard it. Not a word. She was lost in her book. I sighed and headed for the door, but she had one more thing to say.

"One day you'll understand," she said softly, "but I hope that you don't."

Her revelation obviously didn't sit well with me, and I never let her forget it. Kids, I'm not known for holding grudges; I'm known for acting on the grudges that I hold. As time passed, I exacted my unwarranted revenge. When I was in my twenties, I got my private pilot's license; your grandmother went berserk. But I kept her well informed any time I took flight by leaving a message on her answering machine. It usually went a little something like this: "Mom, I'm going to fly in a plane today. In case I die, I love you. And if the plane crashes, just so you know, I definitely suffered. Like a lot. Plane crashes hurt and then you burn alive."

I wish I could say that was the only message I left to remind her of that day, but it wasn't. Here's a list of some of the messages I left on Grammy's answering machine:

- There was the time I went to drive four-wheelers: "Hey, Mom, just wanted to let you know that Ray and I are about to go deep into the woods and ride four-wheelers. The nearest hospital is about forty-five minutes away…by helicopter. You're looking at more like three hours by car, and that's assuming you have four-wheel drive. My friend went to ride four-wheelers the other day, and he broke every bone in his body. Anyway, just wanted to let you know. Oh yeah, and in case I die, I definitely suffered. A lot. Every. Single. Bone. Love you! Bye!"

- That time I bought a cookbook: "Hey, Mom, I bought a cookbook today. My first one. I'm trying out a new recipe for steaks and I'm going to make a baked potato. Going to cook it in the microwave. I've heard that you're not supposed to use metal in the microwave, but I think that's just an old wives' tale. Anyway, if anything goes wrong, I just want to let you know that I definitely suffered because electrical fires are hard to put out. Love you!"

- That time I tried skateboarding: "Mom, guess what? Got my first skateboard today. Can't wait to go flying down a big hill. The guy at the store recommended I get a helmet, but nobody looks cool wearing a helmet. If I get into an accident, I want you to know that it hurt like hell, because I can't think of anything more painful than skidding on pavement for thirty yards. Bye!"

- That time I went to England: "Mom, I thought of you today when I had my first crumpet. Anyway, I'm about to go eat beef Wellington. I know there's an outbreak of mad cow disease here, but I just can't pass up beef Wellington. I read something about it in college, but I can't seem to remember much about mad cow disease…Wait, 'slow and painful,' that's what I read. 'A slow and painful death.' But, I mean, I really want to experience the local culture. Moo!"

- That time I went cliff diving in Mexico: "*Buenos dias, Madre. Yo soy en Mexico*, and I'm about to go cliff diving. Yes, it is exactly what it sounds like. For no reason whatsoever, other than my own need for a rush of adrenaline, I am about to jump off a cliff into a body of water, the depths of which I do not know. So listen up, if the sharks don't eat me — oh, wait. Did I mention that part? I'm about to jump into shark-infested waters. So yeah, if I don't end up as shark bait, then I'll probably drown on account of the riptide. What's that?

Oh, you're so right, it's the rocks that'll kill me. I'll try not to land on any jagged ones. Well, I just wanted to let you know that if I die, whether it be from the sharks, the drowning, or that horrendous fall—or some combination of all three—I suffered. A lot. *Te amo!*"

Naturally, your grandmother didn't see the humor in it. But don't feel bad for her. Eventually, she started firing back in kind. Here is a list of your grandmother's responses to my idiotic remarks:

- "Have fun."
- "Sounds like fun. Would you like an open or closed casket?"
- "That's too bad. We decided to give your sister your burial plot."
- "I have the perfect coffee can to put your ashes in."
- "Love you."
- "You're an idiot."
- "Any shark that ate you would certainly spit you out."

And you wonder where I got it?

———————————

Steve moved. Finally. I heard him rustle forward before I heard the door open. He must have heard the footsteps coming toward us on the other side. I looked up at the door and it opened. Rover walked out, followed by the vet, Dr. Chandra.

"He's going to be okay," the doctor said.

I don't know that happier words have ever been spoken. I wasn't ready to lose a family member. Not that day. Not ever.

It wasn't until a couple of weeks after the incident that things felt normal again. Dr. Chandra explained that Rover had overexerted himself and experienced a serious case of heatstroke and muscle spasms. The diagnosis wasn't as serious as I'd feared, but still I kept a watchful eye over the pup — as did Steve — for the next few months. At first, Steve played the role of the overprotective older brother, and then, only after he felt assured that Rover was in fact healthy, Steve bopped him on the head one day. I was sitting in my chair, channel surfing, and Rover rested on the ground next to me. Steve walked in, went straight to Rover, and tapped him with his left paw. Translation: Never do that to me again. Steve was a gentle soul with a rough exterior.

Your mother and I decided it was better not to tell you what happened that day. We didn't want to worry you. It might upset you to hear that now, but if I could go back and do it again, I still wouldn't tell you. I didn't want you to feel how I felt when I went to talk to Grammy that day. And I should add, it took me some time to understand, but she was right. Please don't tell her I said that. I haven't matured that much. One day you'll understand too, but I hope that you don't.

10 THOSE ARE DADDY'S COOKIES

There comes a time in every parent's life where they become the child—where, true to form, the teacher becomes the student, where Mr. Miyagi becomes Daniel-san—and when it happens, the parent has a choice: accept this change in power with humility or run, run, run...run far away.

For me, that moment happened just after my fortieth birthday. Most adults, when they reach their forties, experience something of a midlife crisis. They dye their hair, undergo plastic surgery, buy an expensive and youthful car, decide to have an affair with someone half their age, or do something equally stupid that reveals their insecurity about this milestone in their life. I have never been one for overt actions that reveal my insecurities, unless of course they're in some way related to my disdain for another person, place, or thing. In other words, I have always been one for overt actions that reveal my insecurities. However, in this case, I managed to pass muster and avoid the inevitable midlife crisis.

That's in large part because I somehow managed to skip a couple of decades, with regard to not my actual age, but rather my mentality. In terms of my emotional outlook, I had something of a Rip Van Winkle experience. I went to bed on the night before my fortieth birthday with the outlook of a thirty-nine-year-old and awoke the next morning with the same mentality as a sixty-five-year-old. Although my closet was not suddenly chock-full of knit cardigans and orthopedic footwear, I was nevertheless donning such garb on a spiritual level.

I'm not sure whether you kids noticed this change in my psyche, but you might remember this period in my life as the time when Daddy grew a beard and Mommy almost divorced him because of it. Your mother thought I'd grown tired of shaving, but the truth is, I just forgot to purchase new blades for my razor and after a week, I came to enjoy the time I saved each morning by not having to shave before work. I used this extra time to make a vanilla pomegranate smoothie — did I or did I not tell you that I suddenly had the soul of a sixty-five-year-old man?

But back to the moment where you, the proletariat of our household, attempted to overthrow the dictatorship: It was a Sunday during football season, which as you know to me is the most important day of the week during the most important time of the year. That morning I had taken both dogs to the park for some vigorous exercise, and when I returned, I was surprised to see that your mother had taken you two somewhere. Where? I didn't know, but it was football season, so you'll forgive me if I decided I would wait until halftime in the morning games to contact the local authorities.

There was another glorious present waiting for me that day. Not only could I enjoy football uninterrupted, but additionally I saw that your mother had been making batches and batches of cookies for an upcoming bake sale that was being held to raise money for cancer research. Your mother had had the foresight to warn me the day before that these cookies were for this special bake sale, and she had also left a note on the Tupperware container itself that read: "Not for you. For the bake sale to raise money for cancer research." Notice that she didn't even have to write my name. Everyone in our household knew her audience.

Now, children, I would like to be able to tell you that I am a man of such strong moral fiber that I would not eat cookies whose sole purpose is to be sold to raise money for cancer research, but alas, I am not. I would also like to be able to tell you that even though I ultimately decided to consume said cookies, I nevertheless possess such strong moral character that that decision took me a long time to make and that I struggled to make it as I was consumed by the guilt.

In fact, I no sooner saw the cookies than I ate them, and after consuming the first couple, the toughest part of my consumption of the cookies was reaching into the back of the fridge to free the milk from its position behind various leftovers and a pitcher of lemonade.

After tasting a few cookies to make sure they were delicious — they were — I grabbed a fistful of them, refilled my glass of milk, and set off for my chair in my den (yes, that's the same room that everyone but me referred to as the "living room"). I took my throne with my loyal steed (i.e., Steve) on one side of me and your loyal steed (i.e., Rover) on the other side of me.

The games had not quite reached halftime when your mother returned from wherever she had been that morning with you two. Upon hearing the door open and close, I quickly destroyed all evidence of my crime. Although I loved having a beard, I had to admit that it acted as something of a smoking gun at times when one wanted to lie about what one had eaten within the previous twenty-four hours. For example, there was an instance during my beard phase when I indulged in a gas station hot dog on the way home from work. As I came inside the house that day, your mother was quick to question me:

"Did you enjoy your hot dog?" she asked.

"I…What? How did you know…?"

"Your beard is riddled with mustard and there's a piece of bun hanging just beneath your chin."

Blast! As you see, the life of a man with a beard is not without its downside.

That Sunday morning I endeavored not to be betrayed by my beard again, and I had a new tool to help me erase all evidence of my foray into the kitchen: a beard comb. I quickly combed out all of the stray cookie crumbs in my beard and then carefully placed all of these crumbs in a napkin, which I concealed in my pocket…

Okay, that's an outright lie. In truth, I combed out all of the cookie crumbs and then deposited them into my mouth. I then used the napkin to wipe my mouth. When I was done, I put the beard comb back in my pocket. It was as if nothing had ever happened.

I heard your mother as she went directly from the threshold to the kitchen. Her movement was followed by the quiet pitter-patter of your footsteps behind her. I didn't leave my stronghold in the den. I was tempted to mute the television so that I could listen and learn whether she opened the Tupperware in the kitchen, but

I refrained, knowing that later at my trial for the larceny of the cookies, my having muted the television would be used against me by the district attorney (i.e., your mother) as evidence of a guilty conscience. Instead I decided to play the role of the innocent party. Accordingly, I closed my eyes and set out to take a nap.

It turns out that I didn't have to mute the television after all. Fifteen seconds into my nap, I heard the television turn off and your mother's footsteps approach my chair. I tried to communicate with Steve telepathically to tell him to attack.

Protect your king, Steve!

But as always, it didn't work. Crap. I had cried "havoc" but "slip" the dogs of war did not. They slept at my side. Damn you, Shakespeare!

"Honey," your mother said to me softly, "I know you're awake."

"What?" I answered with the innocence of a child. I opened my eyes and rubbed away the nonexistent sleep. "You're back. I didn't know where you went."

"Honey, the other day while we were at dinner…"

"Wait. What?" I sat up in my chair and gave your mother my rapt attention. I didn't know where this was going, but I could tell from the concerned tone in your mother's voice that I wasn't going to be happy.

"The other night when we were at dinner…Your pants fell off you when you were walking to the restroom. And do you remember why they fell off?"

"Yeah, the button on the pants came undone."

"No, the button on the pants didn't come undone. You unbuttoned them because they no longer fit properly, and then when you were on your way to the restroom, they fell down. And everyone at the restaurant saw. Everyone."

"So?"

"Honey, I love you very much—"

"But?"

"Kids, come in here."

You two quietly shuffled in, and that's when I knew I was on my way to an execution where I was the guest of honor. Neither one of you could break your stare with the floor, until your mother showered you with encouragement.

"Go on," she said, "it's okay." No, damn it, it was not okay.

Annabelle, you went first. You reached into your pocket and took out a piece of loose-leaf paper. "Daddy," you began, trying to butter me up with affection from the start, "Friedrich Nietzsche once said—"

"Oh, Jesus Christ. Nietzsche, really? Our ten-year-old is about to read me a quote from Nietzsche?"

"She spent a lot of time on this so please let her finish," your mother scolded me.

"Fine," I answered, giving in.

"Annabelle, you were saying?"

"Friedrich Nietzsche once said, 'That which does not kill us makes us stronger.' You will not die if you stop eating cookies. You will live longer. Also, you will not die if you exercise. You need to exercise, otherwise your life expectancy will be shortened. Your car-di…car-di…"

"Cardiologist," I said helpfully, hoping it would quickly bring this exercise to an end.

"Your cardiologist recommends twenty minutes of exercise three times per week."

"You brought Dr. Joseph into this?" I asked your mother, but she ignored me.

"I think you can easily meet that goal. I love you. Please go to the gym."

Then, Peter, you loaded your rifle and took aim at me, removing your prepared statement, which was written in crayon, on construction paper.

"Oh, who are you going to quote? Aristotle?" I asked, fully expecting something akin to a master's thesis.

"Daddy, you love cookies. But you eat more cookies than Cookie Monster. If you don't stop eating cookies, you will die. Please stop eating cookies. I will walk you every day like Mommy walks Steve and Rover. I love you."

For the record, some days I did walk Steve and Rover. Like that day.

"Well, children, that was very touching and I am going to take all of that under consideration. Now, if you'll excuse me —"

"Wait, it's my turn," your mother said.

"Your turn?"

"Yes. I have something prepared too."

"What do you mean you have something prepared? I just listened to two somethings you prepared."

"If you just let me speak, this will all be over."

"Fine." *Et tu, Brute?*

"Honey, I love you so much. We have an amazing life with two wonderful children who we both love dearly. You are the man that I want to spend the rest of my life with. And that's why it's so painful and difficult to see you treat yourself in the way that you do. I'm here to help you. The children are here to help you. But in order for us to help you, you have to want us to help you. Please let us help you. We love you."

"We love you, Daddy," you two said in unison. No doubt rehearsed.

"Well," I said as I stood from my chair. "I thank you all for your very heartfelt speeches. You've certainly given me a lot to think about. I guess I didn't realize how far I'd fallen with the pants and the beard…Excuse me, I need a moment." I started toward the kitchen, and I probably wouldn't have aroused any suspicions if not for my quickened pace.

"Honey, where are you going?" your mother asked.

I stopped midstride and turned toward her. "Just to the kitchen. I'm a little choked up and my throat is dry. I need some water."

Your mother took a step in my direction. "Why didn't you say so? I can get you a glass of water. Have a seat."

"No, that's okay. I'll get the water."

"You're not going to eat any more cookies, are you, Daddy?" Annabelle asked.

"No, of course not." And that's when I went for it. There was no turning back. It's one thing to hit rock bottom. It's another thing not to realize it. Maybe I had. Maybe I hadn't. But one thing I knew for sure. I was going to enjoy the fall. I took off for the kitchen and you kids and your mother weren't far behind. I called for backup. "Steve! Heel!"

Steve did not heel.

I raced through the kitchen, grabbed the Tupperware container filled with cookies, and then exited the house through the side door. I hurdled your mother's favorite rosebushes, kicked the soccer ball that the neighbor's kid had left in our yard, and raced around the big oak tree.

I was a wanted man. I wasn't proud of the fact that I had just stolen cookies that were going to benefit cancer research, but in my defense, the funds from the bake sale weren't going to single-handedly cure cancer. Okay, that's a terrible thing to say. Forgive me. I wasn't exactly in my right mind at the time that all of this was happening, hence my fleeing from you and your mother like a convict escaped from prison. I was just looking for a country where I'd be safe from extradition.

I hit the sidewalk at full speed. I was afraid to glance over my shoulder, but I had to see if you were in pursuit. I looked back. The minivan was just pulling out of the driveway. There was no way I was going to make it out of the neighborhood before you caught up with me. I had to act and I had to act fast. Plus, I had been sprinting—or whatever you call it when you're forty, out of shape, and trying to move as fast as you can; it wasn't so much sprinting as it was disorganized jogging—and if I didn't slow my pace, I was liable to die. Knowing that I wouldn't be able to last much longer, I slowed my pace to a brisk jog.

"You'll never take my cookies!" I shouted. Then I made an abrupt turn toward the house to my right and headed straight down the driveway. I heard the minivan pull up behind me and screech to a halt, but I didn't turn around. I was in too deep.

"Where are you going?" your mother shouted.

"I don't know!" I yelled back. I got to the end of the driveway and ran straight into the back yard. I glanced around the yard and didn't see any sign of an exit. There was a wooden fence about twenty feet directly in front of me, and it went all the way around the yard.

I didn't stop running. I kept moving directly toward the fence. I had to jump it, but it was about eight feet high. This would be no easy task. I was now only a few strides away from it. I took the Tupperware from under my arm and then, using both hands, gently tossed it over the fence. I heard it land softly on the other side.

"Michael Jordan!" I yelled to no one in particular.

I took my last stride with my left foot on the grass. My right foot made contact with the wood, and I used both hands to grip the top of the fence. I hurled myself over and that was it. Easy does it.

Thud.

I landed hard on the other side, right on the Tupperware, which thankfully wasn't harmed by my falling on it.

I was safe. I had made it. I stood up, brushed myself off, picked up the container of cookies, and started to jog again. And I suppose I should give you and your mother credit. That day was the first time I had run in months, if not an entire year. Yes, your plan to get me to exercise had succeeded, though not in the way you intended.

———————————

My throne had been abdicated. The dictator had been removed from power. I wondered if other dictators had suffered a similar experience. Were they too simply enjoying a quiet and relaxing day when the peasants of their time had unceremoniously entered the throne room and tossed them from their restful perch? Is this what it felt like to lose control of a nation?

I had gone from hunter to gatherer. To speak in a language you understand, I had been downgraded from Mufasa to Pumbaa—or maybe even Timon. I'm still not sure what kind of animals Timon and Pumbaa were, but they were certainly several ranks below lion. I mean, they ate bugs, for God's sake. Any animal that eats bugs isn't very high on the food chain. But yes, Scar had thrown me from a cliff into a pack of wild antelope and I lay beaten under their hooves. No longer did I rule everything that the light touches. That's about all of your language that I can speak. To conclude, there was no more "*Hakuna matata,*" there was only "*matata.*" Full disclosure: because of that damn song—whoever wrote that song was a genius—I know that means "no worries," but I'm not sure which word means "no" and which word means "worries," or if it's a package deal. Regardless, the point is I was worried. *Matata!* Big *matata!* (I took a guess; I figured it was fifty-fifty.)

To add to my troubles, every part of my body ached. Turns out when you don't exercise for a long duration and then you try to exercise, it hurts. A lot. I was several clicks from the house, but considering I didn't—and still don't—know what a click is, I'll use a measure of distance that I do understand. I had gone so far from the house that I was pretty certain I was within a different Domino's Pizza regional territory. I estimated that I had run two Domino's away, or converting that to the metric system, five Starbucks from our house—six if you count the one inside the Target.

I stopped to rest in a wooded area somewhere in between our neighborhood and the highway. I found what looked like a comfortable patch of grass, placed the cookies at my side, and waited to be captured like Saddam Hussein, although I didn't go so far as to dig a hole in the earth. But like him, I yearned for my palace, although I would have settled for a reasonably accommodating garage.

For the life of me, I couldn't wrap my mind around what had just happened. Did you just intervention me? You don't intervention me. I helped create you. Every day of your life with me, I intervention you. "Intervention: don't track dirt into the house." "Intervention: don't chew with your mouth open." "Intervention: don't drink from the milk carton; only I am allowed to do that." Or most important of all, "Intervention: don't eat my damn cookies."

I was so upset that I couldn't even bring myself to eat the cookies that I had taken. A level of emotion that—until that moment—I had never known. And I didn't like it.

I swung my fist hard and knocked the Tupperware away from me. It rolled over several times but didn't spill open. It was a useless gesture; I was the only one there to see it.

Had I really let myself go that much? I mean, I had taken the dogs to the park that morning—that counts as exercise, right? I suppose that depends on whether repeatedly throwing a stick over and over and over again is exercise. So, no. But I had been eating smoothies for breakfast! Smoothies! It's what all of the beatniks...the movers and shakers...the hipsters...Wait, what do you call the healthy people who hang out at Whole Foods? Oh, right—it's what all of the people who live off their parents' money have for breakfast, damn it! Granted, my vanilla pomegranate smoothie did include a scoop of vanilla ice cream, but the powdered stuff just doesn't have the natural flavor of vanilla!

So, maybe I had let myself go a little, but I earned every cookie that I ate. Maybe not the smoothies, but definitely the cookies! I may not have gone to the gym and lifted weights or murdered myself on a treadmill (I maintain that humans were not built to run), but every time I was taking a nap in the early afternoon on a Sunday with football on in the background, and you came flying in to tell me that there was a black widow in the bathroom, I charged straight into battle. I saw the bat signal, and I came running.

Okay, there was one time that I invited the neighbor's cat into our house to kill a spider, but that was one big spider. And here's a little something that you don't know about me: I'm afraid of insects, arachnids, and everything in between. And apparently, so was that cat. He said, "Nope!" And he got the hell out of there. Now that cat is a dog. True story. I saw him expressing an emotion that wasn't hatred to the neighbor the day after.

Yeah, I did some work! And it's not my fault if I slipped a little. Honestly, it's not! Kids, let me tell you something that I learned from a Nobel laureate and professor emeritus at my undergraduate university: when one person loses weight, another person gains it. Okay, you got me. There was no such Nobel-laureate emeritus professor, and those aren't the words of Isaac Newton or Albert Einstein or anybody else. I actually read those words on a bathroom stall, which is exactly where I wrote them. Nevertheless, I consider that statement to be an immutable law of physics. Somewhere on this Earth, somebody lost weight, and I gained it. The bastard. I never stood a chance.

I probably should have picked up a weight or two at the gym, but where was the motivation? You just spring in on me on a football Sunday and intervention me?

Sigh. I guess you did leave one or two motivational notes. Here is a list of the places where I found your messages:

- my pillow
- your mother's pillow (I often stole it from her)
- my toothbrush
- the toilet paper roll (in the future, please write all notes on triple-ply paper—Charmin, if you wouldn't mind)
- the tub—note, *tub*—of vanilla ice cream (cruel but effective; I saw it every morning)
- the dashboard of the minivan

- the steering wheel of the minivan
- Steve (he didn't appreciate it)
- several cookies (I still ate them)

Fine. You both tried your best to inspire me. Sheesh. As I said earlier, sometimes you hit rock bottom and you don't know it. But in my case, sometimes you hit rock bottom and then you find a shovel and you keep digging.

Oh my God. Had I really chosen sugary sweets over my family? Crap. I had.

It was time to go back.

But how? I was five Starbucks from our home! Six if you count the one inside the Target!

And I was out of shape. Terribly out of shape.

Despite the fact that I had no idea where I was, I grabbed the cookies — well, I couldn't just leave them — and I started heading home, and by "home," I mean out of the woods.

Eventually, I emerged from the wooded area and found myself in the parking lot of a strip mall. It wasn't the prettiest strip mall in the world, but I didn't have much of a choice unless I wanted to venture farther down the highway. I headed to the closest store, determined to find someone to take me home. In my haste to leave home earlier, I had neglected to bring my cell phone. I could have found a pay phone and asked your mother to come pick me up, but I wanted to do this on my own. And I was certain that someone would help. I was a man separated from his family. Surely, some kind person would give me a lift home.

They didn't. One disputed that I even had a family. One laughed in my face. And the rest simply ignored me. I went from store to store, but no luck. Fed up, I made a mental note to never help a living human being again—only kidding—and tried my last option in the strip mall: Papa John's.

I didn't even know we had a Papa John's. It's like when you see commercials for Sonic, and then you say, "Stop lying to me, television! We don't have a Sonic!"

We really didn't have a Sonic. I don't know why they—whoever makes such decisions—decide to air Sonic commercials in areas without a Sonic.

The Papa John's was a hole in the wall, and inside, already-folded pizza boxes were stacked as high as the ceiling. There were two guys behind the counter, churning out pizzas. It smelled delicious in there—so delicious in fact that for a moment I forgot that I wasn't there to order food. But I quickly remembered; I was determined to live a healthier life.

"Welcome to Papa John's," one of the guys said. His name tag read "Chris." "How may I help you?"

"Hi, yes, I would like a ride home."

"Frank, come here."

The other gentleman stopped dressing a pepperoni pizza and joined Chris at the counter in front.

"Yeah, what's up?" Frank said.

"This guy wants a ride home."

"What?"

"You heard me. He wants a ride home."

Frank looked at me like I was from outer space. "Sir, we sell pizza. We deliver pizza. We don't give rides home."

"Look, I don't think you understand," I said. "I've bought more of your pizzas than Peyton Manning's sold." Not true, but still, I was negotiating. And when you negotiate, you have to fudge the truth a little. Ask any car salesman. You hear that, Carl, you liar you? How dare you sell me a new car with worn brake pads!

Kids, it goes without saying, but make sure that Carl down at Tri-Valley Honda gets a copy of this book. Thanks.

"Look, dude," Chris said, "even if I wanted to give you a ride home, and I don't—"

"I get it," I said. "You're a minimum-wage worker employed in a thankless job, the income of which relies heavily upon tips from often cheap customers."

"Wait. What?"

"Nothing. You were saying?"

"Umm…Oh yeah, even if I wanted to give you a ride home, I can't. Because I'm on the clock. If I give you a ride home, my manager will fire me."

"Okay, fine. No problem. I'll do it your way. I'll call a cab. Can I at least have change for a dollar?"

"Sure thing, boss." Chris took my dollar and gave me four quarters.

"If you don't mind, I'll just take this with me. Never know." I grabbed a menu and some coupons—I was pretty stoked about the existence of a Papa John's near our home. "And thanks again, fellas."

"No problem, man," Chris said.

I left Papa John's and walked across the parking lot to the pay phone. Glancing at the outer shell of the phone, I saw that, sure enough, there was an advertisement for a local taxi company. I inserted my coins, dialed the number, and waited.

The person on the other end of the line answered. "Thank you for calling Papa John's. Can I take your order?"

"Hi, Chris? Yeah, it's me. I'm looking here at your specials and…Wait. I'm getting ahead of myself. What do you recommend?"

"You couldn't just call a cab?"

"What do you want me to say? I'm persistent. And really, it's a win-win. You sell and deliver your pizza, and I get my ride home." There was a long pause on the end of the line, and I could tell he was mulling it over. "And did I mention the part about the substantial tip?"

"Okay. Deal. I like the pepperoni with extra sauce."

Kids, that's how I invented Uber.

———————————

I entered the house quietly with the cookie container stacked on top of the pizza boxes I was carrying. I heard your mother scurrying around angrily in the kitchen, and when I smelled the freshly baked cookies that she had made, I felt a wave of guilt wash over me.

I joined her in the kitchen, and I don't know what shocked your mother more: the fact that I returned home with the Tupperware full of cookies, having not eaten a single one, or the fact that I returned home with the Tupperware full of cookies, having not eaten single one, along with two large pepperoni pizzas and bread sticks. Regardless, her initial response to my return was not one of joy.

"Where in the hell have you been?" she asked. "And there had better not be pizza in those pizza boxes."

"Of course there's pizza in here. What else would you expect to be in pizza boxes? Sushi?"

"You're incorrigible."

"Only when you encourage me."

She started toward the living room, probably too angry to face me in that moment, and I couldn't blame her.

"Wait," I said. "Just give me a chance here." She turned around and crossed her arms over her chest. She didn't abandon me, and you might ask, why? I'll explain: on the off chance that I might add more fuel to her fire, as I was prone to do.

"Annabelle? Peter?" I called up the stairs. "Can you come down here for a moment please?"

You two joined us in the kitchen, and I could tell that you were not happy with me either. "Honey, kids," I began, "I just want to say that I'm sorry. You were trying to do something nice for me because you love me, and I ruined that. You're right. I need to exercise and eat healthier and that means eating less…cookies. So here are your cookies." I placed the Tupperware and pizza boxes down on the bar for your inspection. "You'll notice that I didn't eat a single one. And the pizza is for you. I will not be having any. I'll find something healthier."

Because you are better people than me, you forgave me, and I love you for that. However, I really think you should have offered me pizza, because when somebody does the right thing, they deserve a reward! Plus, the salad I made for myself wasn't very good. Turns out that salads are actually really hard to make. Who knew?

Also, kids, after I finally came to my senses, I wrote a huge check to some foundation that does cancer research, so please don't judge me. Sugar is an evil mistress.

11

THE ENEMY OF YOUR ENEMY
IS STILL YOUR ENEMY

It was springtime, and I was in the front yard caring for the azaleas and rosebushes when the boy encroached upon my private property. By the way, kids, "private property" is what you call your home when you want to shoot your guests. Yes, this was an unwelcome intruder—as if any intruder would be welcome—and one whom I had never seen before.

"Dad, you were 'caring' for the plants? Really?"

Steering the story off topic? I wonder where you inherited that trait.

"C'mon, what gives? Didn't we have a gardener?"

No, *you* had free room and board in a home where the owners—your mother and I—had a gardener. And okay, you win, I wasn't really "caring" for plants. I was pretending to care for plants because it was March and that's when—surprise, surprise—March Madness occurs. Your mother loves this time of year because it's when we "clean everything up and make the house livable again." For me, it's when I do as little work as possible trying to make the house "livable again" and instead focus on college basketball.

Kids, March Madness is my favorite American holiday.

"That's not a holiday, Dad."

I disagree. To me, it is. It's a three-week-long celebration. And unlike the NFL playoffs or the World Cup, I don't really care who wins the final game because by that point, my bracket is already kaput. It's all about that first weekend, the first four days when the "best" sixteen teams emerge from the field.

"Weren't you saying something about a boy encroaching or something?"

Point taken. But anyway, yes, there I was, with some type of gardening tool in my hand—whatever the proper term for a mini-rake is—when the little boy approached. I had my earbuds firmly planted in my ears, and I was listening to the coverage of one of the games on my cell phone.

I'd called in sick at work that Thursday, the first real day of March Madness, so that I could focus on the tourney. Your mother saw it as the perfect opportunity for me to help her with spring cleaning. I obliged but was giving a halfhearted effort. The tournament was only three games in and already my bracket was toast. One of these days I'll fill out a bracket with a perfect Sweet Sixteen. I hope.

The boy walked toward me and I turned down the volume on my phone so I could hear him. I've never been good at guessing children's ages—something I thought I'd become better at after I became a father—but I would venture a guess that the kid was old enough to know how to ride a bike but not yet old enough to ride all of the fun rides at an amusement park. Let's say nine, maybe?

"He wants to see you," the boy said.

"Who?" I asked.

He didn't answer but instead handed me a folded sheet of loose-leaf paper. I opened it and read the words inscribed.

"Fine," I said. "But it's on my terms or it doesn't happen at all. Tell him I'll be at the DQ near the abandoned Blockbuster after school lets out. And if the Michigan State game goes into overtime, I'll be late."

The boy took the note, nodded, and headed off. I didn't know who he was or where'd he come from, but I was curious.

"Hey, kid, why aren't you in school?"

He turned and looked back at me with a wry smile. "I'm homeschooled."

Those poor parents.

I didn't want to tell your mother where I was headed, and thankfully she didn't ask any questions after I told her that I would pick you two up from school. It wasn't long before I realized why she hadn't been disappointed that I assumed her normal duty. The carpool line. I've seen more courteous driving in rural parts of third-world countries where moving violations have yet to be invented.

Somehow, I managed to scoop both of you up, minivan unscathed, and you quickly realized that we weren't headed home. Ah, children. Attentive when you don't want them to be. They'll play their Nintendo and not realize the house is on fire, but hide a Christmas present on the top shelf of the hall closet and somehow it sends a tremor down their spine.

"This isn't the way Mommy drives home," Annabelle said.

You mean safely? No, that's unfair. Your mother is an excellent driver. Don't tell her I implied otherwise.

"We're not going home," I said. "I thought we might stop by DQ on the way home."

You sang a chorus of yays and we quickly arrived at the magical land of Blizzards and chocolate-dipped cones. You unbuckled your seat belts, but I didn't want you joining me inside. It was too dangerous.

"Why don't you stay here? Put on a movie, kick up your feet. I'll go inside and get the Blizzards."

"But we always go inside," Peter said.

"I know, but I'm offering to be your waiter."

I looked up in the rearview mirror and by the expression on Peter's face, I could tell he had been swayed by this offer of first-class service.

"Okay," he said.

I pulled the door handle and started on my way, but, Annabelle, you stopped me. You inherited your mother's intuition. Peter, you inherited your father's sweet tooth.

"Why is James Perkus in there?" Annabelle asked. Your words formed a question, but it was really more of a demonstrative statement.

"What? James Perkus? He's in there?"

"Daddy, don't do it," Annabelle warned.

"Do what? I haven't done anything."

"It's a trap, Daddy," Peter chimed in.

"Peter is right, Daddy. Don't you remember what happened the last time you tried to fight Perkus?"

"I had him beat. That's what happened. Doesn't matter anyway. He doesn't want to fight. He just wants to talk. Now, if I'm not back in five minutes, make sure your mother never remarries."

My palms were sweaty, my mouth was dry, and my heart beat like a steel drum in my chest. The loose-leaf paper hadn't said much, just "We need to meet," and it was signed "JP." I knew that there was a possibility that I was setting myself up for another humiliating moment orchestrated by Perkus, but that wasn't his style. He operated in the same manner as the Vietcong. He preferred to lie in wait and ambush his opponent. He lived in the jungle, not DQ, a place where civilized people enjoy soft-serve ice cream.

They were seated in the back corner of the DQ—he and his unwelcome messenger. I walked as coolly and as confidently as I could across the linoleum floor, then slid into the booth opposite them.

"Well?" I asked.

"Sup?" Perkus said.

"I left my van running. Mind if we move this along? You wanted to see me, so here I am."

"Show him the video, Possum," Perkus said.

"Possum?" I asked. "That explains the homeschooling."

"It's a nickname, doofus," Possum retorted.

"Fair enough," I said, trying to keep the peace. I have to say, with his beady eyes and pointy nose, the little boy did kind of look like a possum. Not the most flattering of nicknames, perhaps, but accurate nonetheless.

Possum reached into one of the pockets of his hoodie and removed his phone. He moved his fingers over the touch screen, then flipped it toward me when a video started playing.

The footage wasn't great. It looked like a student film for an unaccredited, for-profit film school. Frankly, I think Steve and I had created better videos in the back yard using six or seven dog treats to encourage "cooperation." I couldn't make out much of what was going on, but I could tell that it was filmed in a park, during the day, from a low vantage point. On-screen, I saw a figure's back and what looked like Perkus with a pump-action water gun.

"I hit you," the Perkus in the video cried out.

"No one will believe you," a female voice said. Presumably the figure whose back I was staring at.

The camera started to jump around wildly, and I started to feel dizzy. Thankfully the video ended before I experienced motion sickness.

"Great stuff," I said. "Are you going to submit it to Sundance?" I could tell the joke was lost on them. They stared back at me as if I was supposed to have gleaned some divine truth from their shoddy video, and I knew I was sitting across from the students in math class who didn't show their work. "Well?"

"That was taken at last year's Capture the Flag Tournament in Champion Park," Perkus said. "That was me in the video."

Ah, the Capture the Flag Tournament. You kids don't play sports, but you take your capture the flag seriously and I respect that about you. Peter, for many years your sport of choice was eating Play-Doh. Annabelle, don't laugh. For you, it was torturing animals, and by that, yes, I am referring to all of those times you played dress-up with Steve and Rover. The Capture the Flag Tournament was one of the few moments where we bonded as a family and such bonding experience was not: A) against my will; B) forced upon me by your mother; or C) some unnecessarily cruel combination of both A and B.

"Good for you. Do you think it'll warrant an Oscar nod? Maybe best actor, or even best picture?"

Nada. No response whatsoever. How did these kids not know anything about film?

"I hit her and she didn't go out of the game," Perkus continued. "She kept playing! She should've been out!"

"Why don't you just tell somebody?"

"You're such a tattletale."

"Am not."

"Yes, you are."

"Look, only my wife has the authority to argue with me like that. If you're not going to turn this person in, then what do you want me to do about it? People cheat in the Capture the Flag Tournament every year. I don't, of course, but I've seen others do it." I honestly didn't cheat, but if I did, I certainly wouldn't cop to it. You accomplish a lot by cheating, but you accomplish nothing by telling others that you cheat, except making other people think you're a cheater.

"I told you this was a bad idea," Possum said, squinting his eyes like a…well, like a possum. This was a real "chicken or the egg" moment for me: did the kid already look like a possum before he was bestowed with his nickname, or did he begin to look like one afterward? It was unclear.

"This has been fun," I said. "Real fun. Let's do it again sometime. But now I'm going to get my M&M's Blizzard and be on my way."

I slid out of the booth and headed toward the counter to order. I made it about five steps before Perkus spoke up.

"Hey…Where are you going? You can't just walk away!"

I kept walking because I could just walk away.

"Wait…You don't realize who it is, do you?" he goaded me.

I heard a quiet cackle from the booth and I didn't have to turn around to know that it was Possum. That kid even sounded like a rodent. Or are possums marsupials? Isn't that just kangaroos and wallabies? I Googled it. They're marsupials. To be honest, that analogy doesn't really work because I don't know what marsupials sound like. Let me try this again. I heard a quiet cackle from the booth and I didn't have to turn around to know that it was Possum. That kid sounded like a marsupial that had been possessed by a rodent.

"You don't know, do you?" Perkus taunted me again. "Nina George."

Crap.

———————————

I was as cemented in place as the amazing Blizzards at DQ, which when turned upside down defy the law of gravity. I wonder if a Blizzard has ever fallen out of its cup. One must have. What an oddly satisfying marketing strategy.

Enough about Blizzards. I couldn't move. Nina George. The name alone caused my stomach to turn in knots. She was your mother's nemesis. Her very own James Perkus. But arguably much worse.

It had started as the classic romantic tale between two mothers with children in the same year at school. They carpooled together, had joint birthday parties, babysat for one another, and vacationed at the beach together. For one school year, Nina and your mother were inseparable. Your mother even shared some of her secret recipes with Nina — for cookies, no less.

Nina had gone through a nasty divorce, and after winning custody of her children, she'd decided to make a fresh start by transferring her kids to your school. Your mother, an empathetic and compassionate human being, took Nina under her wing and showed her the ropes. That was her first mistake.

The honeymoon ended when the next school year started and Nina betrayed your mother in her hunt for the most coveted position for mothers with children in elementary school: room mother. You see, Nina and your mother had decided to apply for the position of room mother independently and let the cards fall where they might. But that isn't what happened. Instead, Nina told the teacher that your mother didn't really want the position and she was only applying for it just in case nobody else did. Kids, there has never been a room without a mother. Every mother applies. Every mother wants to be room mother. I don't know why, but they do. To me it sounded like an unpaid internship, what with all of the scheduling of field trips, birthday parties, and holiday events. A real headache.

It's implausible that nobody else would apply. Nina assumed the role of room mother and your mother was given the role of…not room mother? I guess there isn't really an understudy for the position. Regardless, that's not to say that your mother would have gotten the position—although everyone loves your mother and Nina is an insufferable bitch, so your mother would have undoubtedly received the position (at least that's the story that I'm legally required to tell unless I want to enter the dating world again).

I'd had my doubts about Nina from the moment that I'd met her. It was a gut feeling, grounded in nothing, but that didn't make the feeling any less real. And, generally speaking, I'm ahead of the curve when it to comes to hating people. I just always got the feeling that I couldn't trust her. The problem with Nina is that she falls into that category of people who don't necessarily do anything horrible—murder, kidnapping, terrorism—but still act in contemptible ways. She'll stab you in the back, but gently. She might even take a cotton swab and dab your back with rubbing alcohol before she delicately inserts the knife between your shoulder blades. Does that make it any better? No. But I think other people struggle with whether or not to dislike her.

By now you kids probably know that if I had my choice, I would live at the International Space Station—far enough away from humanity that I don't have to hear anyone speak, although I would miss nachos, desperately. Maybe they could make some type of astronaut-food nachos? Doubtful, but that would raise my quality of life in space. This dream of mine would work until the dawn of recreational space travel, then I'd have to move. Where? I don't know.

I'd kept my feelings about Nina to myself. I learned early on in my relationships with people that I had to let them decide whom they chose to dislike—as if it's a choice—on their own. Even though I offer this autonomy, I can still stuff the ballot box. However, in this case, given the affinity that your mother had for Nina, at least in the beginning, I opted not to. Though it wasn't long until she hopped onto my side of the fence.

I remember the moment she switched sides. I was sitting in the back yard, getting a bit of midafternoon sun, when your mother came storming out of the house, having just lost to Nina in her quest for room mother.

"That bitch," she raved.

"What?" I asked. She clutched her cell phone in her hand as she paced back and forth across the yard, talking to me but never looking in my direction.

"That *bitch*."

"Who?"

"*That* bitch."

"Oh, Nina?"

"Wait. You think Nina's a bitch?"

"Well…I…"

"Doesn't matter. Because she is."

Phew.

"She just told me she should be room mother because I don't have the time to do it." A tirade followed that went on for a while. It was fully warranted. I don't remember it. Here's the short version: Nina was a bitch.

The thing you have to remember about your mother is she's not one to curse often. Me? I stubbed my toe this morning on the way to the bathroom and I uttered five different curse words in three different languages. If I sneeze three times in a row, I always precede the third sneeze with a frustrated "goddamn it." Sometimes I wonder whether I could go an entire day without cursing. I tried it once. It was really hard, damn it.

For your mother to call someone a bitch, well, that's pretty rare. And there I stood, in DQ, face-to-face with my sworn enemy, who was offering me a chance to get even with your mother's sworn enemy. And I was interested.

I guess it was a testament to the fact that love is a more powerful emotion than hate. I hated James Perkus. He'd tortured and embarrassed me. But I loved your mother, and I would do anything for her. Truth be told, there was never a doubt in my mind that I was going to join forces with Perkus against Nina. I'd already formed the thought; all I had to do was say the words.

I turned around and faced Perkus and his lapdog, Possum. The M&M's Blizzard could wait.

"What about her?"

As far as intra-suburban competitions on Saturdays in the spring go, the Capture the Flag Tournament was the crème de la crème. It was our three-legged race—I don't know when the three-legged race went out of style, but I've lived this long and still haven't done one.

If you remember, this wasn't your standard game of capture the flag with two teams, two sides, and two flags. No, this was all-out war. To start, there was only one flag nestled in the center of the battlefield. And there were numerous teams, each evidenced by their separate colors. Finally, there were no prisons where you could be rescued by teammates. In this game, when you were hit, you were out. Game over. Sayonara. See you next year. Thanks for playing, and don't forget to pick up the free T-shirt on your way out; we've already run out of XLs—they always ran out of XLs!

As for weaponry, each participant had a weapon of their choosing, whether it was Nerf, Super Soaker, or some other instrument of destruction that wouldn't take a life or seriously maim. After all, there were young participants.

Each group started equidistant from the flag, and once the conch sounded, announcing the beginning of the game, chaos ensued and bullets began flying. At first blush, it seemed as if the flag, which was out in the open, unhidden for all to see, may have been an easy grab, but it wasn't. You see, there were multiple teams in this tournament who didn't care about winning the game; their only aim was to prevent others from winning the game, and thus, they had significant control over the eventual outcome. They were the Capture the Flag Tournament's version of anarchists. James Perkus was the de facto leader of these anarchists.

The year I allied with the criminal Perkus, Nina, for her part, had amassed her own team, which, aside from the group of splinter-cell anarchists led by Perkus, was the most powerful group in the whole game. She had grabbed the flag from the resting place at the center of the park several years in a row—I think three at that point, but I hate to even think of it. Hence Perkus's anger when he'd attacked Nina and she'd rebuked him.

As for our group—which consisted of you two, your mother, me, and a few other family-first types—well, we might as well have been playing a different game than Nina and Perkus. Three Slip'N Slides pointed toward the area where the flag rested, and we hadn't so much as made it as far as those Slip'N Slides. We were lucky if we weren't eliminated in the first twenty minutes of play, whether it be from Nina's massive army or Perkus's ragtag guerilla warriors. No one really sought to kill us. We usually died from stray bullets. But not this year. Not this year! *This* was our year.

The conch had sounded. The game had begun. The fog of war was upon us, although it was more like a mist than a fog because of all the water guns. Annabelle, I grabbed your hand, instructed you to do the same to Peter, and so on to your mother, and we ran away from the flag toward cover in some bushes, where we had been instructed by Perkus to wait until his merry group of miscreants cleared out as much of Nina's force and the casual players in the game as they could.

I looked down at my weapon of choice this year. It was a simple Nerf assault rifle with a magazine that I'd tripled in size by taping a few together. On my back, I'd strapped the tank from our weed sprayer. There was enough water in it to keep a small group of cactuses alive for a decade. I had two water pistols resting in holsters at my sides, and each one attached via a hose to the tank. Hidden in my pocket, I had my last line of defense: a small but deadly water pistol, built for short-range combat. Out of the package it'd had one of those triggers that you almost had to use two fingers to pull back, but not anymore. I'd changed out the spring in the gun, and now it had a hair trigger. The damn thing was liable to go off if I coughed. I was armed to the teeth, ready for war. Not only did I have the aid of Perkus this year, but I also had an armory of weapons strapped across my body.

Of course your mother had to approve of said armory before we could leave for the park. She and I had the same fight we had every year before the Capture the Flag Tournament. I spent three weeks in the garage modifying Nerf and water guns, but it was often for naught, as many of my pet projects failed to meet her safety standards. When it came to the manufacturing of weaponry in our household, she held the power of the presidential veto, and I was helpless against it. Your mother wore the top hat and beard.

She was okay with my modifying a gun just so long as said gun passed her simple safety test. I had to stand in front of her at ten paces, raise my shirt, and let her shoot me anywhere on my torso. If, when shot, the round from my weapon caused bruising—or, God forbid, broken skin—then it was deemed "too dangerous" to use in the tournament. If you ask me, it was completely unfair. The weapons I created were child's play compared to some of the weapons parents and children used in the tourney. I swear one year I even saw one of the teachers from your elementary school using a paintball gun. It was like your mother was tying one hand behind my back before sending me into a fistfight.

That year she had stopped the production of my greatest weapon ever: the Cheetah. I named it that because when fired, its trajectories moved faster than the fastest mammal on Earth. This unbelievable speed made it deadly accurate at long range too. The Cheetah was a Nerf gun that would make a person second-guess fibbing about whether they'd been hit during the Capture the Flag Tournament. Sure, say you weren't hit…if you think you can withstand another punishing blow from the Cheetah. It was my greatest accomplishment, and I'll give you one guess as to what happened during our routine test: the Cheetah failed. Why? Because it drew blood. It hurt like the dickens, but it was worth it. It was my version of the Winchester Model 1837 rifle — "the Gun that Won the West." It could have been "the Gun that Won the Capture the Flag Tournament" if your mother had let me use it. But she didn't.

"Absolutely not," your mother had said as soon as she saw the blood trickle down my stomach.

"Oh, c'mon," I said. "Aren't you a little impressed?"

"Mortified is more like it."

"I spent a lot of time on this one."

"Not happening."

"Why do you insist on neutering me? Every year. Every year you do this!"

I made a valiant effort, but the Cheetah was shelved and my hard work nullified in the interest of "child safety," as your mother put it. Still, I put the Cheetah in the back of the minivan just in case. I didn't tell your mother, but I had to bring it. Even if I couldn't wield it, I felt safer knowing it was there.

———————————

It had been thirty minutes since the start of the tournament, and we lay under cover, crouched down near a group of trees at the edge of the park, watching the madness unfold before us. Innocent families, their first year in the tournament, made several desperate attempts to run headlong for the flag, and though some made it to one of the Slip'N Slides, they all received the same welcome: an onslaught of Nerf darts and streams of water. It was useless. Without cover, or some form of help, no one could reach the flag unscathed.

Having witnessed my fateful meeting at DQ, you two obviously knew of my pact with Perkus, but your mother was unaware. That is, until Perkus and his lackey Possum slowly walked by the trees where we hid, completely unaware of our position. We were the lowest form of competitors—campers. Any other year I would have unloaded my Nerf gun on them, then drawn my side pistols and emptied the tank strapped to my back—the highly controversial so-called bonus shot, where one repeatedly unloads on a foe to verify "death." But this year I couldn't. Alas, there would be no bonus shot on Perkus or Possum for me.

"Take the shot," your mother whispered.

The barrel of my triple-magazine Nerf gun was aligned with Perkus's chest, but I couldn't do it. I laid down my weapon and closed my eyes.

"No," I whispered.

"What do you mean *no*?" your mother asked, incredulous. The volume and shocked tone of her voice alerted Perkus and Possum to our position. They looked our way and gave us a couple of waves, then quickly headed off in another direction. "Okay, somebody tell me what's going on."

"Dad and Perkus made a deal," Annabelle said.

"They're not attacking each other this year," Peter added.

That was the last time I ever took either one of you to DQ with me for personal business. Granted, I never conducted personal business in DQ after that. A happy coincidence.

"And just why is that?" your mother asked.

"Well…," I started. "I did it for you."

"For me?"

"The enemy of my enemy is my friend."

"Who's this enemy of your enemy?"

"Nina."

"Who?"

"You know, Nina."

"I know who Nina is!" she exclaimed. Although she would later deny this, I could swear the barrel of your mother's gun started to veer in my direction. Regardless, she didn't need to point her gun at me to telegraph her emotions. They were plainly visible from her expression. "And the enemy of your enemy is not your friend. The enemy of your enemy is still your enemy! They're both your enemies!"

"But I did it for you," I explained again, though it was in vain. Your mother stood up, in the middle of an ongoing battle, and ran off, away from both the flag and us. I half expected her to be shot as she went, and although bullets and streams of water landed in our direction, she managed to stomp off unharmed. I suppose that's part of the mystery of war.

Abandoned, we were now only three. I couldn't blame your mother for leaving. I should have told her about Perkus and included her in my plan. After all, we were a team, and she was an important part of that team. We fought and died together — both when we were on the field of battle for the Capture the Flag Tournament and off it too.

I screwed up. What else is new? Look, I don't want to trivialize your mother's feelings, but damn it, this was war. There wasn't time to shed tears when the bullets were flying overhead. There was only time to bob and weave, and then fire back! We had to defend ourselves against the tyranny of Nina!

We marched forward. Like many a valiant soldier before us, we left a loved one on the battlefield — she was probably waiting in the minivan — and we ventured forth unafraid of what the future held.

Okay, that's not entirely true. We didn't march forward at first. Initially, we remained hidden under the cover of the trees, and we were incredibly afraid of what lay ahead because your mother was an awesome shot. Although we picked off a few stray opponents, we still hadn't made any progress when it came to destroying Nina and laying claim to the flag.

Finally, it came time to play our hand. I reached down to my waist and unclipped the Motorola two-way radio attached to my belt loop. I pressed down on the talk button and spoke.

"Biscuits, this is Gravy," I said. "Come in, Biscuits. Biscuits, come in. Over."

"This is Biscuits. Over," Perkus answered. "We need some help! They're hitting us hard. Over."

"Are you requesting backup? Over."

"Dad, he's clearly requesting backup," Annabelle said.

"Yeah, Dad," Peter said.

"Look, guys," I said, "I'm sorry if I follow the proper NATO procedural protocol for rules of engagement."

"Yes!" Perkus shrieked. "We are requesting backup! Or whatever."

"Let's move!" I commanded. Well, urged. Okay, fine. I said. You happy? I'm no General MacArthur even though I wanted and still want to be.

I took the lead and led us along the edge of the playing field. As it was only the three of us, it would've been too risky to enter the open field, where we could be attacked from all sides. This way we had only to worry about three sides, not four.

There were casualties along our trek to Perkus and his platoon, but we weren't among those lost. I was impressed with the casual grace with which both of you eliminated foe after foe along our path. You were devoid of empathy, and having now seen this stoic side of you, I quietly prayed that you wouldn't mutiny.

We arrived at the edge of the clearing where Perkus lay under siege just in time to see Nina retreat. The three of us set up in prone positions and started hammering away until the siege ceased. After the magazine in my Nerf rifle ran out, I opened fire with both of my water guns and it took about half of the water in my tank to convince the rest of Nina's army to follow after her.

Once they were a safe distance away, we approached Perkus's stronghold—one of the waist-high wooden structures placed on the field for the purpose of providing cover during the tournament. He hadn't been hit, but a "dead" Possum lay at his side, tongue exposed.

"Man down," I said.

"What?" Perkus asked.

"Possum. He's dead."

I no sooner uttered the words than Possum sprang back to life, and thus, I understood the genesis of his nickname. And this whole time I'd thought it was because he somewhat resembled the less-than-flattering marsupial. I was happy to see the little guy still among the participants.

"I'm alive, dude," Possum said.

"Noted," I answered. "That was a close call."

"Yeah, thanks," Perkus said. It was awkward. Like really awkward. I don't know that he'd ever thanked me before—and meant it.

"Where to next?" I asked, anxious to change the subject.

"I heard Mrs. George say that they were heading for the flag," Peter said.

We all looked at you with contempt, as you'd referred to Nina as "Mrs. George." I would've preferred the "enemy" or even "bitch," but *c'est la vie*. If you raise your children to be polite, I suppose you can't complain when they are and shouldn't be.

"I guess that means we should head there too," I said. I used this opportune moment to put a fully loaded magazine in my Nerf gun. It was what you would call a perfect time for "dramatic effect." Sadly, it was lost on every member of your generation. Nevertheless, I felt like a badass, and that's all that truly mattered. "C'mon, let's go before she makes it another year in a row."

We gathered up the stray Nerf darts that lay in the grass around us—an always tedious chore—and then made our way to the nearest of the three Slip'N Slides. Predictably, it was guarded by some of Nina's many minions, but we made quick work of them.

I stared down the length of the Slip'N Slide before us and saw Nina's troops arriving at the inner ring. Thankfully, a separate group of anarchists, not aligned with Perkus, was waiting to greet them, but the anarchists were outnumbered, so we had to move quickly.

"You or me?" I asked Perkus.

"Go on, Gravy," he answered.

"Okay, Biscuits," I said. I was a little uneasy about turning my back to him, as I couldn't be certain that he wouldn't double-cross us, but we'd already made it this far together.

"Dad," Annabelle said. I turned, expecting to hear some last words of encouragement from my daughter. "If you don't make it, I have dibs on your rifle."

"Well then, I guess I'll have to make it."

Yeah, that's not what I said. I thought of that a couple of years later. Instead, I said:

"Okay."

I drew the water pistols from my sides and ran straight ahead for the slide. Both of you laid down textbook cover fire as I went. I'd imagined this moment for so long now: how I'd run toward the slide leading to the flag on my way to certain victory. Unfortunately, it wasn't anything like I'd imagined. At this point, victory was anything but certain, as what awaited me was a throng of other contest participants, none of whom were our allies. But still, I didn't care. I gripped the water guns tighter as I leapt forward and made contact with the slide and then began firing straight ahead, at nothing in particular. I was clearing my path. Anyone who was waiting to ambush me at the end of the slide was sure to be mowed down by the dual spray. As I slid forward, perfectly demonstrating the law of inertia, I heard the sound of you two similarly making contact with the slide, and I knew that I would have to find safe cover immediately.

The end of the slide came quickly, and still gripping the water guns, I put my hands on the ground and barrel-rolled forward until I did a complete turn and landed on my feet in a crouching position. I kept my fingers on the triggers as I made my way to a short barricade to my right. I looked back and saw the rest of the group coming down the slide, and I laid down heavy cover fire. With two guns, I was able to suppress any counterfire. One by one, you mimicked my barrel roll and made it to my side safely behind the barricade.

For five years I'd been playing this game, and not once during that tenure had I ever made it this far. It felt good to finally reach the ultimate level. We were there, so close to the flag I felt as if I could reach out and grab it, but Nina was in our path, along with a few other groups, and we all vied for the same prize.

My moment of quiet celebration was short-lived. Before we could advance from our position, the mortar fire started. Okay, not actual mortar fire, but water balloons. It appeared that Nina had a battalion of troops whose sole purpose wasn't actually to enter the center arena; instead they remained on the outside and pelted those who did come this far with a long-range attack. Nothing in our armory or Perkus's had the firepower needed to reach those operating the water balloon slingshots. I tried aiming all of my weapons in their direction, but it was no use. We were stuck, with front-row seats to Nina's victory party.

I picked up the Motorola radio and made one last call for help.

"Attention, Biscuits and Gravy under heavy enemy fire from mortar attack. Requesting all available units for backup. Enemy artillery strike ongoing. Please report in. Over." We all stared at the radio, waiting for any kind of response. "Please report in. Over," I said again. We watched and waited, but nothing happened. Resigned to our fate, I turned off the radio.

It wouldn't be long now. On the other side of the inner ring, Nina and her army were slowly taking out the last remaining contestants, who had, seemingly by chance, made it this far. They put up a valiant effort but Nina's artillery attack had proved to be too much.

We were doomed. Possum even employed his evolutionary defense mechanism, hitting the ground and splaying his arms out, and that's when I accepted it was over for us. His survival tactic was the telltale sign of defeat. And I gave the speech I had rehearsed in the event that I would have to make one last-ditch effort for the flag.

"I want you kids to know that it has been the greatest honor of my life to serve alongside you in battle. Forgive me, but I will not wait for death to meet me, I will instead meet death."

"What, Dad?" Annabelle asked.

"Don't call me Dad," I said. "I'm John Rambo." I pulled a red bandana from my pocket and tied it around my head. I peeked over the barrier and my gaze was met with a sea of foam rounds. I quickly ducked down.

"Who?" Peter asked.

"Well, not Rambo. More like Willem Dafoe from *Platoon*. Kids, I'm not going to sit here and die in this rice paddy. I'm going to try to make it home."

"What is he even talking about?" Annabelle asked.

"I don't know," Peter answered.

Classic.

I was prepared to meet my maker, to exit the game. We'd tried our hardest, and yet again we had failed. Nina would once again regale us with the story of how she had defeated us. So be it. But maybe I could take out a few of her cronies before that inevitability. I had made my peace with God.

I peeked once more and the bullets came.

This was it. Now or never.

I was ready to charge, but I didn't have to, because something gave me hope.

I recognized the sound of the automatic firing action of the Nerf rifle before I saw it, and I knew that the sun hadn't set on our chances.

"What's that noise?" Perkus asked.

"Our saving grace," I said. "Light in a world filled with darkness. Freedom. Hope. Joy. Whiskers on kittens. Raindrops on roses. Bright copper kettles. Warm woolen mittens."

"He's doing it again," Annabelle said.

"Ugh," Peter said.

"Relax. It's a modified Nerf gun that fires three bullets per second at over seventy miles per hour. It'll decimate everything in its path just in time for recess. Lock and load, kids. Your mother just joined the landing party."

"Nina George!" your mother screamed. I think this might be the appropriate time to lecture you both on suppressing your emotions instead of dealing with them. You see, if you don't deal with your emotions when they occur—and when I say "emotions," I am referring to negative emotions such as disappointment, anger, sadness—well, then, you get what happened to your mother in this instance (i.e., pure, unadulterated rage).

"Should we give her backup?" Annabelle asked.

I shook my head no. "No need. The Cheetah doesn't need backup."

The Cheetah kept firing and firing, taking out enemy after enemy, until the mortar attack finally ceased. The rapid firing also stopped, and after a few long pauses, we heard the quick movement of steps on the other side of the barricade. We readied our arms and looked over the barricade. Your mother was only a few feet away.

"Pancakes reporting for duty, sir," she said as she showed us a Motorola radio. She took cover next to us behind the barricade. "I heard your radio call."

"Mom, thank God you're here," Annabelle said.

"Yeah," Peter said.

"And nice call sign," Annabelle said.

"Agreed," I said.

"Thanks," your mother said. "What'd I miss?"

"Nothing," I answered. "You saved us."

"I did it for you," your mother said. Kids, that was her way of telling me it was okay. You see, your mother and I didn't always say "I'm sorry." She and I were of the opinion that actions speak louder than words. Her actions that day spoke volumes.

"Now," she said, "are you ready to capture that flag?" She pulled back the bolt on the Cheetah. A perfectly executed usage of a gun for dramatic effect. I love that woman. Again, it was lost on your generation. "That is how this game works, right? We capture the flag and we all get to go home afterward?"

Facetious? Yes. Badass? The very definition of.

"Yeah, Mom," Peter said, "that's how it works."

"Okay then. You three go get the flag," your mother said. "And you let me worry about Nina."

"Aye aye, Pancakes," I said. "What do you say, Perkus?"

"I'm Biscuits," he answered. "Are you Gravy?"

"Gravy," I replied. And suddenly, with your mother's help, I felt like I really was John Rambo. To me, she was like whoever the heck was under Bette Midler's wings. (What can I say? It's a good song.)

"Then let's do this," he said as he led the charge toward the center of the playing field where the flag was implanted in the ground. It might as well have been the eighteenth hole at the Masters — that's the way it looked and felt, at least. The road there was long, but it was worth it — so worth it. We went single file, following behind Perkus and Possum until we reached the final group of barricades before the flag. Nina and the remnants of her team lay on the other side of the flag, behind a similar barricade.

This was it. We had reached the final patch of earth that lay between us and victory — sweet, sweet victory. It was so close that I could taste it, and I had to tell myself to focus. It was not the time for pipe dreams; it was the time for action.

Your mother made the first move. In a moment of unparalleled courage, she stood from behind the barricade and picked off three of Nina's most diligent warriors. They sulked as they ambled off the battlefield. Her rifle aimed at the barricade behind which Nina hid, your mother took a few steps forward, unafraid and undeterred.

"Nina George, show yourself!" your mother shouted.

We — the three of us — popped our heads over the barricade and verified what we already knew to be true: your mother had, in fact, lost it. She may not have been insane, at least not in the text-book sense, but she sure wasn't sane. I'm not sure of the extent to which there exists a gray area between the two overused terms, but she certainly was not her normal, genial self. *God help us*, I thought.

"Nina!" she shouted again. She fired several shots at the barri-cade. "Show yourself!"

We were still safely tucked away behind the barricade, and I looked over at the two of you and gestured that maybe we ought to advance our position. Simultaneously, both of you nodded. We lived or died together, but we lived or died together as a family. I stood and walked over next to your mother, out in the open, and you two joined me. To my surprise, Perkus and Possum joined us too.

Your mother was about to goad Nina with another shout, but she finally emerged from behind her safe cover, using one of her team-mates as a shield. She had her gun aimed directly at your mother.

"Are you sure this is how you want it to end?" Nina yelled. There was a certain fear in her voice that I'd never heard before, and for the first time, it dawned on me that we might actually win this thing.

A long moment of silence passed, and our standoff persisted. Nina was joined by other members of her team, who lined up on either side of her. A strong wind blew, and the only sound was that of the flag waving, almost begging us to come and claim it. Finally, your mother broke the silence.

"Kids, you know what to do," she said. "Make Mommy proud."

It all happened in the blink of an eye. If you sneezed, you might have missed it. I dropped my emptied water guns and dove head-long for the woman I loved, while you two, along with Perkus and Possum, unloaded your clips on Nina and her troops. Miraculously, I managed to take your mother out of the line of fire and protect her. As we fell to the ground she grabbed the Nerf gun that hung by a strap around my neck and emptied the magazine, aiming for Nina's head. You see, your mother didn't want to just take Nina out of the game; I'm pretty sure she wanted to take her out...of life. She wanted to redefine the term "bonus shot." But it was jus-tified...kind of. I guess as far as murders go, it would have been on the more difficult side to explain to a jury.

I knew things were going well for us when Possum didn't imme-diately hit the ground and play dead. That little guy is like Punxsut-awney Phil, and this time, he didn't see his shadow.

Out of the barrage of bullets your mother had sent toward Nina, one finally hit. And then several more followed. We were unstop-pable. I felt just like Arnold Schwarzenegger in any movie he did without Danny DeVito. Seriously, those were some horrible col-laborations, although both actors are phenomenal—but separately, not together.

Nina had been defeated. We'd lit her up like the Christmas tree in Rockefeller Center. There was so much firepower you could have seen it from space. Let there be light! And there was. She'd even taken a few steps forward like she might try to contest her elimination, but we just hit her again and again and again, until there was absolutely no doubt. She had fallen. Forget the "did it bruise the skin" standard of safety that your mother had employed on me; Nina had far greater concerns, like internal bleeding and muscle death. I'm talking atrophy, people. Your mother fell to the ground on her knees and began to weep. A bit melodramatic if you ask me—I know, pot meet kettle, right? But still...Okay, fine, I'm being a bit insensitive. She'd defeated her nemesis; she deserved an embellished manifestation of her triumph. Perhaps I was just jealous. I sacrificed having that moment so that your mother could have it instead. But I'd do it again. Every day of the week and twice on Saturday—the Capture the Flag Tournament was on a Saturday, not Sunday.

I glanced toward my left and saw Perkus standing there, looking back at me. Like us, he'd made it through without being hit. I still had a fully loaded water gun in my pocket, and by the looks of it, Perkus had unloaded the entire contents of his clip. I could have taken him out right there and never looked back.

But I couldn't double-cross him. If I did, I'd be no better than Nina. It wasn't my style, and it wasn't his style either. We fought with an inexplicable sense of honor, but honor nonetheless.

"Together," I said.

"Together," he answered.

We walked forward with Possum and you two toward the flag. For the first time since I had begun playing capture the flag, I was going to get close enough to capture it. It was one of those rare moments in life where you actually get what you want. And then when you do, you're not sure what to do afterward. How do I live the rest of my life knowing that dreams really do come true? Minus the part about Perkus and I becoming friends, although I guess that didn't turn out so bad after all.

We grabbed the flag. The five of us. Me. You two. Perkus. Possum. Your mother could have joined us, but her weeping had stopped and she was too busy dividing and conquering Nina's army. She was like a newborn vampire who'd tasted blood for the first time.

You would think that this would have been a seminal moment in my life. That once I'd achieved success after mending a relationship with my sworn enemy, I would thereafter have recognized that success in life can be attained through peace and unity. Such is not the way of the human species. We have not yet evolved to the point where we are capable of apprehending such truths. It is not in our nature. In a world where such truths are written in the sky, we, as a species, don't take the time to look up.

"What do we do now, Dad?" Annabelle asked.

"I don't know…" I said. "Pizza Hut maybe? Isn't that normally where people celebrate championships? I think that's right." I glanced over at Perkus and Possum and figured, why not? "You guys want to come too?"

"Sure," Perkus said. Possum nodded.

Maybe I'm not giving myself enough credit. Maybe I had learned something. Sometimes you have to bury the hatchet…but always remember where you buried it, just in case.

12 DADDY LOVES GOING TO GRAMMY AND GRANDPA'S HOUSE

I hate when the phone rings early in the morning. And I especially hate when the phone rings early in the morning and it's someone asking me to do something.

"I hope this isn't a bad time," the voice on the other end of the line will say.

"Well, actually yes, it is a bad time," I would like to respond.

"Oh, sorry…Death in the family?"

"No, but I haven't had my coffee yet."

I don't know why that's not yet regarded as a socially acceptable reason for someone to call back another time. As far as I'm concerned, every day is Monday until I've had my coffee. Naturally, Monday is still Monday even after I've had my coffee. And Tuesday after a three-day weekend when I've had Monday off is also Monday, and maybe even worse than Monday in some regard because there's the post-Monday-off hangover that I have to deal with. Having Monday off gives one a taste of freedom that one won't have again until retirement…or death.

So let me have my coffee, and then call back, damn it.

Alas, even if allowing someone to have their coffee before asking for a favor becomes the standard of acceptable behavior—let's hope—there is still one person who will always be an exception to this social nicety: my mother.

It was early in the morning before work when I received the call from her that I had dreaded my entire life. To that point, I had thought my day couldn't get any worse, as I'd just spilled coffee on my (mostly) unwrinkled white dress shirt. I hadn't yet had a sip, but my shirt had—so selfish of it. I had showered, carefully selected which clothes I was going to wear—it was really a process of elimination regarding what was and was not clean or wrinkled—and dressed, and was ready to leave for work when it happened. I was dabbing away at the stain with a washcloth soaked in warm water and detergent, causing more harm than good, when the phone rang.

"Hey, Mom, do you mind if I call you back?"

"I need your help," she said. "It's about your father."

"Oh God," I said, dropping the washcloth. "He's murdered somebody, hasn't he?"

"No, he hasn't murdered anybody. But I need your help with something."

"Uh-huh. Go on."

"It's time to take the keys away."

"And you want me to be your henchman?"

"Better you than me."

"Better anyone than you or me."

"I could ask your sister."

"He'd never listen to her."

"That's what I thought."

"Hmm."

"There's nobody else I can ask."

"Mom, I've seen all of the James Bond films. I know what happens to the henchmen. They usually die in the first or second act. And God forbid they should live as long as the third act, because not only do they die, but usually from a very painful and unforgettable method that makes the audience cringe and second-guess buying a ticket for the next installment in the franchise."

"I'm glad you brought that up. It'd also be nice if you could get your father to turn down the TV when he watches those action films."

"One miracle at a time."

"Does that mean you'll do it?"

"You know, during the Second Great War, as he calls it, the Japanese would honor kamikaze pilots with a funeral before their flights."

"I'll make you brownies."

If cookies and cake had a child out of wedlock, it would be brownies. "Look, Mom, I love you. I love Dad. What I don't love is the idea of being stuck between you two over something." Kids, this wasn't my first rodeo. I felt like I was trapped in a rescue boat with two people who might kill each other, and frankly, I was tempted to jump overboard and take my chances with the sharks. A captain should go down with his ship. But the first mate? The first mate should make it safely home and then travel to Hollywood, where he can make a four-quadrant, billion-dollar-grossing film honoring the captain's life. We'll call it *Titanic*. Is that name taken? Crap.

"Please," my mother begged.

It's really hard to say no to someone who has at her disposal a seemingly endless supply of embarrassing pictures of you and who has also offered brownies. And yet I felt like she was asking me to be the second person in a double homicide. It was as if she was falling off a cliff and suddenly thought to herself, *Hey, you know what sucks? Dying alone. Let me grab this poor innocent bastard and take him with me.* But did I hear something about brownies?

"Okay, Mom. I'll do it." It was one of those moments in life when regret doesn't need the benefit of time to sink in. It happened in an instant. Iceberg!

The man you know as your grandfather is not the man I know as my father. He changed. A lot. Like a lot a lot. The thing you won't realize until you're older is that when you're raising kids, you're still growing up yourself—in some cases more than your children. Because—you'll want to sit down for this one—parents aren't perfect…except for your parents. Your mother and I are perfect.
Oh, shut up.

But anyway, there's a side of your grandfather that you don't know. For instance, did you know that Grandpa is the king of de-motivational speeches? Well, he is, which is why it's a good thing he was never put in a position of power while he was in the military. Can you imagine if General Patton said something akin to this before World War II: "Men, most of you will die slow, painful, and twisted deaths that thirty years from now will become preventable with modern medicine. After your demise, the survivors will go home and comfort the women you love. Still, we march forward"?

And then one of his soldiers would respond: "Hi, yes, General Patton? Sir? It just occurred to me that I have flat feet, which might preclude me from serving my country in this manner. Don't worry, if you die at war, I'll make sure to write a really nifty Wikipedia entry for you and the guys."

"What's Wikipedia?"

"Oh, right. Well, it hasn't been invented yet, but it's like a eulogy. Some would even say it's more important than a eulogy."

"Son, if the enemy doesn't kill you, I will."

"Right."

But your grandfather means well. Because, despite the de-motivational nature of his speeches, all of it of course is stated under the guise of "I'm trying to prepare you for life's hardships." I always wanted to tell him, "Dad, sometimes, not always, you are life's hardships."

"Stop being a baby, Dad. Grandpa is a sweetheart."

Oh really, Annabelle? Here's how your grandfather taught me how to swim: he pushed me into the pool and yelled, "Swim!" You want to know what lawyers call that? Attempted murder.

After I nearly drowned, he jumped in after me and pulled me up to the surface. You would think that the experience would have left me permanently traumatized, incapable of ever doing laps in a pool, or even taking a sip of drinking water, again. But shockingly, I don't have a fear of drowning. Plenty of other fears, but not drowning. That, or it is possible that I do have a fear of drowning and that it is embedded so deeply inside me that I just haven't realized it yet, and that one day I'll see a glass of water and it'll trigger something in me and I'll become so petrified that I wet myself. Yeah…Let's hope that isn't the case.

It's not just his swimming lessons. Here is a list of some of Grandpa's favorite "motivational" sayings:

- "Everyone has a six-pack, you just can't see it because of all of the fat."
- "If at first you don't succeed, maybe trying isn't your thing."
- "In the game of life, there are winners, there are losers, and then there are those people who are too stupid to find the stadium."
- "I made a mistake once. It was thinking you would listen to me."
- "When you ask stupid questions, I fantasize about getting a paternity test."
- "Whoever said 'I'm not mad, just disappointed' never met you. I'm mad and disappointed."

Imagine growing up with that. But you can't fault him for it. Grandpa had a harder life than we did. He went to war. And by "war," I mean real war. Blood. Guts. Watching-your-best-friend-die-in-your-arms war. It made him one tough son of a bitch. You know how people go to war and they come back and say, "I saw some stuff over there. Some real shit." Yeah, that was your grandfather they saw. When people come home from war, there's always one question everyone asks them: "Did you kill anybody?" Nobody ever asked your grandfather that. Instead, they asked, "How many people did you kill?" And: "Why'd you use your bare hands?" As you can imagine, the experience made him something of a gruff individual—that's an understatement.

Okay, maybe I am being a little too harsh, but the old man and I just didn't always see eye to eye when I was growing up. My mom always said it was because we were too much alike. How is that possible? I'm not trying to be stubborn here, but if we were too much alike, then we would probably have gotten along better. We wouldn't, however, have argued with each other constantly, which is exactly what we did.

And let me just add, in my defense, that I put up with a lot more than you do, because parenting was different when I was a kid. No, really, it was. This isn't some poppycock I made up, like "Back in my day, 'extracurricular activity' meant working in the mine after school let out, not debate club." Or something about walking to school uphill both ways in the snow. No, parents could publicly maim their children and no one blinked an eye. Okay, maybe not maim, but parents could definitely get away with a lot more.

Be happy you were not a part of my family when I was growing up. We have similar upbringings in the same way that golfers and basketball players are both professional athletes. Sorry, golfers, but I can't imagine any of you taking a charge.

On our drive to Grammy and Grandpa's house, I tried to think of the way in which I would broach the uncomfortable subject of Grandpa's driving record, but I couldn't come up with anything that wouldn't result in my body being outlined in chalk. My brainstorming session was fruitless. We pulled into the driveway of my parents' house, and Grammy greeted us there, as she always does. I was going to have to wing it.

"Where's Dad?" I asked. I knew where Grandpa was. I was just letting the air out of the balloon. Trying to calm my nerves. How'd I know? Grandpa has a level of predictability that is second only to a clock. He would be the world's easiest person to assassinate. At any given time, during any given day, I could tell you exactly where he is, and for the most part, what he's doing, who he's with, and how he's feeling. Having said that, if anyone actually attempted to assassinate him and failed, he would see to it that whoever had been so bold didn't get a second chance.

Grammy led us to his stronghold in the den. We said our hellos and immediately you two started to defy me:

"Grandpa, do you have any soda?" Peter asked.

"For you? Of course I do," Grandpa said.

"Thanks, Grandpa!" Annabelle exclaimed.

"Here, follow me," Grammy said. "I'll get it for you." Like a couple of loyal ducklings, you followed Grammy and your mother into the kitchen, leaving me alone with the man who had given me life, and almost taken it away on several occasions.

I was immensely jealous that your mother and you were nestled under Grammy's wing and taken to safety in the kitchen. She might as well have just put my face on a milk carton. Brownies suddenly didn't seem like much of a reward for the possible kidnapping and murder that would ensue.

Kids, I won't lie to you. I was scared. I felt like a meerkat specialist at the zoo who has just been asked to assist with taming the gorilla. Umm, no thanks? I deal with meerkats. You know, those cute little animals that stand on their hind legs and wouldn't be able to kill me with a single swipe of their paw? But my protest had fallen on ears made deaf by the roars of an angry gorilla. Crap. Gorilla, here I come. Please don't hurt me. I'm a meerkat specialist!

I shuffled forward. Your grandfather had just finished watching the end of his program, a telenovela. He was from a different generation—a generation where men watched soap operas and didn't lie about it.

I didn't immediately sit down next to Grandpa—I still had dreams of possibly absconding to the kitchen and joining you. Sigh. But I had promised Grammy that I would talk to the old man, and that's what I was going to do.

"You're going to let them have soda?" I asked. "I wasn't allowed soda at their age."

"He's not my son. And she's not my daughter."

"What? How does that make any sense? He's your grandson, and she's your granddaughter."

"I'm not the one who's raising them."

There's an interesting dynamic that exists between grandparent, parent, and child. The grandparent, having raised the parent, now witnesses the parent employing different tactics than were employed on him and sees this as a personal affront. As such, the grandparent seeks to undermine the parent at every turn, thus invoking undying love and loyalty from the child, who only seeks to benefit from the insecurity of both older generations. In short, children quickly rise to the top of the hierarchy.

It used to be that a parent could move halfway across the country if they didn't want to deal with backseat parenting from grandparents, but now, with the advent of social media, text messaging, and video chat, there is no moving away. Patience has graduated from a virtue to a necessary dose of medicine needed to heal the ailing parent who cannot deal with the difficult child, or the even more difficult grandparent. Kids, one day you will grow up and realize that "patience" equates to "Xanax." And for my generation, Xanax is a virtue.

I heard laughter resonating from the kitchen, which only added to the dreariness of the den. Grammy and Grandpa were beauty and the beast. She'd had a simple upbringing with humble beginnings, from a family of civilized people who never raised their voices or name-called, and he'd fought in the war so that her family could enjoy that civilization.

"Why don't you have a seat?" Grandpa asked, motioning to the other leather recliner next to his. Ah yes, the "hot seat." That's how Grammy, Aunt Sarah, and I had always referred to this chair. It was the center of my father's web, where he, the spider, would slowly toy with his prey, peppering them with question after question, until he finally decided it was time to suck the life out of them. During my teenage years, I'd avoided this position at all costs. Instead, I willingly ushered in anyone Aunt Sarah invited over to sit there and watched from a distant vantage point as my father fed. Reluctantly, I sat in the chair next to his and hoped I wouldn't suffer the same fate as those before me.

I realize that it must shock you to learn that Grandpa utilized a slow approach in attacking his victims. You would think that your grandfather, given his predilection for abject honesty, would take a direct approach when questioning people, but no. He preferred to lull his victims to sleep before he pounced upon them. You see, he had a time-honored tradition of using the Columbo method to ferret information out of people. I know you haven't seen *Columbo*, so allow me to enlighten you. *Columbo* was a detective show starring Peter Falk — that's the grandfather from *The Princess Bride* — and his character essentially played the role of a blithering idiot who, during the course of a murder investigation, asked various suspects a series of monotonous and conspicuous questions and would conclude each of these interviews with a simple yet devious question that in some form or fashion shed light on the suspect's guilt or innocence. The thought was that he could catch the suspects off guard by making them underestimate him.

The only way to beat this tactic is to Columbo someone back. You have to appear more naïve and unintelligent than they are. It's a game of wits played by idiots. And your grandfather was lord of the idiots.

I knew from the outset that Grandpa was curious about the intent of our visit. It wasn't like us to show up at his house on the weekend on such short notice, especially when it wasn't prompted by a special occasion or somebody's death. Thus, the mission was simple: prevent him from learning of my true objective while at the same time trying to find out as much as I could about his current inability to operate a motor vehicle. It was no simple task, and I certainly wasn't the perfect man for the job, but I was the only man for the job, and that's what truly mattered.

"Mom says you haven't been going to see the fellas lately," I said.

"Just been too busy to see them. Sure is nice of y'all to come visit. We don't usually see you unless it's a holiday or something for one of the kids."

"Always nice to see family. How are the fellas anyway? Getting old, aren't they?"

"Oh, they're fine. So the kids are doing okay in school?"

"They're doing fine in school. Good grades. Lots of extracurricular activities. Mom said something about one of your friends not moving around as much anymore?"

"Chester. Rolled his ankle. But he's perfectly healthy aside from that. The kids making any friends?"

"Yeah, plenty. Perfectly healthy, huh? He sees okay too?"

"Like a hawk. These friends of theirs, you like 'em?"

"I like 'em just fine. So, he doesn't wear glasses?"

"Only to read. And the friends' parents?"

"I like them too. Just to read, huh?"

"That's what I said. So nothing wrong with the kids then? You and the wife okay?"

I could feel the leather in the seat beneath me begin to warm, both literally and figuratively. There was a heating pad in the seat that I'd accidentally turned on when I'd shifted my weight, and also, Grandpa's line of questioning was starting to narrow in on me. I was beginning to circle the drain, and I didn't want to be flushed. We were getting to the point where he would ask "just one more thing," the transitional prompt to his final and accusatory question, à la Columbo—seriously, go watch an episode or two, you'll enjoy it—when your grandmother appeared in the den just in time to rescue me.

"Why don't you two run down the street for coffee?" Grammy suggested.

I told Grandpa that I would drive—I mean, I literally said the words, "I'll drive"—but my statement was ignored. He walked directly to his car, got in, started the engine, and probably would have left without me had I not raced to the passenger seat.

I was a little wary about riding with the old man, but this may have been the best way to arrive at the topic of his driving in a natural fashion. I buckled my seat belt and made my peace with God, which went a little something like this:

"God, I never ask you for anything, but please, spare me. I beg of you." In fact, I often ask God for things, but he has yet to answer my prayers. I'm starting to wonder whether he changed numbers or hasn't upgraded his plan to include call waiting. In any event, I really hoped he would check his voice mail, and soon, because Grandpa set off on the open road with no apparent regard for jurisdictional speed limits.

There's so much derision people feel when they drive. If you want to know what's wrong with the world, you need look no further than a busy street during rush hour — and not at the level of incompetence that drivers show when they drive (although there's certainly plenty of that, and it might explain why there's so much inefficiency in the workplace), but at the way in which people treat each other when granted even the very slightest bit of anonymity (your windows aren't that tinted, guy).

Grandpa is the very essence of road rage. He acts like Dwight D. Eisenhower signed the Federal-Aid Highway Act of 1956 as a grant to him for his own personal use. Everyone else is merely in his way, encroaching upon his private property. After witnessing several instances where Grandpa cursed the families of those driving near us, I finally decided that I couldn't take it anymore. Thankfully my breakdown coincided with our arriving at Starbucks.

"Pull into that Starbucks over there," I said.

"'Pull into that Starbucks over there' what?"

"Really, Dad?"

"Yes."

"Fine. Please."

"That's better."

He turned into the drive-through as I pled my case. "The 'please' was implicit. In my tone."

"We aren't speaking Mandarin. I don't regard tone."

I swear you can gauge the soul of a man by how he orders at a fast-food drive-through. This is one area of life where I am a slave to my own anxiety, as I adhere to rules of etiquette not followed since the sixteenth century. "Pray tell, dost thou have extra sauce of the barbecue for me, m'lady?" Okay, no, I don't really speak like that, but I walk a fine line between being polite and not being so polite that the worker who takes my order interprets it as a form of facetious goodwill. Walking this tightrope gives me high blood pressure, possibly even malignant hypertension. But what can I say? I live in paralyzing fear that whoever prepares—that's the appropriate verb because there is no real cooking involved—my food will add extra flavor to it. And yes, by "add extra flavor" I mean that he or she will spit in it or, worse yet, coat it with some unknown superbacteria that has yet to be classified by the CDC.

Grandpa can't even begin to comprehend this albatross that I bear. The problem is that he's from a generation where people grew up thankful to have a job, any job. They, or the people who raised them, lived through the Great Depression. The notion of "happiness" hadn't been invented yet. It's a concept that my generation invented but your generation perfected. And that's why it was ever so important that I showed appreciation for those manning the grill or espresso machine or what have you, because with entitlement comes happiness. With happiness comes resentment. And with resentment comes spit in my McChicken.

This all goes over Grandpa's midcentury head. He doesn't quite understand that if you're not polite to people in food service, they will gladly spit in your food. I mean, hell, sometimes even when you do show a high level of appreciation for people in the food-service industry, they still spit in your food. But I'm always in favor of playing the odds, and thus, I am a supportive customer.

"Why are we going here for coffee?" Grandpa asked as he pulled quickly up to the menu. "Their coffee is terrible."

"C'mon, Dad! Could you not say that as we're making our approach? It's coffee. It's got caffeine in it. Isn't that all that matters?"

"Could I not say that what?"

"Please. One thousand pleases. And ten million thank-yous. Just behave until the drinks are safely in our hands, and then you may express all opinions, however derogatory of this coffee establishment. Please. This I beg of you."

"Okay, crazy."

He came to a stop and pressed the button to automatically roll down the window. This was my moment. I felt like the above-the-line talent in a Broadway musical, and it was opening night. All right, Mr. DeMille, I'm ready for my close-up!

So, yeah, I'm mixing coasts and mediums, but you get the picture/play.

"Welcome to Starbucks. What can I get for you today?"

"Hi, how are you?" I said.

"What? I didn't get that," the voice said.

Crap. Small talk had failed. When that happens, always go directly to the order. Take the blasters off phase mode. It's time for live ammo, people! And for the record, you should never rely too heavily on technology. Like people, it will disappoint you. "Could I please have a grande Java Chip Frappuccino with nonfat milk, extra java chips, and even though it's a grande, could you put it in a venti cup? With whip and just the tiniest sprinkle of chocolate and a dash of caramel?" I make sure to alter the cadence of my speech so that I speak slower, but not so slowly that it's insulting.

"Does that complete your order?"

"One more thing." I motioned to Grandpa.

"One coffee," he barked. "Large."

"Would you like cream or sugar?"

"No."

"Okay, please pull forward to the window."

Grandpa rolled the window up and I breathed a heavy sigh of relief. It's like when the dentist tells you that you don't have any cavities. Hell yeah, now give me my sugar!

My anxiety reached new heights when we got to the window and Grandpa decided that he and the cashier would be best friends. I don't understand this inclination, but there was nothing I could do about it. After paying for our drinks, Grandpa suddenly—out of nowhere—volunteered:

"He's worried that you might spit in his drink."

"Really?" the cashier asked. He disappeared for a moment, then returned with our beverages and a wry smile. He leaned out of the window as he held a drink in each hand and looked directly at me. "You can have this one and wonder whether I spit in it. Or I can make you a second one that will definitely have spit in it."

"I'll take my chances," I said. With that, we were on our way home, and I was once again confronted with the fear of riding shot-gun with Grandpa. There was a high statistical probability that the Frappuccino would be my last meal. I decided not to bear witness to the car accident soon to occur, and so I focused instead on my cold treat and using the straw to liberate the espresso from the drink. I don't know why Starbucks makes it so difficult to enjoy this beverage. Why have they not yet been able to make a proper milk-shake? I say "milkshake" because we all know that's what it really is. After finally losing patience with the Frap, I looked up and realized that Grandpa had taken a wrong turn.

"Dad...you're driving the wrong way. Home is the other way." How sad. Grammy was right. He'd started to slip. This was surely the end of his driving days. I might have to get a cattle prod to do it, but the keys were definitely coming home with me — to be placed in a locked drawer, never to be utilized by him again.

"I know."

"You know?"

"Yes."

"So you are purposely driving us the opposite direction from home?"

"That's right."

"Okay...And that is because...?" There was no sense using the Columbo method. I needed a quick answer. Something was amiss. I just didn't know what.

"I was hoping to have a second alone with you. Truth is, I've been meaning to call you for a while now. But then you kind of just showed up, and it was perfect." He locked the doors. Wait, this was a trick. What was the old man up to?

"What's going on, Dad?"

"Son, there's something I have to tell you. Something I've been meaning to say all these years but haven't been able to say."

"Dad. No. We have a mutual, unspoken promise that we are never to discuss emotions with one another. Please, I beg of you. Don't break that promise."

"Oh, grow up."

"Never!"

"Son—"

"Unlock the doors! I want out of the car!" *God, please disregard my earlier message. Look, I never ask you for anything — earlier doesn't count because I just said to disregard it — but please, take me now. I'm ready! Here I am. Tell St. Peter to open the pearly gates, I'm coming home! Table for one!* "Why are you doing this to me? Is it because I broke your riding lawn mower in high school and you had to use the push mower?"

"That was you? What in the—"

"I'm begging you. Don't do this. We don't do this. Talk about our emotions. Our feelings. It's not our thing. We prod and make fun of one another. This is Mom's fault. She's gone and ruined the dynamic."

"Son…"

Satan, God isn't picking up right now. I just wanted to maybe see if you weren't busy and had considered building a new neighborhood in hell. We could call it — wait for it — heaven.

"Dad, no."

He had made a couple of turns since he started going the wrong way, and we ended up on a residential road in a neighborhood I hadn't been to in years. He pulled over in front of one of the houses and put the car in park. I could have taken my overpriced coffee and made for higher ground, but something held me back. I suppose you could call it maturity. For the first time since we'd arrived at my childhood home I looked over at Grandpa—I mean really looked at him. I studied his face and remembered the youthful one from my childhood. My heart felt heavy as I suddenly realized how much he had aged over the years, how the contours of his face had grown heavy and fallen, how there was less hair on his head and what hair remained had all but turned white. He had grown into an old man, and this whole time I had failed to see it. To me, he'd always just been my dad in some kind of immortal sense.

"Your mother keeps telling me that we shouldn't wait until the day we die to tell the people who matter to us that we care about them."

"Oh my God…Dad, are you dying?"

"No, I'm not. But come to find out I've got cancer…of the prostate."

"What's the prognosis?"

"It looks good, but still, it's a wake-up call."

"Oh. Do you need some kind of organ donor or something?"

"Do you know what a prostate is?"

"I really don't."

"It's a gland, not an organ. There's no donor for it."

"I think I knew that."

"Don't try to save face. Son, I don't want the only time you hear these words from me to be when I'm lying in some damn hospital bed with tubes coming out of every part of my body, or worse, I don't want you to miss hearing these words at all." He turned toward me and the strap on the seat belt pulled a little. "I love you. And I'm proud of you." These were words I hadn't often heard from my father. It wasn't that I thought he didn't love me or wasn't proud of me. It's just that these words weren't really part of our conversational vocabulary.

"Thanks, Dad. I love you too."

He turned and faced forward again. "Funny, how life is, isn't it?"

"How's that?"

"You're over there filling your body with nearly twenty ounces of processed sugar and I'm the one with cancer."

"You're also older than me. By a lot. And God only knows what you've ingested over the course of your lifetime."

"Nothing like a Frappuccino."

I didn't know what to say. I wasn't used to comforting my parents because they never told me when anything ailed them. That hadn't been the norm in our relationship. Still, I felt like I had to say something.

"Dad, you know how I watch a lot of ESPN?"

"Too much. Those programs give liberal meaning to the word 'expert.'"

"That may be. But anyway, I was watching the other night and they had this special on about this guy James Valvano."

"I'm going to need to hear the shortest version of this story, son. Did you not hear the part where I have cancer? This isn't how I want to spend what may turn out to be borrowed time."

"Just listen. This guy was a basketball coach for North Carolina State when they won the championship in '83—against all odds, I might add. He was just a regular guy. And he had cancer. Anyway, he gave this speech about eight weeks before he lost his battle with cancer where he said, 'Cancer can take away all of my physical abilities. It cannot touch my mind, it cannot touch my heart, and it cannot touch my soul.' I guess what I'm trying to say is that you're a stubborn SOB. And I don't expect cancer to change that. You've served your country. You worked hard all your life to provide for your family. You've been a devoted husband. You've been a loving father. Seems to me that if you and cancer meet, well, cancer's the one that should be worried. Not you. You were a stubborn SOB before cancer, and I expect you to be that same stubborn SOB after it." I moved the straw around in my drink. It had finally melted to the point where I could drink it again, but I no longer wanted it. "He also said, 'Don't give up. Don't ever give up.'"

"I reckon I don't know how."

"I don't know why, but those words stuck with me."

"The good ones always do."

"And I'll add some of my own. Fuck cancer."

"I certainly agree with that sentiment." He put the car in drive and started heading back toward the house. "So you want to tell me the reason for your visit? Your mother didn't tell you about any of this, did she?"

"No, she told me you were having problems driving, but as far as I can tell, you're just as bad a driver as you've always been."

"I'm still and always will be a better driver than you."

"I don't know about that. You did run a red light on our way to get coffee."

"It was green. Maybe yellow. Not red."

"I don't know why people always try to argue over what color the traffic light is. This isn't up for debate. When you went through the intersection, it was red."

"Yellow."

"What happened to green?"

"I'll concede that it wasn't green, but it definitely was not red. So that's what she told you, huh? I'm a bad driver?"

"Yup."

"Your mother playing God again I see. Did she bribe you with anything?"

"Brownies. And wait…Are you saying…? So, she tricked me and in doing so forced us to have a talk about our feelings?"

"She's a devious woman, your mother is."

"And she acts all innocent too."

"Don't I know it."

And that's when it occurred to me. Maybe Grammy was the one I should have been comparing to Columbo.

Grandpa and I returned, and in our absence, your mother and you had laid claim to Grandpa's den—if I had done that, he would have killed me. He went to join you, and I went to collect from Grammy.

"I believe I was promised something," I said to her.

"Yes, of course. Right this way." She scurried off to the kitchen and I followed. It was hard to be mad at her. Technically, she hadn't done a thing, but at the same time, she was the most devious apron-wearing person I had ever known in my entire life. We turned the corner into the kitchen, and the strong aroma of baked goods encompassed me. It was glorious.

"They're actually cookies with little brownie bites in them," she explained as she held out a plate of cookies, which had been dusted with powdered sugar.

"Such a thing exists?"

She nodded. We sat together at the kitchen table, and I delved into the treats she'd made me.

"You know, you could have just told me to come here. You didn't have to make up some—"

"Wouldn't have been right. That was his information to share, not mine."

"Yeah, I guess." I took another few bites. She had outdone herself. They were delicious. "You know you can call me if you ever need to talk about anything. I don't want you to think that you don't have anyone you can speak with. That is, if you need someone to talk to."

"I know, but I'll be okay. It's your father who really needed somebody."

"So you're fine, but he's the one who needed support?"

"That's right. I would have thought that by now you realize I'm the stronger one of the two of us."

"He's fought and killed people, but you're the stronger one?"

"I am. He's much more sensitive than I am. Just because he doesn't always show it, doesn't mean he isn't."

"Never shows it is more like it." I finished the first of what would be several cookies, and my mouth was parched. "You have any milk for these cookies?"

"Yeah, I do, and I keep it on the same shelf I have for the last fifty years."

"I thought I was your guest."

"You're not a guest in my house. This is still your house, and members of this household get their own milk."

"Geez."

I opened the fridge, and sure enough, there was the milk. The same place it'd been for my entire life. For as long as I could remember, I'd been opening and closing this fridge and getting milk, and never once did I consider that activity a source of comfort — save for the part where milk washed away the cookie crumbs in my mouth. But that day, it was different. Opening the fridge and seeing the milk was a source of great comfort to me. I would miss that regularity, that safety. I didn't want to live in a world where I couldn't stop whatever I was doing, race home to my mother's kitchen, and find the milk sitting there on the top shelf. Sure, I was a so-called adult with a wife and two children of my own, but I wasn't ready to grow up and leave that world behind. Not yet. As quickly as I had opened it, I closed the fridge, leaving the milk behind, and turned and hugged my mother.

"I love you, Mom."

"I love you too."

13

THE DOCTOR IS NOT GOING TO HURT YOU

Peter, I have a confession to make. You are not my son. Your mother and I found you in the middle of a field near our farmhouse — by the way, yes, we used to have a farmhouse. Believe it or not, you're actually an alien from a foreign planet and you have superpowers.

Annabelle, as for you, well, I'm sorry, but your mother and I are your parents. I have the certificate to prove it, which is more than I can say for your brother.

And yes, Peter, I know that's the origin story for Superman, one of your fictional heroes.

Here's the life story of one of my heroes — note how I don't say "fictional" for my hero. He's a simple man who works hard and takes good care of his family, and then, when his kids go off to college, he sells everything he owns and moves to the Caribbean, where he spends the rest of his days drinking beer and deep-sea fishing. Recognize that person? I would be shocked if you said yes, because I actually met that guy at the hardware store. He was in town visiting his daughter. But he's a hero, damn it, because he's living his — and my — dream.

Okay, fine, Peter, your mother and I are your real parents too. Sorry to disappoint, kids, neither one of you was adopted. You are both members of my gene pool. And what a dirty pool it is. Let's hope your mother has more dominant genes than I.

That wasn't the confession I wanted to tell you. Here goes: Peter, when you were a little boy, we almost lost you. I don't mean at Walmart or on the merry-go-round at the mall food court. I mean lost as in gone…forever. One-way ticket. No forwarding address. In the "we keep Peter on the mantel" kind of way.

"Very funny, Dad."

No, seriously, Peter.

"Hold on. Seriously?"

Seriously.

"What the…Really?"

Yup.

"I almost died? Oh my God! How could you and Mom almost let me die? You're horrible parents!"

Well, that might be true for other reasons, but with regard to this topic it's at the very most debatable. We may have our shortcomings as parents, but we did not almost kill you — not this time.

"Tell me what happened!"

I'm glad you asked. I'm getting to that. And please withhold your judgment — and your call to social services — until you've heard the full story.

"Fine. Go ahead."

'Twas the End of Summer Festival, which cometh round this time every year, usually one morrow before the first day upon which school once again begins anew.

"Dad, why are you writing like that?"

Dang it, Peter. I was trying to channel Shakespeare or some other tunic-wearing writer, but I'll drop the act if it makes you happy.

"It makes me happy. It makes me very happy."

Sigh. Okay, damn it. I bite my thumb at thee!

"Dad!"

Peter!

All right. Anyway, yeah, it was the End of Summer Festival, which gives children the opportunity to have one last hurrah before returning to school again for another year. Consequently, it also provides the opportunity for parents to celebrate the happy return of their children to school. But that's not why I loved it. Yes, I said "loved." I know I use that word sparingly, but here's one time where I absolutely mean it. I loved it because among the many booths at this festival, which included face-painting, balloon animals, carnival games, and odd fried concoctions, there was also a sundae booth. Yes, a booth where one — I — could make one's own sundae.

I know the question you want answered: why didn't I just go out and purchase my own ingredients for a sundae booth and have it at home? Well, I don't have a good answer for you. You're right. I could have done that. That's the benefit of adulthood, I suppose. Every day could be the End of Summer Festival, and every night

I could have a sundae booth. But your mother wouldn't let me eat sundaes every night, and also, that would cheapen sundaes.

That's a lie. Nothing could cheapen sundaes.

This End of Summer Festival, unlike the previous ones, was of particular importance for our family because this was the year that young Peter was to begin the first grade — the first real year of schooling, because we all know that kindergarten is nothing more than disorganized finger painting with a daily nap. Peter, you had come to love this routine and were quite worried that it was coming to an end.

But not to fear, for your sister was there to comfort you during this pivotal moment in your young life, to provide you with some sage wisdom and advice. Here's what she offered up when recounting her own recollection of the first grade:

"Oh, prison? Yeah, prison's great. Unless you're somebody's bitch. And everybody is somebody's bitch."

Okay, that logic doesn't really add up, but it doesn't matter because that's obviously not how she described first grade to you. It went more like this:

"Nobody paints with their fingers in first grade."

"Oh my God. What do they use?" Peter asked.

"Brushes."

"No."

"Yes."

"No, not brushes. The horror."

Okay, that wasn't it either. It actually went something like this:

"Kindergarten is over. First grade is tough. You have homework. Mrs. Smythe made somebody cry last year."

Thanks, Annabelle. Really making my job easier there. Imagine my surprise when later the same day, on the eve of the End of Summer Festival, I came home to find this note from your brother:

> I am runing away from home. I dont want to go to
> furst grade. Bye. Petar.

Lovely.

Admittedly, I was pretty worried when I first saw the note, and it is only now, when I possess the knowledge of what happened after Peter ran away, that I am able to joke about it. But yes, you didn't have the requisite skill set to run away from home. As stated, at that point in your life, you had only just graduated kindergarten. You could: finger-paint, nap, and walk in a mostly straight line. Our search lasted all of two minutes. We found you in the back yard playing with blocks. I don't know whether it was your intent to possess our back yard and declare it your own homestead, or whether you honestly thought that we would never find you there. Regardless, you were easy to spot. And here's a list of the things you took with you when you ran away from home:

- blocks
- gum
- a blanket
- cookies (When will you learn that taking my cookies is an act of war?)

- a pillow
- a flashlight
- coloring books
- Steve's favorite toy (and you're lucky he never found out; I don't think he would have believed the lie that you were just bringing something with you to remember him)

A malnourished house cat would have stood a better chance at surviving than you. It wouldn't have been long into your search for food that you would have become another creature's food. Such is the way of the food chain, and the world. Thankfully, we found you before you experienced this harsh reality.

I estimated that with no means of creating shelter and on a diet of cookies and gum, you would have died within fifteen minutes, maybe twenty if you were lucky. Don't get me wrong; it was partially my fault for failing to prepare you for life in the outdoors. But in my defense, I always figured it was my duty as your father to put a roof over your head, not the opposite.

Once your mother and I had you back in our custody, we brought you down to the precinct (i.e., the kitchen) for questioning. You crossed your arms over your chest and said what everyone already knew.

"I don't want to go to first grade."

Again, thanks, Annabelle!

I knew exactly how to handle this. It's as if I had prepared my entire life for this one moment. As if everything I had done to that point, every decision, good or bad, had been leading up to this one second in time in my existence. And thus, I gave you the best advice I've ever given any human being:

"Peter," I said, "life is a series of doing things you don't want to do and then you die."

Stitch it on a pillow.

Okay, I obviously didn't say that. Instead, I said:

"It'll be different at first, but you will love it. Remember when you didn't want to go down the slide? Now when we go to the playground, we have to tear you away from it. It's going to be just like that. You're going to go to first grade, and you'll never want to leave."

Naturally, you looked to your mother to verify what I had said. I don't know why you kids always did that. It's like you were getting a second opinion from a doctor and making the first doctor watch as you did. Hmm. Actually, that's not such a bad idea. We might have better doctors if the medical industry worked that way.

"Daddy's right. You're going to love it."

And that's the story of how you almost died. For fifteen, maybe twenty, minutes you ran away from home and almost starved to death. The end.

"Dad!"

Okay, fine. That's not the end. If that were the closest you came to death, I would have at least five years added back on to my life.

So, yes, after some convincing, we managed to calm you down and you decided that you weren't going to move out.

The next morning came and I awakened with the same unadulterated joy that a child awakens with on Christmas. It was sundae day—that's kind of fun to say. Coincidentally, it was also Sunday. Not even the corniest of double entendres could ruin that day for me.

We arrived at the festival, and before I had time to conjure up an excuse to separate from the group, your mother suggested that I embark on my mission.

"I know you," she said. "You're going to be absolutely intolerable until you've had your sundae. So, go. Get the sundae. Then meet up with us later."

"Do you mean it? Do you really mean it?" I would like to say that I waited around long enough to ask that, but I didn't. I was already gone. *Adios!* By the way, I don't really speak Spanish, but sometimes I pretend to. Oddly enough, people seem to understand me when I do.

We parted ways, and like a hawk circling its prey, I found the sundae booth. There was a new twentysomething working it that year. He didn't know me, or how I operate at sundae booths, but soon, he would. Muahahaha. Muahahaha. Not many people have an evil laugh for when they go to a sundae booth, but I do. And, kids, you just have to ask yourself one question right now. One important question. Have you ever been more embarrassed by me?

That's what I thought.

I waited patiently in line at the booth and then when it was my turn, I went straight into my pitch.

"You've been working hard all day, making all of these parents and children delicious sundaes," I said. "Maybe it's time you should grab a break and let me take it from here. Okay?" I started to step around to the other side of the table between us, but the young lad stopped me.

"I don't think my boss would like it if I let you make your own sundae."

"Your boss?"

"Yeah, my boss."

"Ah, I see. And just where is this boss of yours?"

"Uh, he's not here."

"Oh. So what's the big deal? You wanna make sundaes the rest of your life or something?"

I could tell I had swayed the kid. Truth be told, I think that if the annals of history have taught us anything, it's that it doesn't take much to corrupt the minds of our youth.

"Fine. You want to make a sundae for yourself that badly? Go ahead. Be my guest."

"Now we're talking." I ran around the edge of the table and surveyed this year's assortment of toppings and other delightful options. It was good fare, a nice take, the kind of sugary substances that would have put even the most resolute of health fiends into a steady diabetic coma. Huzzah!

Kids, I don't dabble much in the art world. By that, I mean I can't tell you what it's like to run a brush over a canvas or mold wet clay with my bare hands. I don't have the mind for it. But I can tell you this with firm certainty: art is about vision. There has to be something inside you, whether you know it's there or not, wanting to come out, trying to free itself from the depths of your soul. That is art. And my art is sundaes.

The typical construction of a sundae is as such: two or three scoops of vanilla ice cream covered with chocolate syrup, oftentimes nuts, possibly caramel, and whatever other toppings your heart desires, finished with whipped cream and a cherry.

It's lazy. I won't stand for it.

The secret to a good sundae is layers. Why should all of the ice cream be at the bottom and everything else on top of it? What purpose does that serve? *Nein.* First, I start with a cookie. Alas, I surveyed the offerings before me, and I didn't see one.

"I don't see cookies here," I said.

"We don't have cookies."

"It's okay. I brought my own." I removed a Ziploc bag from my back pocket.

"You travel with cookies?"

"You don't?"

Through a slow, careful, and delicate process, I constructed the best ice-cream sundae that the End of Summer Festival had ever seen. I moved tirelessly from layer to layer, filling every empty crevice with some form of topping. When it was complete, I adorned my creation with whipped cream and a cookie. I don't much go for cherries. Well, not the bright red ones that the sundae stand had. Real cherries, sure, but there weren't any there.

I marveled at my work. Did da Vinci feel this way the first time he stepped back and viewed the Mona Lisa? Is this the same joy that coursed through Michelangelo's veins when he stood in the middle of the Sistine Chapel and turned his head to God?

I wasn't the only one overcome with emotion. There were several onlookers admiring the creation before them. And why wouldn't they? Next to me, the worker had made more than ten sundaes in the time it took me to create my one.

A father in the front of the line was frothing at the mouth. He either had been attacked by a rabid animal or had been waiting for this day for an entire year like me.

"I want him to make my sundae," he said.

"I'll see you next year," I said to the worker as I left. I scurried away before anyone else could request my services.

At last! A year I had waited for this moment. I was about to take my first bite when it happened.

There's something odd that changes inside you when you become a parent. Yes, you grow older, and slowly your body deteriorates until you reach the point at which you wish you were dead because you can no longer do all of the amazing things that you used to be able to do, and also because your jeans will never fit you in the same way they once did — come on, now, that's a given — but despite this slow decomposition of your body, you also develop a well-attuned sixth sense that allows you to know when one of your children needs you. It's an internal alarm of sorts.

Before spoon touched glorious sundae, I felt this sixth sense come alive. I didn't think anything of it at first, because I'll be honest, I worry about both of you more times than there are seconds in the day, but I heard the alarm sound on full alert. And it was real.

Everything inside me told me so. Something was wrong. I felt it to my very core.

Let me tell you something about my not-so-youthful ears. We could be together in a crowded room filled with children screaming variations of "Dad!" or "Daddy!" and I would be able to find you blindfolded. I know the way you say my name. It doesn't matter whether you shout or whisper it; I know it's you. And when I hear this call, I answer. That day, that moment, I heard the call.

"Dad!" Annabelle shrieked.

My head popped up and I quickly surveyed the scene of parents and children enjoying the festival.

"Dad!"

I dropped the sundae and ran. I must've covered ten feet by the time it finally hit the pavement. I moved in and out of the massive crowd in front of me, trying not to hit anybody, but at the same time not caring if I did. I didn't know why, but I was needed. I heard your cry several more times, and each time it grew louder and more frantic as I moved closer to you. Finally, I cleared the last group of festivalgoers and saw you, Annabelle, with your mother kneeling on the ground next to a still, lifeless Peter, who was lying on his back, his head cocked to one side with a few of his long locks covering his eyes.

Your mother heard me coming and her head turned toward me. "His heart's not beating," she whispered.

I reached out, grabbed Peter's hand, and held it in mine.

It was a freak accident. A couple of older kids were playing a game of catch on a field nearby. One of them threw a wild pitch and it hit your chest at the exact place and moment it needed to in order to cause an irregular heartbeat and send you into cardiac arrest. *Commotio cordis*, that's what it's called. That's Latin for "agitation of the heart." It's rare, and often fatal.

Thankfully, there were paramedics on duty at the festival. They saved your life with a defibrillator. They pushed their paddles together, yelled, "Clear!" and shocked your heart over and over until it started beating again. They rushed you to the hospital, and after one sleepless night, you were discharged.

Yours was not the only heart that stopped beating in that moment. Nothing else in this world or in this life meant a damn to me. By God, Peter, you almost got your wish; you almost did not attend first grade. For several minutes, losing you was a very real possibility, and I can honestly say, unequivocally, that those were the worst minutes of my entire life.

What came next was an easy choice. I decided from that point forward that you would never again leave my sight. And I was really excited about repeating the first grade, although I was upset that I had missed kindergarten, if only because of the mandatory nap time. Admittedly, I was also a little afraid of painting with brushes. Finger painting seemed a lot less intimidating—especially for someone like me, who had been out of the watercolor game for a long time.

Annabelle was right. It was tough. We almost didn't pass first grade, which for you would've been acceptable, but I went to college and have an MBA. Since when do people need to know how to spell? Microsoft Word does it for you.

Okay, so no. I didn't go to school with you, although I would have loved to, but I did help you with your homework and often-times received embarrassing grades from your teacher, which really made me wish that I wasn't the only parent helping his child.

Our home life experienced noticeable change. From that point forward, the most commonly spoken phrase in our household was "Where's Peter?" There was nary a moment without your mother and I worrying about exactly where you were and what you were doing. And it was tough too, because you moved around a lot. But we were steadfast and determined. There were helicopter parents, and then there was us, those who made helicopter parents look like those cool parents who let their kids throw parties where alcohol is served. Here's how most conversations in our revised house-hold—where martial law governed—went:

"Oh my God, hon," I'd say, "did you see that the NASDAQ dropped five points? Wow, and where the heck is Peter? Oh my Christ! We almost lost him once! Find him! Why doesn't either one of us know where he is?"

"I don't know," she'd say. "We have to find him! Now!"

Okay, I wasn't quite that neurotic. Still, I was neurotic. And the extra layer of neurotic behavior inhibited my friendships with other parents.

"What? You? Dad, no."

Oh, shut up. I know I'm not the easiest person to get along with. I mean, I have only three friends, and one of those is a dog and the other is your mother.

But it was a difficult time for me. I mocked overprotective parents…until I became one. I should have joined one of those anonymous support groups for help:

"Hi, my name is Dad and I'm an overprotective parent."

"Hi, Dad!" a chorus would respond.

"Sometimes, I wake up in the middle of the night and go check on my son even though I know he's there and he's fine, but I'm just worried."

"Nobody's judging you!" a man will shout.

Thanks, "nobody's judging you" guy, for always being there for people like me. You're a necessary cog in the machine of my enablement.

This borderline-psychotic behavior never manifested itself better than at Anna Stacia's birthday party a couple of months after the End of Summer Festival. I don't know what you remember about her, but Anna Stacia's parents had means, which I recently learned is a cool way to say someone is really rich, not just rich. And her birthday might as well have been the End of Summer Festival, Part Two. It wasn't as big, granted, but there were booths, although no sundae booth — that takes real wealth to acquire, more than just means.

At the party, your mother and I were like the US Secret Service detail for the president. I made eye contact with her, and she nodded. Translation: she had eyes on Peter. It's a beautiful thing when you're a neurotic parent and your partner is also neurotic and willing to enable your neurosis. We were like two drug addicts sharing a needle. Yeah, I didn't have to worry about watching my son's every move because your mother, whom I trusted implicitly, would be doing that.

I nodded and walked off to watch a clown make balloon animals. Little fact about me: I hate clowns. So do all normal, well-adjusted human beings. We have that in common, me and all of the normal, well-adjusted human beings—that makes one thing. I decided to mess with the clown by paying children at the party to ask him for oddly specific balloon animals: three-legged tortoise, elephant with a pollen allergy, blind tiger with an overbite, etc. I was having a pretty good time—the clown wasn't—and dare I say, I was even starting to enjoy myself for the first time since the End of Summer Festival, when I heard another cry.

"Dad!" Annabelle shrieked.

It's always when you drop your guard that life decides to screw you. I abandoned the balloon-animal-making clown and relived my nightmare as I hightailed it for Annabelle. When I got there, I saw Peter lying on the ground. Your mother on one side, and Annabelle on the other. It was the same scene as before. *Not again, God. Not again. I can't go through that again. I know that the human heart can withstand a lot of stress, but I can't withstand this.*

I saw Peter's chest rise and fall, and mine did too. He was breathing. He was awake. He was in one piece. And by all accounts, his heart was beating.

I checked again. And again. He was definitely conscious. In fact, he was clutching his knee.

"What happened?" I asked.

"I cut my knee, Daddy," Peter said, wincing in pain as he did.

"It'll be okay, sweetheart," your mother said. "We just need to stop the bleeding." She put up a positive front for your benefit, but I could hear the worry in her voice. It was the same worry I felt then too. My eyes found hers and she nodded. Peter was truly okay.

But I didn't feel okay. I was still worried. But at least I knew that my worry was ill founded, which was oddly comforting.

"Isn't there a damn doctor here?" I asked.

Barry Feldman, MD, stepped forward. Oh, brother. Kids, there's a reason that there aren't any hour-long-drama television shows loosely based upon the life of Barry Feldman, MD. It's because each week there wouldn't be a mystery to solve. We would already know who the murderer was: Barry Feldman, MD. Cause of death: treatment.

"Step back and let me have a look at it," Barry said.

"No," I answered. "Isn't there a doctor here?"

"I'm a doctor. You know I'm a doctor."

Now, look, I have kind of a sordid history with Barry Feldman, MD. You see, I was once a patient of his, and I mean that both in the sense that it was a long time ago and in the sense that once with Barry was enough. My experience with him was not a positive one. First, there was the runaround that his receptionist gave me. I called her and told her that I'd been having stomach issues, among other symptoms, and that I needed an appointment immediately, but she didn't appreciate my need for medical attention. I suppose we can't fault medical receptionists for that. After all, answering phones at a doctor's office is a lot like going to medical school.

But seriously, never anger a receptionist. They are the gatekeepers to the doctor.

"I need to see the doctor," I said. I was lying in bed, curled up, and I had the phone placed awkwardly on my ear.

"He's all booked up for the week," Barry's receptionist said. "I can get you in next Tuesday."

"I've had diarrhea for the last four days, and it just escalated to vomiting. I need to see the doctor today. Please."

"Well, there is a twenty-four-hour virus going around."

"That would've been a viable theory…about seventy-two hours ago."

"Are you having diarrhea still?"

"I wouldn't quite call it diarrhea."

"Is your stool loose, sir?"

"It's somewhere on the spectrum from loose to solid, but not quite diarrhea."

"Okay…"

"Look, I wouldn't put it on my fridge and say I was proud of it. That is to say, it isn't a good example of what stool should look like, but still, it isn't diarrhea. So, yeah, I think I've passed all of your tests. So, can I see the doctor?" It was like being at an award show where the presenter opens an envelope and names the winner—the moment of truth. "For what it's worth, I'm not the type of person who runs to find a doctor at the first sign of trouble. I'm the guy about whom they say 'It's too late. There was nothing we could do.' Okay?"

I would like to tell you that my plea wore down Barry's receptionist until she finally agreed to fit me in that day, but it didn't. Somebody canceled. Regardless, I got what I wanted: an appointment with Barry. My first. My last.

After I spent a significant amount of time in the waiting room — that seems to be the industry standard; I mean, show me a doctor who's on time and I'll show you a nurse or at best a physician's assistant — the exam started and I shared with Barry my laundry list of symptoms, which included the aforementioned bowel troubles. Barry, to his credit, seemed to listen, or he was just really good at pretending to listen. He examined me — this included a series of uncomfortable pokes and prods — and then delivered his analysis.

"I need to give you a prostate exam," he said.

"I want a second opinion."

"I haven't even given you a first opinion."

Kids, it wasn't pretty. And that's all I have to say about that.

"But, Dad —"

That. Is. All. I. Have. To. Say. About. That.

But, Peter. Son. If you only ever take one bit of advice from me, let it be this: find a urologist with small hands. You're welcome.

Rest assured, Peter, I wasn't going to let Barry misdiagnose you too. I kept one hand wrapped around yours and with the other I motioned for Barry to stay away from us.

"Barry, you're like that crocodile in *Peter Pan*. You've already had a bite and now you want seconds."

"You're just going to ignore the fact that I'm a doctor and that your son needs medical attention?"

"You're a general practitioner. You're basically a nurse; you shouldn't even be allowed to call yourself a doctor. You don't practice; you malpractice. If anybody breaks a nail or somebody gets something stuck in their teeth, I'll ask for your help. Now, if you even so much as lay a finger on my child, I'm going to hire Marty over there to sue you for malpractice. Did you hear that, Marty?"

"What?" Marty asked. Marty Scott, Esq. He was a high-priced attorney. I didn't know much about him or his practice, but I knew that he sued people for a living and that he wore really nice suits with thin pinstripes. And cool socks. Really cool socks — he had a habit of pulling up his cuffs and showing them off. And in that moment, that's all that really mattered to me — the fact that he sued people, not the socks.

"Marty," I said, "I'm putting you on retainer if Barry tries to commit malpractice on my child."

"I'm a corporate attorney," Marty said. "I don't do med mal."

"My wife has a trust fund."

"Then I'm your attorney," Marty said. "Barry, stay the hell away from his children."

Kids, let the record reflect, I know how to talk to lawyers.

"What's going on over here?" Ronald Massey asked. Another doctor. But more importantly, a better doctor than Barry.

"Oh, Ronald, thank God," I said. "Where have you been? Peter fell and scraped his knee."

"Poor little guy," Ronald said. "You should have Barry look at him."

Barry gave me a dirty look. "Ronald," I started, "what's your area of practice again?"

"Dermatology."

"Isn't that one of the most competitive residencies? Only the best students become dermatologists, right?"

"I mean, it is, but—"

"Enough said. Why don't you take a look at Peter's knee?"

"Well, I guess I could. You know, this sort of thing really isn't in my area of practice," Ronald said. He kneeled down and surveyed the damage caused by Peter's fall.

"Just put a Band-Aid on it and he'll be fine," Barry said. Such a backseat doctor.

"You know, this looks pretty bad. Could get infected," Ronald said.

"What?" your mother asked.

"This is worse than it looks. He's going to need stitches," Ronald said. "And I'd recommend making an appointment for a tetanus shot."

"Great prognosis, Barry," I said. Hack!

I saw Marty shoot him a dirty look, which I was certain he was going to bill me for. But hell, it was worth it. The fewer people Barry treated, the less death there would be in this already cruel and messed-up world.

"I'm going to run out to my car and grab my medical bag," Ronald said. "I'll be right back."

"Thank you so much," your mother said. She was ready to order a battery of field tests for our young Peter. Ronald's words were music to her overprotective ears. And mine too.

We had some time to kill until Ronald returned, so I decided to make amends with Barry. And of course by "make amends," I mean goad him further.

"Here's a joke for you, Barry," I said. "What do you call the person who graduates last in their med school?"

"Very funny," Barry said. "I've heard that joke before too. You call them doctor."

"No, you call them defendant."

Kids, I can't really explain my actions, but see above where Dr. Feldman gave me an unwarranted prostate exam. I was too young! It was before my time. You have to be careful with doctors. Don't be fooled by the white coat, the stethoscope, and the eleven years of education. They're not all good at what they do. Some doctors do more harm with a prescription pad than North Korea would with a nuclear weapon. Maybe I shouldn't have goaded him on like that—I definitely shouldn't have and I apologized right after Ronald stitched up your knee and I calmed down—but there was no way I was going to let him treat you. Your health and well-being were and are far too important to me. When either is compromised, it turns me into a crazy person. I deprive myself of my favorite vices (sundaes) and I treat people whom I perceive to be a threat to you (Barry) rudely.

So, no, Peter, you didn't die that summer before first grade. You lived. And you did love first grade, as you do most things in life.

I don't know what your mother and I would do if anything ever happened to either one of you, and I'm glad we never found out. So, please, I'm begging you, no more close calls. Okay? I don't know why the world keeps spinning when a heart stops beating, but I don't like it. And when your heart stopped, my world didn't spin.

14 ALWAYS TAKE THE HIGH ROAD, BECAUSE THAT'S WHAT I DID

If you ever talk to anyone who was alive in the early half of the 1960s, they can tell you exactly where they were when President John F. Kennedy was assassinated, and that conversation usually goes a little something like this:

"There I was, in the middle of English class, not paying attention. For the life of me, I couldn't tell you what we were discussing that day, and then, all of a sudden, the principal made an announcement over the loudspeaker. 'The president has been shot,' he said. Because you see, at first we didn't know that he had died. It wasn't until later that they pronounced him dead."

And then of course you'll have to hear three hours of conspiracy theories from the tinfoil-hat guild, and my advice to you there is to nod and smile, because there are no answers for some of life's questions.

That's exactly how I felt one Saturday afternoon. I was in the kitchen making myself a peanut butter and jelly sandwich when my world came crashing down. It's why I remember, vividly, exactly where I was and what I was doing when it happened.

Kids, the thing about peanut butter and jelly sandwiches is that I can go six years without eating one, but one day, for no apparent reason whatsoever, I want one and I can't live the rest of my life until that craving is filled.

I had just delicately—and by that I mean evenly—spread the peanut butter and jelly onto my sandwich when I heard footsteps behind me. Normally that wouldn't have concerned me, but I had just finished off the jar of peanut butter and I was worried that one or both of you might demand all or part of my creation. It's not that I'm selfish, it's that I really didn't want to share my sandwich with either one of you. Okay, fine, I guess that does make me selfish. But selfish people have to eat too!

"Dad…," Annabelle said.

"Yes?" I asked as I glanced over my shoulder while trying to keep my torso still. I admit I was attempting to hide any view to my beloved treat.

"Can I talk to you about something?"

"Sure, honey."

"It's about Max."

No. No. No. "What's that?"

"It's about Max."

"The boy from school?"

"Yeah, the one I've been dating."

No. No. No.

Yes, I knew who Max was. I knew exactly who Max was. Frankly, everybody who lived within two houses on either side of us and across the street or catty-corner from our house, in addition to anybody who had eaten at any of the restaurants we dined at regularly or had even dined next to us within the last several months, had heard of Max. That is to say, you spoke about him, Annabelle. All the freakin' time. So much so that when you'd stopped talking about him the week prior to this kitchen rendezvous, we were worried.

Who was worried? Well, everybody who lived within two houses on either side of us…You get the point. Mostly, your mother and I were worried, but other people too. It had gotten to the point where people not only asked me how Annabelle and Peter were, they also asked me how Max was. And you told me so damn much about him that I actually knew. I would say, "Well, he sprained his ankle in last week's game, so he's sitting out for a couple of practices. Fingers crossed." Or: "Coach Grisson benched Max in favor of a freshman player who he likes at point guard more. We're hopeful he'll regain the starting job before the end of the season. Fingers crossed." Or: "Damn that Coach Grisson, he still hasn't given Max his starting job back. Maybe that freshman point guard will be caught in a doping scandal…Fingers crossed." Halfway through answering these questions I felt the strong urge to vomit all over myself. Why? Because I'd unintentionally and inexplicably become the publicist for a high school basketball player—and he wasn't even in the starting rotation!

When you abruptly stopped mentioning him after every breath, I was relieved, but your mother quickly ruined that feeling for me.

"Something's wrong with Annabelle," she told me.

It's not that she wanted to hear all about Max's sprained ankle, performance in practice, or otherwise illustrious basketball career (yes, that's sarcasm); believe me, we had heard enough about all the above, and I still think Coach Grisson should have kept Max in place as the starter and benched the more talented freshman because it totally ruined the team chemistry…Oh. My. God. Do you see what you've done to me? No, your mother knew you too well. You shut down when you're upset, and that makes her anxious because she's afraid she won't be able to reach you.

Your mother would have been elated that you were suddenly willing to speak about Max again. It's just too bad she wasn't in the kitchen with us. It was moments like these, when you were hurt, wearing your heart on your sleeve, that made me wish your mother had a Bat Phone like in the old Adam West version of *Batman*. But she didn't. I was left to my own devices. And my devices were peanut butter and jelly, not dating advice.

"Is something bothering you?" I asked.

"I'll tell you, but first promise me that you won't tell Mom."

"What?"

"Promise me that you won't tell Mom."

Don't tell Mom? What do you mean, don't tell Mom? Mom is my wife and I tell my wife everything about my children.

And then it dawned on me. I had raised a sociopath. Clearly, this was an elaborate plan to ruin my marriage so that we would get divorced and then you kids would get two Christmases — every child's dream. Well, not *every* child, but definitely the ones who would try to ruin their parents' marriage.

Why couldn't you just want the sandwich?!? *Have the peanut butter and jelly sandwich! It's yours. I don't want it anymore. Take it! Please!*

You didn't take the sandwich. The conversation continued. What joy. It's not that I didn't want to be there when you needed me. Just the opposite. But this was one time where your mother would have been more helpful.

"You won't tell her, right?" Annabelle asked.

It's not often in life that you look back on a moment and say, Yup, that's where I went wrong. Right there. Had I just done everything differently from that point forward, everything would have been fine, everything would have turned out differently. For me, this was that moment.

I have replayed this conversation over and over in my head numerous times, similar to how athletes watch game tape to correct their performances. I couldn't help but torture myself in this way. No matter how hard you try, you can't change the past. If I had a time machine, I would go back in time and counter with: "Honey, your mother and I don't keep secrets." But I don't have a time machine. Where are Doc, Marty, and Einstein when you need them? Or should I say, *when* are they? Get it? Because they traveled through time?

If I had a time machine, I also wouldn't have made that lame joke. I'm better than that. Where were we? Oh, right. Here's what I said:

"Sure, honey, you know you can always tell me anything." Sometimes, I make Benedict Arnold look like Mother Teresa. Not often.

But when it happens, it's usually because I'm hungry. Hunger is a powerful emotion.

"Dad, Max and I broke up."

"Oh...I'm sorry to hear that."

"Thanks."

"Was it...mutual? The breakup?" Okay, look, once I was in, I was in. If you give a mouse a cookie, he's going to want to know more about the breakup. Plus, maybe I had underestimated myself? Maybe I could handle this conversation with you? After all, I am a parent. I know things. Some things. Not all things. But things, damn it! Yeah, I could definitely handle this conversation. Piece of cake.

"Kind of. He like wanted to break up and I guess I didn't want to at first, but now I do. I don't know. I guess I don't really know what I want...Dad, I'll tell you what happened, but you have to swear to me that you won't say or do anything."

"Of course. I swear." Oh, crap. What have I done? Sometimes you give a mouse a cookie and then he asks for a glass of milk, and then, after eating that cookie and washing it down with the milk, he gets hit by the crosstown bus on the Friday before a holiday weekend. And he never sees it coming. God help me.

"He dumped me."

"What?" I was wrong! I could not handle this conversation. I was in over my head. Way over my head. Where was your mother? *For the love of God, call the National Guard! Declare a national emergency.*

"Coach Grisson didn't bench Max because Devon —"

"Who's Devon?"

"You know, the freshman who plays…whatever position—"

"Point guard."

"What's point guard?"

"That's the position."

"Yeah, right. So anyway, Coach Grisson didn't bench Max because Devon is better at point guard. He benched Max because he was failing English. And Max wanted me to write his final English paper for him so that he would get a good grade, and when I wouldn't do it…"

"He dumped you?"

"And started dating someone who would. She wrote the paper for him and now he might be starting again. I didn't even know he was dating someone else because on his Facebook profile he made it so that I couldn't view everything on his page and then he—"

"What are you saying?"

"You know in the privacy settings how you can select who can and can't view what you post?"

"Huh?"

"Well, you can. And he did. But I didn't realize that until my friend Alice told me about it, and then I found out I was kind of like blocked. Not really blocked, but like not really friends either. And we are—were just dating so that was kind of weird. I didn't even know but…" You went on to explain the various technicalities of the privacy options on Facebook, and I listened halfheartedly. Okay, not even halfheartedly. I didn't listen at all. And you know why? Because my baby girl had just told me that someone had broken her heart. I felt like I needed a bulletin board from one of those cop shows to lay out the facts of the case. Ironically, Facebook sounded like a digital version of such a bulletin board. I don't know. I didn't use it and still don't. Social media has many charms, none of which are for me.

Eventually, you took notice of my distant stare, and you stopped droning on about Facebook.

"Remember, you swore you wouldn't do anything."

I took a moment to think about it. I guess I had, hadn't I? "Honey, I swear. I won't do anything. All I care about is that you're going to be okay. You are, right? Going to be okay?"

The tears formed quickly in your eyes, and I wrapped you in my arms and hugged you. Sometimes all we need is a hug. I let you go and wiped the tears from your cheeks.

"And now I don't know what to do. I miss him. Do you think he'll come back to me?"

"You want my advice?" You nodded. "Don't be the girl who sits at home waiting for Prince Charming to come and rescue her. That's never been your style. Go out there and kick some ass. Find a new, better boyfriend and forget about this Max kid."

"But you always called me your little princess. I like that."

"There's nothing wrong with being a princess. You're a still a princess. You're just a princess who kicks ass. Your mother and I didn't raise you to be the type of girl who needs to be saved. Promise me you'll never be that girl."

"I promise. And you promise me you won't do anything to Max."

"Of course. I promise."

Kids, when you're shopping for guns, the thing to remember is that you want something that is safe but also packs enough firepower to accomplish whatever you want it to, whether that's an immediate killing blow or just a moderate-to-severe wound that will eventually take the life of your target. I wanted the latter because my purpose was simple: I wanted Max to suffer a slow and painful death. You know how in every spy movie the villain fails to kill the spy just before the climax and instead chooses to focus on world domination, leaving that one loose end untied? Yeah, to heck with that. The climax of this story would be when I killed my enemy.

Because I didn't seek something meaningless like world domination. No, I sought revenge on the man — nay, the boy — who had hurt my baby. Nobody, and I mean nobody, hurts my baby.

Let me tell you something about me. I am crazy. Straight loco. I realize that there will be times in your life when people hurt you, whether that's someone you love, a boss, a friend, a teacher, a coworker, or just some random person on the street. And I can't fight all of your battles for you, but moreover, I shouldn't fight your battles for you. And promise me now, as you read this, that you'll always remember: You are strong. Stronger than you will ever realize. Strong enough to deal with all of those people and any other people who might hurt or upset you.

Yes, Annabelle, I lied to you. To your face. I swore to you that I wouldn't do anything to Max, but one day, when you have a daughter or a son of your own, you'll forgive me. Okay, "forgive" probably isn't the right word. You might never forgive me, but you'll understand. I hope.

Kids, in life, there's the high road and there's the low road, and when it comes to my children, I follow the low road. You don't need to give me directions to the high road. Simply put, I ain't takin' it. To hell with the high road. That's for another time and place. On that day, I was not worried about saving face or trying to make sure nobody's feelings were hurt—that's high-road jargon. No, I was concerned only with retribution. Because if you mess with my children, you suffer the consequences.

Look, maybe this will explain it (i.e., here's why I may not actually be crazy): Go watch *Scent of a Woman*. It stars Al Pacino, the guy who plays seemingly every mobster in every movie ever, but not really, because that's Joe Pesci. But seriously, watch *Scent of a Woman*. It's one of my favorite movies. Here's the plot: A poor kid, played by Chris O'Donnell, at a ritzy, upscale boys' boarding school faces expulsion after he refuses to snitch on two rich, spoiled brats. And the headmaster of the school, who's played by the same actor who always plays the guy you hate in seemingly every movie, wants to expel O'Donnell. But at the end, Al Pacino gives an epic speech and defends O'Donnell because he has honor and won't rat out the rich, spoiled brats. And everyone cheers. And the poor kid isn't expelled. Yay! It was great. Really, it was.

I'll be honest with you. I don't really care about *Scent of a Woman*. I only told you about it so that I can tell you what really matters, and that's what happens in the sequel. In the sequel, Al Pacino gets a machine gun and kills everybody who crosses him, from the rich, spoiled kids to the headmaster. The movie? It's called *Scarface*. In life, there's a time and a place for speeches like in *Scent of a Woman*, and when those fail, sometimes inevitably, well, thank God for *Scarface*.

"*Dad, we've seen* Scent of a Woman. *You made us watch it, and there is no sequel...*"

What do you mean, Annabelle? Yes, it's *Scarface*. Al Pacino realized that taking the high road never works and so he decided to do a lot of drugs and shoot a machine gun. Everybody knows that.

"*I'm going to have —*"

You too, Peter?

"*Yeah, Annabelle is right.* Scarface *came out before* Scent of a Woman. *And that's not exactly what happened in* Scarface..."

Fine. Whatever. I didn't realize I had raised two film buffs. Are you going to start using words like "lexicon" now? And as long as we're on the subject of movies, I hope you both realize that your skewed view of reality is 100 percent Disney's fault.

I hate Disney movies.

But wait, you'll say, I saw Daddy watching *Aladdin* that one time I was supposed to be sleeping but I decided I wanted a cookie — correction, one of Daddy's cookies — as a midnight snack. Yes. Daddy did like *Aladdin*. The first time he saw it. Daddy did like *Aladdin* the second time he saw it. And the third. And the fourth. And the...ninety-seven times. Ninety. Seven. Daddy has seen *Aladdin* ninety-seven times. Daddy has seen *Aladdin* so many times that he can recite every line by heart. Daddy has seen *Aladdin* so many times that he has nightmares about talking parrots. Daddy has seen *Aladdin* so many times that he is now fluent in Arabic. Daddy has seen *Aladdin* so many times that if he found a magical lamp with a genie who gave him three wishes, he would use all three wishes to unsee *Aladdin* ninety-six times. And finally, Daddy has seen *Aladdin* so many times because he misses Robin Williams.

Daddy likes Westerns. Daddy likes cop movies. Daddy likes ironic cop movies. Daddy likes movies with children in them, but only if the children don't have speaking parts, with one exception: *Home Alone*. Daddy likes Al Pacino. And Meryl Streep — only inconsiderate people without any taste don't like Meryl Streep.

If it were up to me, I would have used the parent function on the TV to block the Disney Channel. Why? Because you made me watch it so much…and because life isn't a fairy tale.

And I mean that. Life isn't a fairy tale, but that doesn't mean you should stop believing in happy endings. For example: Max hurt you? I was going to kill him. That's a very happing ending. Maybe the happiest of all endings. It was just like the lyrics to one of those Taylor Quick songs. You know, the girl who sings about all of the boys who broke her heart? Yes, I know it's Taylor Swift, not Quick, but I kind of like Quick better.

Well, I aimed to add another verse to one of Taylor Quick's songs: this boy broke my heart, but I still love him, and then my father killed him. Remix.

I'll be the first to admit it. It's possible I had a misconceived sense of justice. I had to consult somebody I trusted, so I called a man who suffered from the same ailment I did (i.e., a father raising a teenage daughter): Pradeep.

"She's my baby girl. Pradeep, I don't know what to do. What do you think?"

"It's simple. I would kill him."

"You're Hindu. Aren't you supposed to be a peaceful people?"

"We are a very peaceful people. I, however, am not a peaceful people. I am a violent man when it comes to protecting my family."

"Yeah. Makes sense." That was code for "I don't know what to do." I was between a rock and a hard place. (For the record, I have no idea where that saying comes from or what it means. A rock is a hard place. So I guess you put me between two rocks? Crap, I don't know. I was paper and you were scissors, and scissors always beats paper. That's a much better way of saying the same thing and it doesn't use any rocks.)

It was the shortest consultation I have ever had. I thought that it would be like some sort of Socratic dialogue where we discuss the meaning of justice and talk about a cave metaphor or moderation or some other deep stuff like that, but no. To paraphrase Forrest's mother, "Life is like a box of chocolates, you never know what you're gonna get..." Except I did, because I kept a gun in my box of chocolates. Honestly, who would ever look for a gun in a box of chocolates?

I knew what I had to do.

My plan went into action on a Friday night. You kids were busy doing whatever it is that you kids did back then—wait a second, it's kind of scary that I don't know what you were up to. Was I a negligent parent?

I'm only kidding, and you better not have answered yes to that. You were both staying at friends' houses that night. Annabelle, you were having something of a girls' night, and Peter, some nerdy video game—I apologize for the obvious redundancy there—came out that weekend and you and your friends were celebrating its launch. Is it just the plight of our youth that they're destined to celebrate meaningless feats? Yes, yes, it is. I sent your mother off to spend some quality time with Gwenyth, and for the first time in as long as I could remember, I had the night to myself.

You see, kids? A parent's job is never finished—especially when said parent doesn't play by the rules. I was a rebel with a cause. Take that, James Dean! Seriously though, he was such a great actor. Rest in peace, James Dean. The world could use more actors with your talent.

I was ready for action. Locked and loaded. There was just one problem. Your mother didn't go out that night. Well, she went out, but she came back. Her plans fell through at the last minute. Thank you, Gwenyth, for once again failing to come through when I needed you most. I was behind the wheel of the minivan, engine started, when your mother pulled into the garage next to me. I rolled down the window just as she got out of her car.

"No Gwenyth?" I asked.

"She's not feeling well."

"Ill, huh?"

She smirked. "Where are you headed?"

"Grocery store. Need anything?"

She thought for a moment. "I'll just come with." She opened the passenger door and got inside.

Crap.

I didn't move. How could I? I wasn't going to the store. I was going to kill Max. The neurons fired quickly in my brain. I had to get rid of her. But how?

I did what any responsible spouse who wants to remain in a happy marriage would have done in my situation. I lied.

"Honey, look, I'm not going to the store. The truth is I'm going to buy you a present." Kids, let this be a lesson: "the truth is" almost always precedes a lie. People who tell the truth just tell the truth; they don't need a precursor to qualify their words.

"A present? What for?"

"Anniversary."

"That's not for seven months."

"I mean birthday."

"Five months."

"First time we ever met?"

"You're getting closer. Three months. You want to tell me where you're really headed?"

Kids, another life lesson: if you lie, make sure that the lie is something more believable than the truth.

"Why won't you tell me where you're really headed?" your mother asked.

"I can't."

"Why not?"

"Because I can't."

"That's not good enough. You have to give me some idea of where you're going."

I placed my hand on her hand and squeezed. "I can't. You just have to trust me."

"Honey…Please…"

"It's…" I shook my head. "I can't tell you."

"It's about Annabelle, isn't it?"

"Oh my God. I thought you were going to say I was cheating on you or something."

"I would never because you would never."

"I wouldn't."

"I know. That's what I just said."

"Okay. Well, good. I'm glad you know that."

"I do. So, it's about Annabelle, isn't it?" she asked again.

"I feel like we just shared a beautiful moment together, and you're ruining that by changing the subject…"

"Fine. Don't tell me. I'll guess. It's about Annabelle and Max. You're going to talk to him? To try to fix whatever's going on between them?"

"I can't tell you."

"Why not?"

"Because Annabelle asked me not to."

"She asked you not to tell me?"

"I've already told you more than I should have."

"What do you know that she won't tell me?"

"That's all I'm going to say."

"Did he hurt her?"

Annabelle, I want you to know that what I'm writing here is the God's honest truth. I didn't betray your trust. You may argue that even telling your mother that you asked me not to tell her something is a violation of your trust, and there would certainly be some merit to that argument; however, I didn't tell her. I didn't have to. You know why? Because she read it in my expression. You see, there's a certain look a father has when he learns that his baby girl has had her heart broken. I think they call it psychotic. Maybe. Just a guess...No, that's definitely it.

"He did," she said quietly.

"I'm going to go now," I answered. "I'll be back soon."

"No."

"Honey, I know what you're going to say and—"

"You don't know what I'm going to say. I hate when you say you know what I'm going to say. You can't possibly know what I'm going to say if I haven't said it yet."

"Fair enough. I don't know what you're going to say, but I think I know what you're going to say. I have a working theory. May I share it with you?"

"Go ahead."

"Okay. I think you're going to tell me not to go and that I can't fight her battles for her. Any other time I would welcome your wisdom and your insight. I really would. You do such a great job of keeping me grounded by lending me perspective, which at times, I'll admit, I am completely devoid of. But this isn't the time for perspective. This is the time for revenge. Right now, I have no need for perspective. I have to go take care of something, and that something is Max. The little shit crossed the line. And as for perspective, well, I left perspective back at the gun store."

"You didn't actually go to a gun store, did you?"

"No. I meant it more as a euphemism of sorts."

"I see."

I gave her a moment to digest my words and then waited for her to pull me back from the edge of the cliff. It's one of the reasons that your mother and I are perfect for one another. I'm a raving lunatic and she keeps me sane. I run to the edge of the cliff, and she pulls me back each time. She keeps me from jumping. From going head over heels into rock-solid earth. From making regrettable choices. From losing what little sanity I do have.

"That's not what I was going to say," she said.

"What were you going to say?"

"Did you turn on the alarm? Because we shouldn't leave unless it's on."

"You want to come with me?"

"You said you didn't go to the gun store, right?"

"No, of course not. I'm not a murderer."

"Okay, good."

"But you're coming?"

"Let's go kill him."

"Oh my God." I smiled. "I don't think I've ever loved you more." Kids, there is no greater aphrodisiac than mutual hatred. Not oysters, not chocolate, not a romantic weekend in Paris. Nothing brings two people together like mutual hatred for a third. I threw the minivan into reverse and lightly tapped the gas pedal, then turned the wheel to the left and hit the brakes.

"Where we're going…We don't need roads," I said. I shifted down into drive and then hit the gas pedal while simultaneously pressing the garage door opener—how's that for multitasking? Right before the end of the driveway, I jerked the wheel to the right and cut over a patch of our neighbor's yard—later, I would apologize for that badass maneuver. Kids, if you've ever wondered why minivans have sports drive, well, it's for times like that—when somebody's broken your daughter's heart and you want payback.

"That's your plan?" your mother asked. I had just brought her in on my grand scheme, explaining the many ways—way, really—in which I was going to wreak havoc upon Max's life.

"I mean, it was either that or Plan B."

"What's your Plan B?"

"Second-degree murder."

"You're going about this all wrong. You don't need to kill the kid. You don't use a flamethrower to start a forest fire when all it takes is a match."

"I think your words might have just killed Smokey Bear. And to be clear, you don't need a flamethrower, but it helps, right?" It took a moment, but I swallowed my pride. "Fine. What do you suggest?"

I learned something about your mother that night, something I never knew about her. She is a mastermind of wit and deception. It was just like that movie *The Usual Suspects*. To the unknowing eye, she was Verbal: sterile, hapless, nonthreatening, not meant for jail, let alone prison. Sure, she'd had a fair number of disputes with people, but those usually ended with her silently boycotting a person for two months, never once telling said person that she wasn't speaking to them, until one day when she finally lifted her boycott, and the person was never the wiser. I didn't think she was capable of malice aforethought. But that was when I thought she was Verbal. I didn't realize I'd married Keyser Söze.

"Your problem is that you want revenge," she said. "Revenge is pointless. How about you stop the murder before it occurs? Frankly, I don't care what you do to my murderer after I die. And do you know why?"

"Is that rhetorical?"

"Yes."

"Okay. Just checking. So…why don't you—"

"I don't care what you do to my murderer because whatever you do won't bring me back to life. Revenge is a day late and a dollar short. It doesn't do me any good. Revenge isn't for the dead; it's for the living."

"Okay, fine. You think you can come up with a better plan?"

"I do."

"You drive then."

"Fine. I will."

I pulled the minivan over, and your mother and I switched places. She pulled the seat forward and started off in sport mode again.

"We have to make one stop first," she said.

"This is your rodeo now, cowpoke."

"What?"

"Nothing. I watched *City Slickers* last night."

Your mother made her stop, and I waited in the car. She drove for a while after, and it gave me time to think. She hadn't said what I thought she was going to say, but that didn't mean that all of it wasn't true. I can't fight your battles for you…but I can kill your ex-boyfriends—or at least maim them. Well, that's not entirely true. I can fight your battles for you; I just can't let you know that I'm fighting your battles for you, otherwise you may not be able to fight your own battles. So it turns out, Annabelle, you're not the one who's a sociopath. I am. But the thing is, I'm also a loving father. So it's complicated. But many things in life are. Was what we were doing wrong? I didn't have an answer to that question, and before I could think of one, the minivan came to a stop on a residential street. It wasn't the one I had thought your mother and I were headed to.

"This isn't Max's house," I said.

"I know."

I knew this neighborhood. I knew these houses. But how? It took me a moment, but I remembered. "Is this Coach Grisson's house?"

"Yes, we came here a few months ago for a potluck."

"Oh yeah. But…are we even going to Max's house?"

"That's next. To plant the evidence."

"What evidence…? Oh my God. You are evil."

"He hurt my baby girl. Time to make the first domino fall."

"Max isn't the first domino?"

"No. Save the best for last."

———————————

The next morning we had breakfast as a family. It was Saturday morning, and on Saturdays we almost always had breakfast as a family. I thought I might go crazy waiting for an update, any update, and finally, halfway through my ham and cheese omelet, your phone, Annabelle, started to go crazy with text message after text message. Oh how the mighty had fallen.

"Sure is a lot of text messages for a Saturday morning," I said.

"Oh my God!" Annabelle said. "Alice says that Max just got in trouble for rolling Coach Grisson's house and vandalizing his car. He said he didn't do it, but his parents found empty toilet paper rolls and shoe polish in their trash. He is so getting benched for that."

"What? Really?" Peter asked. Always the skeptic.

"Don't believe me?" Annabelle asked. "Here, look!" Annabelle showed us the pictures.

"Wow," Peter said. "What a moron. Forget getting benched, he'll prolly get thrown off the team."

"And he wrote something on the car too," Annabelle said. "Cantank...Cantank..."

"Here, let me see," I said. I glanced at the phone and read the word in the picture. "'Cantankerous.'" Pretty big word for a person who was failing English.

"I have to call Alice! She's blowing up my phone."

"Go ahead," your mother said.

You raced off to your room, and your mother and I started clearing the table and doing the dishes. She scrubbed the plates and I dried them after. We were the perfect team.

"Do you think we should ever tell her that it was us who rolled Coach Grisson's house and then planted the evidence at Max's?" I asked.

"One day. When the time is right."

I smiled at your mother, and she smiled back. My loving accomplice.

I know what you're thinking. No way. No — don't even think about saying that word — way. No way your sweet and darling mother helped me vandalize Coach Grisson's house and car.

Well, kids, it's like this: You're right. It's shocking. If I hadn't been there to witness it myself, I wouldn't have believed it either. I asked her about it before we got out of the minivan, and here's how our conversation went:

"You don't have to go through with this," I said. "We can turn the car around and just head home."

"What's your biggest fear as a parent?" she asked.

"What?"

"Your biggest fear as a parent. What is it?"

"Geez. There are so many things. It's hard to name just one."

"Besides the obvious stuff I mean."

"Well…"

"Can I tell you mine?"

"Go ahead."

"That Annabelle will have all of my worst qualities and none of my good ones. That she'll be haunted by all the same things that haunt me. That the faults I have don't go away after a generation. That I'll be so concerned with making sure she isn't like me, I'll make her something worse. And that's just chapter one in the book of things that keep me up at night — that of course being the volume on our children. There are plenty of other volumes in the series."

"So you're going to do something completely insane because…?"

"Because she's not like me. She's too good for that. All the things I said I have to worry about? I don't have to. We raised an amazing daughter. And an amazing son. They're better people than we are. She would never do this, but I will. So, you ready?"

"Let's do this."

Sometimes karma gets it wrong. But still, it's true that what goes around comes around. It's just that sometimes, what comes around is your mother and me.

15

I'M HAPPY YOU MOVED OUT OF THE HOUSE AND ARE GOING TO COLLEGE

It hit me on a Saturday. The first Saturday after your mother and I dropped Annabelle off at college. We ventured to Home Depot that day as I wanted to purchase a new power drill and your mother was in need of rust-free gardening supplies. I needed the power drill to build a workbench. Why a workbench? I was going to use it to build other stuff. What other stuff? I didn't know yet, and that was assuming I could even build a workbench to begin with. It was a test, a threshold project. I figured that if I couldn't build a simple workbench, then woodworking wasn't for me. And yes, children, I did already have a drill, but I had burned out the motor on it within fifteen minutes of use. I needed a professional drill, not the kind you use to build IKEA furniture when you fail (i.e., neglect) to follow instructions properly. No, I needed the kind that contractors built homes with.

This is what my life had become in your absence. I had hobbies. I don't think I've ever had a hobby in my life. Well, that's not entirely true. I had a hobby for eighteen years. It was called parenthood. But that hobby had ended — or was going to end soon when Peter graduated high school—and there was going to be this massive, unfillable void in my life and I had to fill it with something. Your mother suggested a hobby.

I rejected this solution at first. A hobby? What is a hobby? You guys were my hobby. Eating cookies and watching sports were my hobbies. Those qualify as hobbies, right?

Apparently not—so your mother told me. She had been delicate when explaining that she and I were at an important period in our lives when our home would transition from a family home to a Laundromat with good Wi-Fi and free food. Some parents made this transition in life gracefully. I was not one of those parents. It's not that I was incapable of—or opposed to—change, it's just that I appreciated the comfort of a steady routine. Taking on a hobby seemed like an underwhelming distraction. I'm losing my children, who have been the most important part of my life for the last eighteen years, and your solution is to take up bowling? Great idea...That's like using a Band-Aid for a bullet wound.

It helped that your mother was following her own advice and had decided to pick up a hobby too. I don't know why, but she chose gardening. It seemed genuinely challenging, and by that I mean it was literally backbreaking labor. I just wanted an excuse to play with power tools; I think she actually wanted to do something rewarding with her time. We even went so far as to fire the gardener so that she would be solely responsible for maintaining our lawn and flower beds. He wasn't pleased:

"Was it something I did?" he asked.

"I don't know," I responded. "Are you on the admissions board at my daughter's college?"

He wasn't. He didn't get it. People don't really have a sense of humor when you're firing them. I can't say I blame them.

Standing in the middle of Home Depot, I felt like Pablo Picasso staring at a blank canvas. There was so much hope in those aisles. I was overcome with inspiration. Dreams of vast accomplishment flittered through my mind: "I could put in a new washer/dryer." And: "I could install ceiling fans." And: "I could build a picket fence and have some poor sap paint it white for me." It was a land of endless opportunity. A happy place.

But I was distraught. Your mother and I had essentially been fired from our full-time jobs as your parents, and there I was, left with no coping mechanism save for retail therapy.

I pushed all other home repair projects out of my head and focused on the task at hand as I made my way to the power tool section. I knew next to nothing about the reliability or the utility of the various power drills, but I used an age-old shopping method — an ancient art form that existed before the dawn of the five-star Internet review. I picked the coolest-looking power drill on the shelf without regard for price or brand. I figured there was a strong chance I wouldn't be good at woodworking, but that didn't mean that I couldn't look awesome while failing. Content with my selection, I made my way to the wood aisle.

I was back at square one all over again. My lack of knowledge about power drills is second only to my lack of knowledge about wood. I didn't know how to pick out wood for a workbench, but, in my new life, I picked out wood. Or should I say "lumber"? I didn't know. What was the difference? Or was there not one? Desperate for answers, I flagged down one of the sales associates and asked for help.

"Hi, I'd like to buy some wood for a workbench."

"You're in luck," he answered. "We sell wood."

I hate when salespeople try to be cute with me. You're supposed to laugh at my jokes, not the other way around. This isn't Friday night at the comedy club, and I really don't want to hear your stand-up act.

"Is there any particular piece you're interested in?" he asked.

"Yes, what type of tree did this one used to be?" I pointed to a random piece of wood.

"What type of tree?"

"Yes, what type of tree? Wood comes from trees, you know. Paper too." I can be cute too, guy.

"I don't know, but I'll find out."

He went off to fetch some help, and I turned to the box with the power drill. There had been a time in my life where I was too timid to open a product in a store before I purchased it, but that was before I met either one of you. The two of you taught me that opening a product in a store is not a heinous act. No, you, my children, had committed far worse acts, such as opening products and then destroying them, or opening food items and then consuming them and littering with the remains. I had been softened by years of watching you run roughshod over social convention.

I opened the cardboard box and started going through the items within. The drill. The bits. The instructions. The safety guide — thank you, lawyers. There was something missing. Where was the chuck key? I searched and searched, emptying the contents and then returning them, but I couldn't find it.

How could a company sell a power drill without a chuck key? It didn't make sense. Everybody knows that a drill needs a chuck key to change out each of the individual bits. A drill couldn't exist without the chuck key. The drill would be worthless without it.

And that's when it hit me. That's when I realized why I had come to Home Depot in the first place and how everything in the past eighteen years in my life had led me to this aisle of wood and this drill without a chuck key.

I took one deep breath and lost it. I certainly wish I could blame it on sawdust, but that wasn't the cause. I was broken. There was a part of me missing. Like the drill with the missing chuck key. That part of me was you, Annabelle. You'd moved out and gone to college. And there I was, in Home Depot, searching for some new purpose for my life. I don't know what causes a person to reflect unexpectedly on his life and all of the decisions he's made when he's running what would otherwise be a routine errand, but I wish I could eradicate the part of my brain that initiated such reflection. I had no need to face my emotions, and I especially had no need to face my emotions while shopping for wood at Home Depot.

The waterworks came and I knelt down then crawled over a short stack of boards on the shelf in front of me. On my hands and knees, I moved over to an adjacent shelf with long boards piled high. Nestled there behind the stack of lumber, I was safely hidden from view. Numerous shoppers passed by unaware of my presence in the secret alcove. Eventually, the sales associate returned with one of his coworkers, but they didn't see me cowering behind the stack of wood, silently weeping. Praise be.

"This is where I left him," the first sales associate said.

"What did he want again?" the second sales associate asked.

"He wanted to know what type of tree this wood was."

"Good lord, Justin. Go back to work."

"What? I was —"

"He probably got his wood and left. He was messing with you."

It was me or Justin. And I chose to let Justin take the fall for me. I could have run out there and told the second sales associate that there really was a man waiting to hear more about wood, but I didn't. I couldn't. So, thanks, Justin. You're more than just a sales associate. You're a silent hero. Because there was no way that I was going to face the world, especially the Home Depot world, given my emotional state.

Let me tell you an immutable fact of life, kids: if you're suddenly going to have a nervous breakdown, you do not want to be at Home Depot when it happens. You would much rather have a nervous breakdown at Bed Bath & Beyond. You can wipe your nose on almost anything at Bed Bath & Beyond. Best Buy would be rather unfavorable too. There are too many cameras. Some inconsiderate teenager would probably record the most heartbreaking moment of your life and then share it on social media for the world to see.

The sales associates left, but I was trapped. I couldn't walk around Home Depot crying. I made shelter. I couldn't stand to face the other shoppers. I wouldn't let them see me in this fragile state. This was the end of my workbench. How would I make a workbench if I couldn't come to Home Depot anymore? I could go to Lowe's, but Home Depot was closer to the house and I didn't feel like driving the extra twenty minutes. That's forty minutes round trip.

I hid behind that stack of wood and wept for what felt like hours. It was something closer to fifteen minutes. I know because your mother called me and informed me that she had been looking for me for about that much time.

"Where are you?" she asked. "I've been looking everywhere for you."

"The wood aisle."

"Are you okay? You sound like you've been crying."

"I'm fine." *No. I'm not fine.*

"I'm coming there right now."

Your mother didn't have any trouble finding me in my hiding place. She crawled through the gap between the stacks of wood and sat down next to me. I looked at her handheld shopping basket and saw that she had collected quite the assortment of gardening tools. Good for her. It was nice to see that at least one of us hadn't been emotionally crippled by shopping at Home Depot. Yes, she seemed ready to start her new life. I wish I could have parroted that sentiment.

"What's the matter?" she asked.

"Nothing…" *Everything.*

"Tell me."

I motioned toward the opened power drill box in front of me. "The drill doesn't come with a chuck key to remove the bit. The drill can't work without the chuck key. It needs the chuck key. How can they sell a drill without a chuck key?"

"Really? That's what you're upset about?" She placed her arm around my shoulders. "Because if it upsets you that much, I'll do something about it. I'll call the manager. Just say the word."

"Fine." I took a long breath. I couldn't reasonably expect her to believe that. Or could I…? No, I couldn't. Time for the truth. "I'm upset because I don't want Annabelle to go to college."

"You don't want her to go to college?" Your mother didn't roll her eyes, but that was only because she had years of practice conditioning her reactions to my absurdities.

"That's right. Just hear me out."

"Okay."

"If she goes to college, when are we ever going to see her again? Thanksgiving? Christmas? A few months during her summer vacation? What about after she graduates? The same few holidays minus the months in the summer? And what happens after she gets married? We'll have to compete for her time with her spouse's family. And God forbid she should marry someone we hate. Our little girl isn't going to college; she's starting a new life without us."

"You've really thought this through."

"I can't help it. It's all I can think about. Parenthood is such a losing proposition. We, the parents, sacrifice arguably the best years of our lives—and our time and our money—giving nearly everything that we have in this world to our children, and then just when those children reach an age when we might actually enjoy spending time with them, they move out and leave us behind. Of course this is often punctuated by a phase where said children blame us parents for all of their shortcomings and disappointments. Instead of being thankful for these monumental sacrifices, they bear unwarranted resentment. Who in their right mind would sign up for that?"

At the time, it was unclear to me how anyone could go through that process—child-rearing—and arrive at a different conclusion. Parenthood had taken much from me. Here's a list of all the things that I could have purchased with the money I spent on you two over the years:

- A country.
- A second family.
- A fleet of warships.
- A space program.
- A research university.
- A professional sports team.
- Possibly even a third family.

And of course there was also the list of my prized possessions that you had ruined:

- My wedding ring (okay, fine, I lost that one on my own, but I blamed you, Annabelle).
- My second wedding ring (I pinned the blame for this one on Peter).
- My Rolex watch. The warranty doesn't matter if I can't find it.
- My cookies. Death by consumption. Too many of them.
- Several of my Nerf guns.
- My baseball signed by Babe Ruth. (Fine. So I didn't have one of these and I stole the idea from that movie *The Sandlot*, which is one of the few children's movies that I don't actively hate. Regardless, if I did have one, I bet you would've ruined it.)
- My third wedding ring. (Just kidding. I still have it, and I'll never lose it.)
- Several TV remotes.

There in our makeshift cave there was just enough light for me to see the blank expression on your mother's face. It could have gone either way—your mother's reaction to my diatribe. For a moment—and I mean one bloody second—your mother looked at me with all of the strength in the world, before she, too, lost it. Lost. It. But no judgment. I had invoked this reaction, and you know what's better than having a shoulder to cry on? A companion who knows exactly what you're going through.

"We spend all of our money on them," your mother said, "and we raise them and love them and they just abandon us? Our children are so coldhearted. So coldhearted. I don't understand why anyone would want to bring children into this world. Tell me. Why?"

Seeing her lose it…Yeah, I lost it. Again. "You can't cry right now," I said. "This is my moment."

"Our baby's going to college," she said. "College!"

"I know. I'm so happy for her, but at the same time, I'm so sad for me."

"I'm sad too."

"Why did we push her so hard in school? We shouldn't have helped her with her homework. We could have had another year with her. Maybe even two."

"We could always stop sending in checks for tuition."

"Then she'd just get student loans. There is no shortage of lenders who will make her a prisoner of insurmountable debt."

"You're right. What're we going to do?"

Before I could tell her my plan to make Annabelle fail out of college and move back home, a new sales associate interrupted our crying powwow.

"I'm sorry, but is there something wrong?" he asked.

"Something wrong?" your mother said, lashing out at him. "Why doesn't this drill come with a chuck key? Why would you sell a drill without a chuck key?"

"I can call the manager over if you—"

"Forget the manager. I want to send a message to corporate!"

"Ma'am, I can also get you a chuck key. We sell chuck keys."

"It's okay. We'll learn to live without it. I don't know how, but we will."

"Okay, ma'am. I'll leave you two alone. If you need anything…"

He left before he could complete the thought. Frankly, I couldn't blame him. That's exactly what I would have done if I'd stumbled onto a Dumpster fire. I would have run — fast and far.

"Ready to face the world again?" I asked as I motioned toward the person-sized gap between the stacks of lumber.

"No. But I don't think I ever will be." Your mother headed for the aisle, and I followed right after.

My legs ached when I finally stood up. We were disoriented at first, uncertain of what to do next, but we soon received instruction. Your mother's phone rang, and it was you, Peter. She answered and listened for a moment, then quickly hung up.

"What did he want?" I asked.

"He asked if we'd pick up food on the way home."

"Well…" I looked at the power drill and the basket of gardening tools resting on the floor in front of me. "If you want to go now, we can always come back later to buy the rest of this —"

"Let's go. We can't let our child starve."

"What kind of parents would we be if we did?"

"Exactly. Also, we should probably call the gardener and hire him back. I felt a little overwhelmed in the gardening section."

"I'll do it first thing tomorrow."

We headed toward the exit, our pace quickening with each step. It felt good to be needed, even if it was only in an Alfred Pennyworth kind of way.

———————————

There's a movie your mother told me to watch—made me watch—after our heart-to-heart talk at Home Depot that day. It's called *Cinema Paradiso*. She thought it might help. It didn't. It only made things worse. If you have any inclination to watch it, now is the time to stop reading, because I'm about to spoil it for you. Even though it didn't comfort me, that doesn't mean I didn't enjoy watching it, because I did. It's a great movie. It has one of the most touching moments I've ever seen in a film. Right up there with Forrest Gump asking Jenny if his son is smart, Sean Maguire telling Good Will Hunting it's not his fault, and Andy Dufresne crawling three hundred yards through sewage to freedom. In the film, there's a boy who grows up in a small town on the island of Sicily and dreams of one day being a film director. When the boy finally matures into a young man, his mentor, an old man who's spent the latter part of his life watching the boy grow, tells him, "Forget us, never come back." The old man knows that the young man will never accomplish his dreams if he doesn't move away from the small town, so he tells him to leave. And that's exactly what the young man does. He leaves, accomplishes all of his dreams, and forgets about everyone in the small town.

Cinema Paradiso is a beautiful story. It reminds me of another movie I love: *Taken* with Liam Neeson. Kids, if you forget your mother and me and never come back, I will find you, and I will embarrass you. Not kill, embarrass. But that's the skill set I possess. I expect you both to come home for every major holiday until your significant other prevents you from doing so, and when that happens, I expect routine phone calls.

No, *Cinema Paradiso* didn't help—because it only made me sadder. But my conversation with your mother in the nook at Home Depot did. There's a little part that I left out, before Peter called. You see, it was within that nook next to your mother that I realized what I had to do. It was she who led me here, and if you've read this far, well, I guess you're probably wondering how it all started.

There we were, hidden safely behind the pile of wood with your mother waiting patiently for me to talk. I took a couple of breaths until I was certain that when I attempted speech I wouldn't start sobbing. You know that feeling? It's similar to the feeling you get right before you sneeze. You're completely helpless, but still, you try to stop it. Breathe in. Breathe out. Okay. Ready. Speak.

"I don't know what to do," I said with a careful cadence. "You think that they know I love them? That I really love them, and that there isn't anything in this world I wouldn't do for them? That they're my life? And that every time my heart beats…it's…?" By the time I approached the end of that sentence I had lost all the composure I had gained by breathing in and out and was choked up again.

"It's for them?" your mother asked, finishing my thought. She took a couple of deeps breaths and then she spoke again. "Yes, I do."

"So what do I do?"

"What's that metaphor you always tell me when I'm upset? The one about how if I don't deal with my feelings, they'll only get worse?"

"The acorn and the oak tree."

"Right. That's it. It applies to you too. If you don't deal with what's bothering you, it's only going to get worse and bother you more. It's like you're planting an acorn that will eventually grow into an oak tree. When you ignore what's bothering you the first couple of times, that's you watering the acorn. And every time you neglect to face those feelings thereafter, that's you fertilizing the acorn, helping it grow. Pretty soon all of that watering and fertilizing leaves you with an oak tree. That's it, right?"

"I really hate when you quote me to me."

"Why? It shows that I listen." She gave me her best impression of the Cheshire cat's grin.

"I know. And sometimes I wish that you wouldn't listen. Then I wouldn't be held accountable for everything I say."

"Well, I think you ought to do something about your oak tree."

"What about the acorn?"

"We're way past the point of acorn. That oak tree has been chopped down and right now we're hiding behind a pile of it. You know good and well you shouldn't suppress your emotions. You should face them. Deal with them. Show the kids how much you love them. How much you're going to miss them. Because if you love somebody, you tell them. But more importantly, you show them."

Kids, your mother was right. Most people go to Home Depot and they know what they want to build. They know what they need to build it. They buy the necessary tools and materials, and they leave. I knew I needed to build something, but I didn't know what.

Not until your mother helped me. So, here's the oak tree. I hope you liked it.

Never forget, I love you just as much on your worst day as I do on your best day.

Love,
Dad

PS: Stay away from my cookies.

ACKNOWLEDGEMENTS

Writing is a lonely endeavor. It's like being marooned on an island without the comfort of a volleyball. The only cure for such loneliness is the help and support of editors, friends, and family—I include animals in that last one, of course.

This book would not have been possible without the help of some amazing people. Thank you to Lauren Harms for her cover design which captured the essence of these stories.

Thank you to my proofreader Mike Waitz for his keen ability to spot errors and his suggestions for improvement.

Thank you to my editor Aja Pollock for being incredibly knowledgeable about so many different topics and for her diligent attention to detail. She made every part of this book better.

Thank to you my friends and family for their encouragement and support over the years and in the time leading up to publication.

In particular, I would like to acknowledge my parents and my brother and sister-in-law. When you tell someone that you want to write a book and their immediate response isn't, "You? Really? Wait…You mean one with words, or one with pictures?" Well, sometimes that's all the confidence you need to begin typing.

I especially have to thank my mom who read every page of this, numerous times, making good use of her "delete" button. I couldn't have done this without her.

Any and all mistakes are my own.

ABOUT THE AUTHOR

ALEX SHAHLA is a graduate of Haverford College and Pepperdine University School of Law. He currently lives in Santa Monica, California.

AlexShahla.com

CPSIA information can be obtained
at www.ICGtesting.com
Printed in the USA
FFOW03n1552210217
32713FF